EDITORIAL REVIEW

Dragoria: The Lost Dragon Realm
Book Three

DRAGON BREEZE

"Apprentice sorceress Samara needs to liberate the dragons and dragon elves so they can oppose the despotic Sacred Flame coterie of magic users. But she must also protect her family from the Flame's wrath. With help from her invisible familiar, the dragon Ulrieg, and a few trusted friends, she moves closer to her goal." Kim H., Proofreader, Red Adept Editing

"The stakes for sorcerer's apprentice Samara, her dragon familiar Ulrieg, and their allies are higher than ever as they continue trying to save the dragons of their world while evading the suspicions of those responsible for dragon persecution. Fans of the Dragoria books and new readers alike will enjoy this third entry in the series, full of intrigue, danger, and magic." Mary M., Line Editor, Red Adept Editing

DRAGON BREEZE

DRAGORIA: THE LOST DRAGON REALM
BOOK THREE

KATRINA COPE

COSY BURROW BOOKS

DRAGORIA: THE LOST DRAGON REALM BOOKS

Part One

Dragon Moon

Dragon Heart

Dragon Breeze

Part Two

Dragon's Royal

Royal Alliance

Royal Resistance

Dragon Moon
Ebook first published in USA in January 2024 by Cosy Burrow
Books
Ebook first published in Great Britain in January 2024 by Cosy
Burrow Books

www.katrinacopebooks.com
Text Copyright © 2023 by Katrina Cope
Cover Design Copyright © art4artists.com.au

ISBN: 978-0-6455102-8-7

❋ Created with Vellum

To all the people who nominate to be organ donors after they leave this earth, thank you. It's because of people like you that people like me can live. As for the people who donate organs while still living, you are a special kind of angel.

BLURB

Danger lurks everywhere, as hope blows in the breeze.

Sorcerer's apprentice Samara is elated by the rescue of the dragons, but that feeling is soon squashed as the risks of being caught increase. Not knowing who in the Sacred Flame coterie is involved has Samara on edge, especially when she and her dragon, Ulrieg, are spotted in places they shouldn't be.

Powerful head sorceress Callista embarks on a journey to find a sacred crystal to add to her collection, taking Samara and a couple of other apprentices. Samara discovers shocking truths along the way as Ulrieg scrambles to sabotage the mission.

What unfolds when they return to the coterie base will unexpectedly change their future.

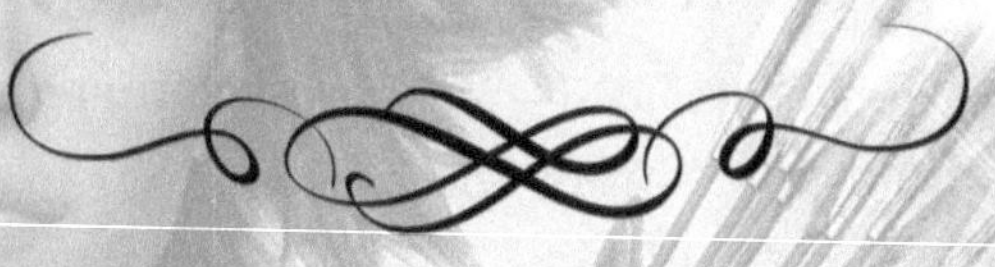

CHAPTER ONE

Hey! *Let me see.* Ulrieg scrambled up his bonded's back, his talons digging into flesh left unprotected by thick leather.

Samara braced herself under the extra weight as her leather pants and sleeveless fitted top groaned in protest. Her dragon was half her size, and it took all her core strength to hold her petite body steady with the aid of the doorframe as Ulrieg settled his front talons on her shoulders while his hind talons clasped the leather on her back.

They peered through the small gap into a secret underground cave to which only a few Sacred Flame coterie members were granted access. Samara squinted, pushing away the ominous feeling that this cave brought with it. The bright-orange light of the orb inside contrasted starkly with the dark, dingy corridors of the catacombs they had passed through to get here.

Ulrieg shivered, rocking Samara's entire body. *Ergh! That orb gives me the creeps. There's something very* wrong *about that thing.*

The cave was spotless, fully illuminated by the orb without any sign of the carnage that had taken place the night before. Images haunted her memory of bloody trails on the floor and gruesome scenes in the smaller caves off the main area.

Samara shook her head to rid it of those thoughts. She must keep her mind clear, or they could end up discovered because of a simple mistake.

Something black shifted near the far side of the cave, and when Samara's eyes grew accustomed to the bright glow, the dark shape morphed into Mystique, the familiar of Callista, head sorceress of the Sacred Flame coterie. The black jaguar sat cleaning herself, licking her front paw before running it over her ear. Mystique paused momentarily as movement apparently caught her interest, and her yellow-slitted eyes focused on Kellam. The senior sorcerer stood before the orb, his arms stretched toward the magical glowing light. Mystique's eyes narrowed.

Within moments, Callista entered the cave. The

head sorceress nudged the sorcerer's shoulder with her fingers and waved him away, her crystal-blue eyes hard, the only hint of expression on her always unreadable face. After watching him retreat to one of the smaller rooms, the sorceress stood at the side of the glowing sphere with her arms wide and her back arched as though soaking up the magical power the orb seemed willing to give her. The gold on Callista's diadem shone under the light, and the beige of the long leaf-patterned dress that hugged her torso and draped to the ground in soft waves seemed to glow gold as well. She looked radiant and unstoppable.

A minuscule line of orange light burst from the orb, circling it before embedding itself into Callista's chest. The sorceress arched back farther, stretching her arms wider.

Samara blinked with disbelief. *Did you see that, or are my eyes playing tricks on me?* she asked Ulrieg.

Yep. I definitely saw it.

Even though Samara knew that the great sorceress had consulted with the orb in the past, her thoughts on this had changed since hearing Ulrieg's stories. The sight made her cringe. *Isn't that orb supposed to be filled with the magic of the evil sorcerer who was overcome by the dragons and dragon elves from the land of Dragoria?*

Ulrieg slightly shifted his weight. *Yep. And it should be quite powerful after all those sacrifices offered to it last night. Maybe that's what gives it the strength to temporarily pierce a tiny hole and release some energy.*

A chill returned to Samara's body, and her body convulsed, rattling Ulrieg and causing him to dig his talons in deeper. She grimaced.

Ulrieg leaned forward. *Doesn't seeing this make you think she's guilty of what has happened?*

She groaned. *I can't say it paints her in a good light, but I can't see any evidence of what was in here last night, so we still haven't proven her to be responsible.*

Ulrieg's hot breath warmed her face. *I swear your stubbornness over making sure you have proof that someone is evil will get you killed one day.*

And what? The only way I will avoid that is to be as distrusting as you?

If it keeps you safer, what's wrong with that?

She peered up at where she thought the dragon's face would be. *Not everyone has sinister motives. And if I were like you, we would probably never have anyone on our side. But now we have Paxton and Forgrac.*

Samara wondered how her friend and fellow apprentice, Paxton, was coping this morning. It had been the first time he had witnessed the aftermath of the happenings in the cave. She'd spotted him from her window earlier as he headed into the forest, moving toward where they had left Daena the dragon elf and Byzarid's injured sister. He was probably going to finish healing Byzarid's sister so they could leave the coterie-occupied area.

Ulrieg's cousin, Byzarid, was still missing, which was why Samara and Ulrieg were visiting the catacombs during daylight hours. Samara's stomach growled. She'd skipped breakfast to try to beat the two senior sorcerers to the underground, yet she and Ulrieg had failed. They needed to find evidence of where to find Byzarid. He hadn't been seen since he left Daena to try and help the dragons, and he hadn't been in the carnage of the previous night. Byzarid's sister was the only one still alive.

I can't see him in there nor hear any dragon noises. Ulrieg's voice pulled Samara back into the present.

That's probably a good thing, she told him. *Hopefully, that means he's still alive and well. I wish I knew who cleaned the place up before this morning. It makes me wonder how close we were to being caught in there. Have Vexx, Kellam, or Zofia been in there already this morning, or did they just miss us last night?*

Samara shifted, ready to back away from the door, when Callista began to speak to the orb. The words were too soft for her to hear. She turned her ear, straining toward the room. *Argh. I can't hear what she's saying. Can you?*

She's not speaking loudly, although I wouldn't be surprised if she's thanking the orb for its counsel.

Samara grimaced. *I hope you're wrong, especially if you're right about the type of magic that the orb holds. If Callista turns out to be evil, I'm doomed, and so are Paxton and our families.* She backed away from the door quietly, pulling the door closed.

Ulrieg jumped to the ground and turned visible, his red eyes etched with sorrow.

Samara squatted down to his height. *I hope it's good that we didn't see your cousin there. Maybe he avoided capture and is out in the forest somewhere.*

Ulrieg gazed at the ground, his body shaking slightly. *We'll see.*

Samara's heart melted. Ulrieg wasn't as shaken as he'd been the previous night, but he still wasn't his usual self in these catacombs. She cupped his muzzle, careful to avoid the horn under his chin. *What are your moon senses telling you?*

Something is still not right down here. I hoped it was what we saw last night, but I'm not sure. The impending sense of dread remains. Ulrieg took a deep breath and straightened his spine. *But there was nothing in the cave.* He headed back the way they had come. *We should check on Paxton and the others.*

Samara followed him, pausing when he stopped halfway down the corridor by a door. *What is it?*

He sniffed under the door before pulling away. *I wish I had a stronger sense of smell. A strange feeling floods me when I'm in front of this door.*

Samara tried the handle, but it wouldn't budge. She looked for the Sacred Flame coterie emblem around the lock but didn't find one. Holding her palm near the handle, she readied to cast the opening spell when she heard a *click* from down the corridor. Startled, she glanced at the cave door she had closed only moments before to see light streaming through the corridor.

CHAPTER TWO

Ulrieg turned invisible as Samara extinguished the torch and pressed against the door, forcing herself to remain still. She was lucky that the doorway was slightly indented in the wall, but although she was thin, it wasn't enough to hide her completely. She hoped her dark leather tunic and long pants would blend in with the shadows behind her and her brilliant-pink hair would stay out of sight.

The cave door opened slightly, and the orb's orange glow illuminated long, lilac hair as Callista's head peeked through the opening. She appeared to study the corridor, casting a partial shadow over Samara.

Samara gripped the handle, taking all her tension

out on the brass knob and using its stability to help her keep balance. It was a struggle not to run. She hoped the corridor was long enough and the distance would help her camouflage in the shadows. Holding her breath, she waited, her heart thundering against her rib cage.

Eventually, Callista retreated back into the cave, closing the door and leaving Samara and Ulrieg in darkness once again.

Relief flooded Samara's body. *That was close. Ulrieg, are you still here?*

Of course. Talons scraped the stones only a couple of feet away from her.

Would you mind reigniting the torch?

She held it out, and he breathed a plume of fire over the end. The torch embers ignited, filling the corridor with a glow duller than the brilliant light of the orb.

Body visible again, Ulrieg started for the exit. *Let's get out of here. That was too close to being caught. It makes me wonder if Callista saw us earlier, but if she did, you would think she would call us out.*

Samara followed. *Maybe her opening the corridor door was her way of saying that she knows we were there and that she's on our side.*

Hmph. Whatever! I'd be amazed if you're correct.

Whether the cave is clean or not, it still places her in the suspect category if she consults the orb as she does. No ordinary sorcerer could do that. If she had good intentions, surely, she couldn't talk to an evil magic, let alone accept any of its light.

Samara glowered at Ulrieg even though she knew he wouldn't see it. *There are still so many things we must prove.*

Yeah. Yeah. You will only say someone's guilty once you have the proof. Ulrieg wobbled his head.

They climbed the stairs, and Samara placed the torch back into the holder on the wall then nearly tripped over Ulrieg when he stopped without warning. Her boots slipped on the lingering rainwater, skidding her down to a lower step.

Samara grabbed the cracks between the rocks on the wall and righted herself. *What's wrong?*

I just have a bad feeling about that room. We should try again to see what's in there.

Clenching her teeth, Samara squatted to Ulrieg's level. *If we go back now, we could get caught. Just because I'm not willing to say Callista is evil doesn't mean I trust her to be good. She or anyone else in that cave could check this corridor anytime. She may even send someone else out here to look. Is your "bad feeling" pressing enough to risk being caught? They would know Byzarid's sister is missing, and someone broke into the cave again.*

The horns on Ulrieg's forehead bunched together as he frowned. *I don't know. I understand what you're saying. But what if it's something urgent?*

Samara tugged at the hair near her temple before heading back down the stairs. She would never be able to live with herself if she didn't check behind the door and found out later that they could have saved someone. When she heard Ulrieg's talons behind her, she stepped into the corridor again as a door clicked open down the way. A stream of orange light filled the corridor. She quickly retreated into the darkness surrounding the stairs. *Ulrieg, can you see who it is?* A gust of air brushed against her face, feeling like the light breeze from the pump of a wing.

It's Kellam, and his monkey familiar is with him. We should get out of here.

Quickly, Samara tiptoed up the stairs, keeping her boots quiet on the stones, before climbing out of the hole into the daylight and darting behind a shrub. The bush covering the entrance rustled briefly before she heard Ulrieg, invisible now, land on the ground next to her.

That was too close. Samara peered around the bush, checking to make sure no one was around, before darting to the side of the building. After another quick glance through the wild-grass plain surrounding the building and a scan of the edges of the pine forest, she walked casually to the front door of the building.

Yes, that was, Ulrieg agreed. The flowers blooming on the tall grass waved as the invisible dragon walked beside her.

Samara wiped away the perspiration beading on her forehead. *We'll have to try again later. The inner circle of the Sacred Flame coterie seems to be on high alert after last night. We shouldn't be surprised, seeing we were the reason they lost another dragon.* She worried her lower lip with her teeth. *I'm glad we found your other cousin, but I wonder why she was the only one alive.*

Perhaps something else grabbed their attention. Like Byzarid. Ulrieg snorted, and a small patch of grass in front of him withered.

Samara ran her hand over some of the flowers. *I hope not.*

They climbed the stone stairs to the coterie building, and Samara opened the front door. Inside the large gray-stone building, the common room bustled with apprentices hurrying from breakfast to prepare for their first lesson. Seeing some of them coming from the direction of the dining hall, Samara decided to try her luck at grabbing a few items to eat before heading to class.

When she was only a few feet away from the

dining hall entrance, Vexx's yellow snake familiar, Mara, slithered across the floor in her direction. Samara diverted course and headed to the stairs that took her to the level of her room. She would rather go hungry than get the attention of the senior sorcerer, Vexx, and have him find out that she behaved differently from the way most apprentices acted in the morning.

On the other side of the common room, she noticed Paxton taking the stairs up to his side of the building two at a time. The sight of him made her breathe a sigh of relief only to be jolted to a stop when someone ran into her. She found herself looking into Kaine's blue eyes. Vacant of the alluring charm usually residing in them, they were instead filled with a confrontational hardness. He reached to touch her skin, and she jerked back, determined to not fall under his magic-accentuated charm.

Maybe she'd only thought she saw hardness in his eyes, but her personal experience instantly hardened her heart against him as she remembered what he could do.

Samara sidestepped him and ran into his familiar, Ginger. The fox's nose was high and nostrils flaring like she was sniffing for evidence of Ulrieg. Samara wasn't sure if Kaine had told Callista about

Ulrieg and what the two of them had been doing in the forest with Paxton.

Samara didn't know if Kaine knew exactly what Ulrieg was, but she hoped their brief relationship would inspire some kind of loyalty in Kaine to keep her secrets even though he hadn't been included. He was upset that she hadn't included him, she knew, despite her reasoning. She wished she had the time to talk to him and try to sort things out, but after what happened in the forest in the last lesson with weapons master Zofia—and the defensive-arts lesson with Devi—she suspected nothing she did would smooth things over.

Samara attempted to pass by both Kaine and Ginger to climb the stairs, only to find the fox baring her teeth. "Kaine, please call Ginger off so I can pass."

When she met Kaine's eyes, Samara flinched. It wasn't her imagination. He had turned hostile since he had discovered her secret. "If you want, come to my room, and we can talk further to clarify things. I never wanted it to be like this. It's all been because of misunderstandings." She reached out to him and, at the last second, withdrew her hand before touching his skin, reminding herself of his charm power that seemed to lure people into telling deep secrets like a siren would sing a sailor to crash into the rocks.

Her retraction wasn't missed by Kaine, who sneered down at her. "Going to your room is the last thing I want. You had your chance to tell me, and you didn't."

Samara withdrew, pressing her back against the stair railing. Kaine had changed so much in a short time, and even her saving his life earlier seemed to mean nothing to him now. Not that she wanted him to treat her above others because of it, but she thought it might lead him to give her a second chance to explain everything.

Come, Samara. Ulrieg snorted. *Forget him. He's just proving how selfish he is.*

Samara glanced up the stairs toward her room, but she looked back to Kaine when she sensed him moving. Kaine moved aside and down the stairs, Ginger following him. She didn't know what changed his mind, but relief flooded her, and she rushed to her room.

Grabbing the handle of her bedroom door, she glanced quickly back at the stairs, hit with an overwhelming sense of doom. Life in the coterie was becoming very tricky. She and Ulrieg could end up in great danger if she wasn't careful and the wrong people discovered her secrets.

She turned the handle, and the door released its usual groan as it swung wide. As she glanced inside, she halted, a cold dread filling her. Her belongings were strewn all over the floor, her mattress tilted against the wall. Her owl, Gray, sat wide-eyed on her desk despite rarely leaving his perch.

Samara's room had been ransacked.

CHAPTER THREE

Who *would've done this?* Ulrieg asked the question that whirled in her mind. His talons clicked on the floor, the sound loud in the quiet room.

Samara followed him in and shut the door behind her. "I don't know. Maybe it was Kaine. I don't know why he would do this, unless he thinks I'm keeping more things from him." She rubbed her fingers together. "I hope it wasn't one of the senior sorcerers."

Ulrieg turned visible, his red eyes serious. *In all honesty, would it be any better if it was Kaine?*

Samara lowered her mattress to place it back on the bedframe and started remaking her bed. "It would only be better if Kaine was still susceptible enough to change his mind."

As if that's likely, after what you experienced on the stairs. He shouldn't have even been on the stairs. His room is on the other side of the building.

Fluffing up her pillow, Samara placed it at the head of her bed. "Unless he was visiting Luna's room." She was surprised to find that the jealousy that had plagued her every time she thought of them together seemed to have mellowed. Only a twinge still remained.

A knock sounded on the door, and as soon as Ulrieg turned invisible, Samara opened it to find Paxton in the corridor, his frog, Jojo, sitting on his shoulder. Dark circles framed Paxton's eyes, and his shoulders stooped slightly. Her heart warmed. Once again, Paxton had helped someone else, sacrificing his own strength and safety.

She opened the door wider and indicated for him to come in. "You're back!"

His footsteps halted momentarily after he walked in, his eyes widening as he surveyed her destroyed room. "Did you know that I had gone?"

Ulrieg perched beside Gray on the edge of her desk. Samara closed the door then smirked at Paxton, indicating the window. "I saw you from here. I figured it was best you went alone in case we drew more attention by leaving the building together."

Paxton noticed Gray on the table and put Jojo in his pocket, out of sight from the owl's intense gaze. "What happened here?"

Shrugging, Samara straightened some papers on the bench. "I don't know. We just found it like this. I passed Kaine on the stairs on my way up, but that doesn't mean it was him."

Jumping onto Samara's bed, Ulrieg wrapped his tail around his body and sat up straight. *We think it might've been someone looking for more information. Who knows? The perpetrator could have been looking for evidence of what happened to Byzarid's sister. How is she?*

A satisfied smile crossed Paxton's face. "I'm happy to say she's mostly healed. She has a few minor wounds, but all the serious ones are fixed."

Ulrieg tilted his head to one side. *That's great! You look tired but must be getting stronger. Are you going back to heal the rest later?*

Without answering the dragon's question, Paxton placed his hand in front of Gray's chest, and the owl climbed on. Paxton chuckled, his eyes brightening. "I've always wanted to do that."

Samara leaned against the wall. "He must be getting used to you being around."

He grimaced. "I understand why you always wear gloves while handling him. His claws are sharp and surprisingly strong."

Gray lurched toward Paxton and let out a short cry.

"Ow!" Clenching his teeth, Paxton thrust the hand holding the owl away from himself. "Oh no, you don't! You're not eating Jojo."

Samara pushed off the wall and came to take Gray. "On the other hand, maybe it's his fondness for your familiar and what the frog might taste like that has his interest."

Releasing a sigh of relief, Paxton took a quick peek at Jojo. "Good. You're safe and unharmed." He glanced apprehensively at Gray, perched on Samara's arm, then back to Ulrieg. "In answer to your question, my strength for healing magic does seem to be growing, or maybe I'm learning to not expel so much energy every time I use it. However, I'm not going back to heal your cousin. I've sent both her and Daena away. They wanted to wait to find Byzarid, but I told them that we would continue looking, while they needed to get away from here to avoid being recaptured. I think a second capture for them could be deadly."

Ulrieg's jaw dropped. *I'm glad for them, but that's not great news for Byzarid.*

Samara placed Gray back on his perch. "We don't know if Byzarid has been recaptured. Hopefully, he's not. But that's the best thing Paxton could do for the others. It'll also give us more time to look for Byzarid if we don't have to worry over or look after them."

Ulrieg lay on his stomach and rested his chin on a front talon. *I guess you're right. I trust your judgment.*

Samara moved beside Ulrieg and touched his front leg, hoping to comfort him. Then she faced Paxton, asking, "Did Daena say where she is going? Is she going to try to get through the border to return to her home?"

Paxton picked up some books strewn on the floor and placed them on the desk. "She was certain her chances of going home to Clialarion were shattered when she bonded with Kaida. Daena will be on Vexx's wanted list until she's dead. I think she's planning on staying with Ulrieg's cousin, and they plan on keeping each other safe."

"That's probably a good plan." Samara squeezed Ulrieg's leg.

Yet they are still stuck in Wraeyanor, the land of the sorcerers and the realm where most Sacred Flame coterie members reside.

"Isn't that where you are based?" Samara pulled back to study Ulrieg's discouraged face.

Yes, but I have the ability to turn invisible. They don't.

"I'm sure there are plenty of places to hide if they're smart." Samara petted Ulrieg's leg then picked up some clothes thrown on the floor during the disruption of her room. Her stomach growled.

Paxton looked at her. "Are you hungry?"

She rubbed her stomach. "I missed breakfast. We went to check on the cave and see if we could spot evidence of Byzarid."

Paxton bent to pick up Samara's feathered quill and ink pot, placing them on the desk. "I have some food in my room. I'll grab it for you as soon as we're finished here. Did you find anything underground?"

Samara straightened her back. "We ran across Callista almost worshiping the orb."

Ulrieg nodded. *It was weird.*

"Yes, very disconcerting," Samara agreed. "Especially when a small sliver of the orb's magic seemed to break free and enter Callista."

Stroking his chin, Paxton nodded. "That *is* odd. Do you think she knows about what's been happening to the dragons?"

"I honestly don't know. The cave was clean, not a trace of blood. I didn't see a lot, but Kellam was down there. Kellam and Callista almost discovered us in the corridor on our way out."

Paxton frowned. "What do you mean?"

"We stopped in front of a door in the corridor that was giving Ulrieg bad vibes. We were about to unlock it with a spell when the door to the cave opened and Callista peered down the corridor. I don't believe she saw me, but not long after, Kellam peeked out with his monkey familiar." At Paxton's look, she sighed. "I'm sure he didn't see us. But we were close to being caught. Needless to say, we didn't go back to check behind the mystery door. It was too risky. We'll have to go back."

"It sounds like you've had an interesting morning." Paxton turned to Ulrieg. "Have you tried to talk to Byzarid?"

Ulrieg pulled back his lips, exposing his teeth. *Of course. Wouldn't you think that's the first thing I'd try? My mind talk only works if the other dragon is in close range and conscious. If he is so ill or wounded that he can't answer, it wouldn't be any different than if you were calling out to him.* He blew out a plume of steam, heating the center of the room.

Paxton backed away, raising his hands in the air. "I was only checking. After all, we all have moments of stupidity, especially when we're tired. Even if we're extremely intelligent."

Ulrieg's glower lessened slightly.

Paxton shifted closer to the door. "When you're ready, we'll get that food from my room before we go to our next lesson."

Nodding, Samara picked up Gray's stand from the floor. "Just give me a moment." She catered to the owl, ensuring he had enough food and water to last through the day, then grabbed her stuff, ignoring the last few things in the room that needed straightening.

They traveled through the corridor that held most of the females' rooms and passed across the joining balcony overlooking the common room on one side and the internal courtyard on the other.

Warning! Vexx and his snake are in the corridor.

Heeding Ulrieg's words, Samara peeked over the railing and glimpsed Vexx's spiky red hair. Quickly, she shifted to the courtyard side of the balcony, followed by Paxton. If Vexx was on the hunt for the people who stole his last dragon, they needed to be out of his sight for as long as possible. They scurried along the corridor that mostly held the males' rooms.

Paxton turned the door handle to his room before looking at her with a slight bashfulness. "Um, I would ask you to excuse the mess, but I guess you've already seen it when you were searching for the potion to get me out of that stupor from potions class."

Gently, Samara touched his shoulder, and a surprising warmth traveled through her arm and into her body. "I wouldn't call your room messy.

Cluttered, yes, and full of useful items, but not messy."

Jojo stuck his head out of Paxton's pocket and croaked.

Paxton smiled. "Jojo says it's perfect for hiding."

Paxton and Samara chuckled, and they entered his room. When Paxton closed the door behind them, Ulrieg turned visible and climbed the stone wall to blow fire onto the torch. A dull light filled the room, and memories of the last time Samara had been here filled her mind.

Potions were still strewn across his desk and filled boxes on the floor under the desk and at the bottoms of the bookshelves along the wall. Educational books, mostly, filled his bookshelves, stacked until they were almost overflowing.

Running a hand over the spines, Samara asked, "Are these all your books, or are they from the library?" She pulled one from the shelf without reading the title and flicked through the pages.

Paxton took something off his desk and glanced over his shoulder. "Some are from my home and some, the library. Some are borrowed from different instructors."

He placed a hand under hers and took the book from her, his hand warm as it held the back of hers, lingering a few moments longer. Sensation fluttered through her hand and up her arm. She swallowed, confusing emotions passing through her. It was such a gentle touch, and although Paxton couldn't boast the charm that overflowed from Kaine, this simple gesture made her legs suddenly unsteady.

When she looked into Paxton's eyes, they were filled with the warmth she had come to know recently. His quietness had been etched away with every secret they shared and with the aid he'd given her and the dragons. When he smiled, she almost lost her balance. It was the most genuine smile she had seen in a long time. Nothing could surprise her more.

Only when the sensation changed as something was placed into her palm did Samara realize she was staring openly. Embarrassed, she glanced down at her hand as Paxton folded her fingers over something. She gaped at the large chunk of bread in her palm, blushing as she chastised herself for her stupidity. They had come here for food.

"Thank you," she blurted.

Paxton squeezed her hand before releasing it. "I have some dried fruit and nuts in a bowl on my desk if you would like them as well."

Glad for the distraction, she went to the desk and took a handful from the bowl, her back to him and the room.

"How have you and Kaine been?" Paxton asked. "Has he settled down and realized he's overreacting?"

Sighing, Samara faced him. "No. I don't think he's ever going to get over it. Even though we haven't talked about it, I think our brief relationship is over. I think he's moved on with Luna." She placed some nuts and dried fruit in her mouth, waiting for a quip from Ulrieg, but none came.

Paxton sat on his bed. "Honestly, I think you can do much better than him."

Samara scoffed. "Oh, really?"

He leaned back on his hands, his eyes never leaving her. "You are kind, caring, and beautiful."

She sucked in a breath, and a piece of nut stuck in her throat. She coughed, and he poured her a cup of water and handed it to her.

Paxton watched as she tried to wash her throat clear. "You deserve someone who will treat you better."

She swallowed more water, not knowing where to look. *Aren't you going to help me here, Ulrieg?*

Ha! And why would I do that? You already know my opinion. It hasn't changed, and I'm sure not going to discourage him.

Glaring at Ulrieg as he climbed on the bed, Samara leaned against the desk, setting the cup beside her. She didn't know how to respond. Paxton had proven himself to be a loyal, kind-hearted person, but her emotions were a mess with everything going on. To keep herself busy, she finished her water.

Paxton rose from the bed and placed a palm on her shoulder. "Are you ready to go to our first lesson?"

Warmth flooded through her again from his touch. Samara stood, scooped up the last of her food, and nodded.

CHAPTER FOUR

Paxton and Samara were on their way to their first lesson when Callista's magic summoned them to a meeting. Changing direction, they headed toward the meeting hall with a flood of apprentices.

Samara found each step more difficult than the last. She hoped it was only a coincidence that this meeting had been called the morning after she, Paxton, Daena, and Ulrieg had taken the last living dragon from the underground. If it wasn't, that meant she may have been spotted by Callista or Kellam in the catacombs.

Her heart pounded rapidly against her rib cage as the crowd entered the large hall. Instructors lined the side of the room under the large, high windows, their familiars either sitting at their feet or on their person. Zofia, the weapons master, stood close to the front, her sun bear, Jet, sitting proudly near her.

With Mystique by her side, Callista was seated at the front of the room in her throne-like chair of interwoven branches. The backrest displayed a fresh arrangement of flowers magically enchanted by the head sorceress.

Callista wore a green leaf-patterned dress and sat with her back straight, legs crossed at the knees, and arms draped on the armrests. She adjusted her golden diadem, pressing it firmly against her forehead as though ensuring the crystals under the headdress were in contact with her skin.

Something seemed different about the head sorceress. Her expressionless face almost seemed to glow, and Samara wondered if it was from her visit to the orb.

Then Samara's eyes caught a movement that made her want to retrace her footsteps out the door. Vexx and Kellam hovered in one of the room's front corners as though having a private conversation, Kellam's snub-nosed monkey at his feet and Vexx's yellow snake slithered around his shoulders. The sorcerers' eyes landed on Samara and Paxton, and goose bumps ran across Samara's neck. She hadn't brought Gray, and although Ulrieg was somewhere close in his invisible form, she suddenly felt bare and exposed.

Vexx and Kellam marched over to join Callista, their long dark-brown cloaks billowing out at the sides, hoods down and exposing their brilliantly colored hair. They stood on either side of Callista, their faces distorted in scowls and fingers flexing by their sides.

Worrying her bottom lip and trying to ignore the sorcerers, Samara led Paxton down the short aisle to the second row of chairs. Even if they weren't responsible for the dragon disappearing from the cave, it would be challenging for Samara and Paxton to act innocent when they were constantly under the sorcerers' unwanted scrutiny.

Kaine sat at the front on the opposite side, one arm wrapped around Luna's shoulder and the other draped over the back of Mist's chair. Mist's crow, Okak, sat on the wooden rafters, while Ginger curled up at Kaine's feet and a rabbit familiar, Coco, sat on Luna's lap. The younger apprentices filled in the remaining chairs.

Waiting for everyone to settle unnerved Samara, and she picked at her nails, jumping when Paxton placed a gentle hand on her fidgeting ones. She met his gaze, calmed by the depth showing in his brown eyes. She suspected that he was concerned, yet his touch filled her with peace that flowed from her hands through her body as though he was working some kind of calming magic. She drew from that peace, conjuring up a weak smile and squeezing his hand before turning her attention back to the front of the room, dreading the fear that might flood her if she let go of his hand. He didn't pull away as he faced the front of the room.

Once the final apprentice entered, Callista raised her hands, silencing the soft hum of conversation. "I've called you all here this morning to make an announcement. Vexx and Kellam have agreed that some of the senior apprentices are ready. The chosen apprentices will be taken to the borders to spend time learning to defend our kingdoms. It's the perfect opportunity to have their training expanded by the senior sorcerers' expertise in real-life situations."

Face unreadable despite the announcement of her apprentices' advancement, Callista observed the room. "The chosen ones will be the senior apprentices who have discovered and enhanced their additional unique magic powers. They would have shown their growth since bonding with their familiar."

Samara's fingers tightened around Paxton's as alarm coursed through her. His powers of healing and manipulating plants had grown. Although he had kept it a secret from the others, she wondered if Ginger had informed Kaine of how Paxton had healed Byzarid, and Kaine had told Callista. She didn't want to lose the only fellow apprentice she could trust, the one she would need if they found Byzarid again and he required healing.

Callista turned to Vexx and Kellam. "Go to your selected apprentices and inform the rest of your reasoning."

The snub-nosed monkey paced the floor around Kellam as the sorcerer approached the apprentices in the front row on the opposite side of the room. Kellam's nose turned up as his gaze fell on Kaine. His disgust at Kaine's humanness cleared before Kellam turned to Mist. His back straightened as he fixed his gaze on the elf and addressed her by her formal name. "Kanara, you have shown that your magic not only creates a thick fog but has also grown to wield lightning strong enough to cause a being a considerable shock, robbing its victims of their immediate functions. I have chosen you to be my understudy."

Okak cawed from the rafters as Mist stood, her shoulders pulling back and pride filling her face. She inclined her head, her sword knocking against her chair. "I promise I will work hard not to fail you."

Kellam led her to the front of the room, and Okak landed on her shoulder, the crow's head held high.

Vexx moved then, and Samara's body stiffened as he seemed to head toward their seats. His gaze wandered over the gathered students, stopping at Paxton, only to change direction as he reached the short aisle. Instead, he approached Kaine, his hand outstretched. "Kaine, I have chosen you to train under me, for you have increased your ability to charm others into telling you anything, including their secrets. It is a powerful weapon when assessing a subject's true intentions."

Kaine grabbed Vexx's hand, and Ginger sprang up as Kaine let Vexx pull him to his feet. His steps were sure, exuding confidence, as he followed Vexx to the front of the room. Only slight remorse shadowed his face when he gazed at Luna.

Raising her chin, Callista projected her voice above the chatter circulating through the crowd. "Vexx, Kellam, Mist, and Kaine will leave today to further their training." She nodded at Mist and Kaine. "Learn well. The kingdoms are relying on you."

The senior sorcerers led their selected apprentices out of the room, all four familiars following them, as all eyes tracked their departure.

Samara breathed a sigh of relief. She mustn't have been spotted in the catacombs. "For a while, I thought Vexx was going to take you," she whispered to Paxton. "I admit, I'm selfishly glad you weren't chosen."

Paxton retrieved Jojo from his tunic pocket. "Jojo said he's glad I kept my advanced magic a secret. He didn't want to go with the evil sorcerers."

Jojo croaked, catching Samara's attention.

"I'm glad too," she confessed. "I was worried about what I would do without another apprentice to consult with. I'd miss your company. This way, you'll be around to heal Byzarid if he is found wounded again."

So much for Pretty Boy's loyalty. You saved his life from the trolls, and he can't even say goodbye with a smile. By the look on Paxton's face, Ulrieg had also projected this comment to him.

Samara met Paxton's eyes before looking up at the rafters. "There's no use worrying about what Kaine does anymore. I'm certain we are finished. And the way he's been acting lately, I wouldn't expect anything more, whether I saved him or not."

Three loud claps cut through the chatter of the remaining apprentices, and everyone turned back to Callista. "The rest of you can leave to attend your normal class, except the older students who have bonded with a familiar. I need all of them to remain here."

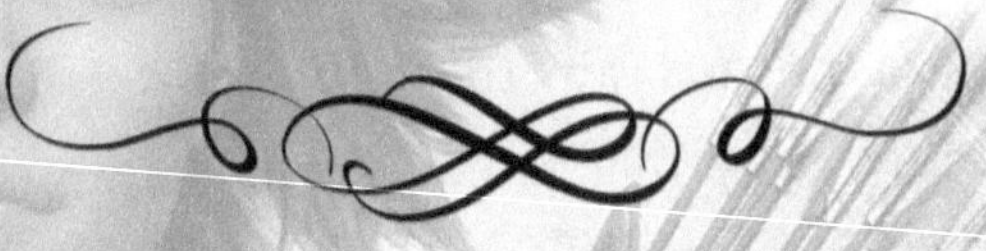

Tension seized Samara's neck. "I hope this isn't another talking-to like we had before we bonded with our familiars. Either we advance, get kicked out, or prove ourselves some other way, like going up against an unfair number of trolls."

"At the moment, if it weren't for my family's protection being removed, I wouldn't mind getting kicked out," Paxton whispered. "They were constantly in danger before I joined."

She nodded. "That, and I'd love to know if there's a way to protect the kingdoms."

Sure there is. Just find Dragoria and lead all the dragon elves to the land of the dragons, and they'll fight for the people. Ulrieg's voice was filled with love and wonder, a far cry from his usual sarcastic tone.

Samara's heart warmed. "Your optimism is

inspiring, except somehow, I doubt it will be that easy."

"It's not a bad idea." Paxton rubbed one arm. "We'll still need to ensure our families won't suffer first."

Samara pushed air through her teeth. "Don't forget how risky that journey will be, especially if we're working against Vexx and traveling across his borders."

The room fell silent as the last of the younger apprentices departed, leaving Peadar in the middle of the first row, one row up from Paxton and Samara, while Luna remained on the other side of the aisle.

Callista glanced over them. "Come to the front of the room. We have a lot of work to do."

When it didn't seem as though the head sorceress was going to threaten them, the anxiety eased from the room. It appeared no one was being removed from the coterie at that moment.

Samara and Paxton moved to the front next to Peadar, shoes shuffling on the stone floor.

Callista rose from her chair and approached them, Mystique prowling behind her. "We need to activate your special gifts from your familiar bond." Callista's long gown weaved around her legs as she walked.

Peadar scooped up Ziggy and scratched the raccoon behind his ear. "Head sorceress, what is your special gift? You seem to have so many."

Callista's mouth rose in the slightest of smiles. "It is true. I have many because I consult with the orb and the three crystals in my office. But my natural gift from my familiar bond is amplifying the crystals' magic, and with this gift, I am able to call you from a great distance to meet me at a designated meeting spot."

"But can't Vexx and Kellam also call us with their magic?" Paxton asked.

The head sorceress waved her hands out to her sides. "Yes, that is true. But their call isn't as strong as mine and can't reach as far. It may seem comparable when you're within the same building or area, but I assure you it isn't." She paced in front of the seats, her eyes trained on the apprentices. "Have any of you noticed an elevation of your natural gifts since bonding with your familiars?"

The room remained silent, as if each apprentice's senses were fine-tuned for the slightest movement of their colleagues, all of them curious about whether the others had managed to outperform them.

"Anyone?" Callista cupped Luna's chin and lifted it. "What about you?"

Luna shook her head, her eyes downcast.

After Peadar shook his head, Samara willed herself not to look at Paxton when the head sorceress focused on them. It was up to Paxton to tell them when he was ready. Her eyes met Callista's briefly as Samara shook her head. While it appeared that the head sorceress hadn't spotted her in the catacombs earlier, Samara's relief was washed away by the shame that, once again, she hadn't progressed as quickly in her studies as she was expected to.

The head sorceress nodded. "All right. We have a lot of work to do. That's why I've retained you four here. There may also be the possibility that your magic talent has expanded, but you haven't realized it yet. That is what happened with Kaine. He is already extremely charming and has such confidence that when his magic powers expanded on that charm, he was unaware of its additional effect."

Ulrieg shifted. *Dragon dung! He knew. He was just making excuses for his bad behavior.*

The edges of Paxton's mouth lifted slightly as he struggled to keep the smile from his face, forcing it down before Callista's eyes landed on him.

It was difficult to tell if Callista was upset with them when her face remained expressionless as she observed each of them in turn. "Having a small class will allow me to work with you all individually." She stopped in front of Peadar. "What are you naturally good at?"

Peadar clasped his hands behind his back and kicked the floor with the toe of his house shoe. "Being clumsy."

Ulrieg's raucous laughter traveled through his bond with Samara. *He's got that right!*

Don't be mean, Ulrieg. It's true that he's clumsy, but he's got to be good at something. Besides, he seems to have a good heart.

I know, I know. He can't hear me. I'm just surprised that he hasn't sliced himself with his machete. At least he knows how to hold it right.

Callista placed a hand on Peadar's shoulder. "I know that has often been a problem for you. Has it improved at all since you bonded with Ziggy?"

Peadar shook his head, then his forehead creased. "Although maybe I'm less clumsy while using my weapon."

The head sorceress pursed her lips. "I don't think that is it. Let's ponder your gifts as I converse with the others."

Callista headed toward Luna, her crystal-blue eyes assessing the beautiful elf as she neared. "How about you, Luna? What is your enhanced magic going to be?" Dipping her hand into a hidden pocket at her hip, she pulled out a few crystals and tossed them in her hand.

The tall elf gazed at Peadar, and the male approached her, his eyes clouded with admiration. Luna shrugged. "I'm ashamed to say I don't know."

Callista watched as Peadar passed her by and stood beside Luna. She scowled and turned to Paxton. "Does Luna draw you toward her as though she has a rope tied around you and is pulling you close?"

Paxton glanced at Samara before returning his attention to the head sorceress. "I'd be lying if I didn't say that she is gorgeous, and something about her is alluring. But for me, it's not uncontrollable."

"Paxton seems to be able to see the reality of what's happening before others," Samara explained. "He could see through Kaine's charm well before I could. I can confirm that Luna certainly grabs Kaine's attention and obviously Peadar's."

Callista nodded. "What about you, then? Does Luna draw you as well?"

Samara shook her head. "To be honest, I haven't been around her much, but she hasn't in the past. She seems to grab many males' attention, though, which I thought was because she is beautiful and likes to hug them."

She didn't miss the look of distaste Luna sent her

way. Whether it was because what Samara said had offended Luna or Kaine had told Luna something about Samara, she didn't know. The beautiful elf covered her emotions with a giggle and wrapped her arm around Peadar's shoulders.

Callista's lips pursed. "That's true, but I feel there is more to this than her looks. She doesn't have charm like Kaine but still has a siren-like effect on many males, possibly even females, if taught properly."

Then Callista approached Paxton. "What about you?"

Jojo stuck his head out of Paxton's pocket, his throat bobbing as though he was having a conversation with his bonded. Paxton fiddled with his fingers before clasping them behind his back and looking Callista in the eye. "It's not that impressive, but I've been able to manipulate plants."

Callista arched one lilac eyebrow. "Interesting. What do you mean?"

Paxton gripped his hands together tightly. "Well, when Blade died on the field trip Zofia took us on, I didn't want to leave him to be eaten by animals. So I manipulated the roots of the nearby trees to create a natural coffin."

The head sorceress's eyes widened ever so slightly. "That's very caring—and certainly out of the norm. You have a natural ability to care for plants, and it's laudable that you can get them to do things for you."

Peadar looked impressed. "Wow! That's a fantastic gift. I wish I could do something like that." He seemed to have come to his senses now that Luna had shifted away from him.

Samara noticed that Paxton didn't tell Callista about his healing ability. It was probably a good thing, seeing as how those powers were responsible for saving and healing the dragons.

Callista shifted her attention to Samara. "How about you?"

Samara expelled a sigh. "No. Nothing has changed."

The head sorceress looked around the room. "Where is your familiar?"

"I've left him in the room to catch up on some sleep."

Callista leveled her gaze at Samara. "You need him for lessons like this."

"I'm sorry. I didn't know he was required when I heard your call."

After a beat, Callista nodded. "I imagine not. I didn't give any warning." She strolled a few steps away as Mystique watched her from the other side. "You do have a special gift that no one else has."

Samara frowned. "What do you mean?"

"You can spell your arrows to do different things. None of the other apprentices or magic wielders I know can do this. It is a special gift." Callista paused. "Perhaps you should go to your room and retrieve your familiar and your bow and arrows."

"Now?" Samara stiffened.

"Yes. I think that is best."

Samara turned to leave, hearing Callista's voice behind her saying, "Luna, I'm certain your gift is as I discussed. Now that you know, you only need to practice it. I won't need you or Paxton any longer, so the two of you may go to class. I will focus on Peadar while I wait for Samara to return."

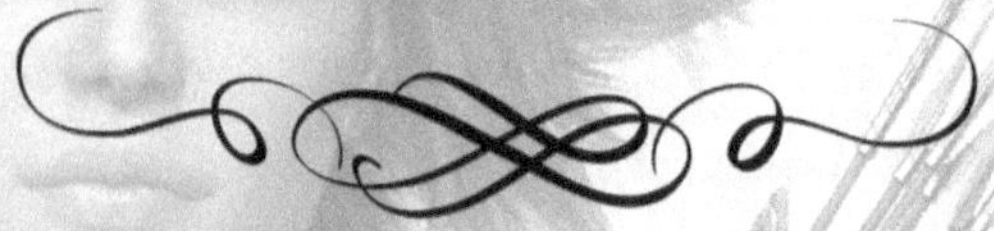

CHAPTER SIX

Samara wasted no time grabbing her bow and quiver, taking a little longer to collect Gray. He wasn't happy about being pulled off his perch so early in the morning, and it took a little coaxing before he slowly climbed onto her hand. Her boots drumming down the steps and Gray's claws digging into her shoulder, Samara quickly returned to the hall where Callista was working with Peadar, only to find him heading toward the door.

She paused a few feet inside the room. "Are you finished already?"

Standing in front, Ziggy chattered at her, his eyes flicking to Gray.

Peadar crouched low to pick up his familiar, telling him, "She can't understand you, but I like how you're proud of me."

Samara smiled. "Of course he's proud of you. You're his bonded."

"And he also knows how clumsy I am." Paxton played with Ziggy's paw as the raccoon's masked eyes watched his bonded.

"Still, he has every reason to be proud of you." Callista was making her way toward them. "Come, Samara. It's your turn to find out what your unique magical power will be."

Apprehension flooded Samara, and she jumped slightly when talons climbed up her leg and onto her back. Gray's wings buffeted her over the head as he settled, his feet secured by the invisible Ulrieg.

Don't worry. If I get too heavy or in the way, I'll get off you, but I can feel your apprehension, so I'm getting closer to see if it helps.

Samara raised her hands to block Gray's blows. The dragon's invisible form probably startled him as well. *Thanks, Ulrieg. I feel a little nervous, knowing I will be alone with Callista.* She turned to find Callista focusing on her. *And clearly, I'm going to be under her scrutiny.*

Although the head sorceress's face was expressionless, her eyes held a distinct curiosity, as though she was amused by what was playing out in front of her.

Samara didn't know if Callista's reaction was

because she knew what was happening or because she was trying to assess Gray's restlessness.

Callista tilted her head to one side, watching the owl. "You have quite a free spirit there. Don't you?"

Samara straightened her back and tried to simultaneously act both confident and relaxed.

Raising one purple eyebrow, Callista added, "I'm not surprised you are struggling to find your stronger, unique power. Often, magic wielders with strong-spirited familiars will eventually hold stronger magic once they have sorted out their bond. Mystique was very strong-willed, and I was like you. I didn't excel in my unique magic instantly. It took some practice and a lot of determination."

Mystique sauntered to Callista's side, watching Samara. The jaguar's yellow eyes narrowed as she gazed at the shoulder that carried the invisible Ulrieg. Samara couldn't help turning slightly to pull that shoulder away from the leering jaguar.

The way the large cat sometimes scrutinized the area around Ulrieg, it almost appeared as though she could see him. Most likely, the reason was her acute sense of smell. But the thought of Mystique suspecting Ulrieg's existence caused panic to surge through Samara. If Mystique knew about her dragon, then surely, Callista would also know about him. But whenever she met with the head sorceress, she never let her knowledge of Ulrieg show.

More likely, Samara was overly paranoid over Mystique, and Callista simply didn't know that Ulrieg was her dragon familiar.

"Now, what can you do with your arrows? I've seen you conduct some incantations on them to make them act differently from normal ones. I've heard you can make beings freeze into statues or have nightmares—or really, daymares. You can make people see their biggest fear and many more. This is a special gift." Callista studied the tip of the bow showing over Samara's shoulder.

Knowing her every move was being watched, Samara reached over her shoulder for the bow, carefully avoiding Ulrieg and Gray. She turned it over in her hands.

At the whooshing sound of Callista's gown, Ulrieg pushed off Samara's shoulder, his sudden shift in weight causing her body to sway. Gray's wing hit her over the head as Samara pretended to wave her bow to counteract the unusual body movement. After giving a hoot of displeasure, Gray flew up to the rafters.

Her soft house shoes skimming the floor, Callista reached over Samara's shoulder where Ulrieg had been sitting only moments before, grabbing an arrow from the quiver.

That was close and random, Ulrieg muttered.

Yes, it was. Samara studied Callista's face. Even this close, it was difficult to tell what was going through the sorceress's mind.

The head sorceress twirled the arrow shaft in her fingers before she handed it to Samara. "These are all very unique incantations."

Samara grabbed the arrow from Callista. "Yes. But this was magic I was doing before I bonded with my familiar."

"Just as Kaine was charming everyone he could before he bonded with Ginger. Perhaps there is a way to strengthen this magic, or you can conduct other spells on the arrows that weren't possible before." Callista pursed her lips. "After you have used the arrow for its enchanted purpose, do you have to enchant it again, or does it keep the enchantment forever?"

Samara scratched her temple. "I must enchant it every time, or it will be an ordinary arrow."

"So no one else can pick it up and benefit from the arrow's enchantment?"

Samara fiddled with the tip and shook her head. "No. That way, the spell can't be used against me because it's already been used."

"What if you used it to create an opening through a wall or other surface?"

Samara frowned. "Through a wall?"

"Yes, of course. Have you not tried that?"

"No. I've only considered incantations that can be used against beings without seriously hurting them."

"There's something new to try. It could be classed as advancing your current skills, although I imagine it would only work on a surface vulnerable to an arrow. I assume it wouldn't work on stone."

Samara waved a hand over the arrow. *"Aperti."* She then nocked and raised it, pointed it at a chair in the front row, and let it fly. The arrow hit the chair's back, and the wooden rest disappeared, the arrow hovering horizontally where the chair rest had been only a few moments ago.

Now that's something! Ulrieg sounded astonished.

Samara stepped over the chair seat and put her leg through the invisible back. Her leg didn't connect with anything, nor did the chair topple like it usually would if she had kicked the back.

After she had stepped through, she reached back and yanked the arrow out. A split second later, the back of the chair reappeared. She blinked in astonishment.

"Why don't you try the door?" Callista crossed

the room and closed the wooden door before standing back and watching Samara expectantly.

Muttering the incantation, she nocked and shot the arrow, her mouth twitching into a wry smile moments after the expected thud. A hole grew large enough around the arrow for her to climb through. The arrow once again hovered in midair.

Is she sure she should be teaching you something like this? It almost seems she's teaching you a way to escape if things go astray.

After glancing at Callista and pondering over what Ulrieg had said, Samara climbed through the hole, struggling with the height she had made. It was about half a foot too high for her legs. She would have to remember to embed the arrows lower in the future. *If she is doing this on purpose, then perhaps there's still hope that she doesn't support Vexx and Kellam's treatment of the dragons and dragon elf.*

She ignored Ulrieg as he grunted and climbed through, grabbed the arrow, and pulled it free, ensuring she removed her arm from the unnatural hole before the wood returned after a few breaths. "What would happen if part of my body was still in the gap when the solid material closed back?"

"We should find out." Callista pulled a large leaf from her floral display on the back of her chair and waited as Samara created another hole in the door.

Callista balanced it on the bottom of the opening, and Samara pulled the arrow out of the door. The hole filled in, leaving the leaf stuck in the door, one end sticking out on their side, and when Callista opened the door, the other end was sticking out the back.

"I'll try to get it out." Samara enchanted the arrow and aimed for the spot she thought she had hit earlier. The hole reappeared, and the leaf fell from the door, cut in two. She cringed. "I'm guessing if that was my arm, it would also be cut in half."

Callista's mouth thinned. "It looks that way. I wouldn't recommend you try it."

This would be so spectacular if it worked on the walls, even though they're stone. Ulrieg couldn't restrain his enthusiasm.

Keen to try again, Samara enchanted the arrow and eyed the wall. "So far, I've only tried wood. Are you sure it wouldn't work on the stone wall? It has so many joints. What happens if the arrow embeds in one of them?"

"Why don't you try? Your aim must be accurate or lucky to get in the cracks."

Samara aimed for one of the joints, but she missed it by a finger's width, and the arrow bounced to the floor. Grabbing another arrow from her quiver, she tried again, this time slightly embedding the arrow in the joint. The arrow wobbled, threatening to fall, until it stilled and created a hole big enough for her to climb through.

She raced over and peered through the hole. There was a slight drop off the side. It was surreal, sticking her head through the stone wall, and she pulled back, dislodging the arrow and gathering the first arrow off the floor as the stones sealed off in front of her.

Callista looked pleased. "I believe you already have your gift, and it's growing stronger."

Samara frowned. "But I've basically been doing the same thing, just with a different idea and spell."

Callista clasped her hands in front. "And that's what happened with the others. Over the next few weeks, I want you to use your imagination and come up with more spell ideas to use on your arrows. I'll check back with you later."

What she says seems to be true, Ulrieg confirmed. *Like she said, Kaine was already charming, but after he bonded with Ginger, he appeared to be almost obsessively charming, especially when he touched someone he wanted to extract information from.*

Samara scowled at the thought of Kaine but pushed it aside. "All right," she said to Callista. "I think I see what you mean."

"Wonderful! Now you can see if you can join the others in your regular class before it finishes."

Samara packed her arrows away in the quiver and hooked the bow on her back before calling Gray down from the rafters. She turned to leave.

"Oh, and Samara."

She turned back and faced Callista as the head sorceress came over to fiddle with some strands of Samara's hair. "Yes?"

Callista rubbed Samara's pink strands between her fingers. "You need to emboss your hair with its magical color again. The pink is fading."

Samara nodded, unsure how to take Callista's touch. She wasn't usually an affectionate sort. "I'll work on that on my way to the lesson."

"Yes, make sure you do that."

Samara turned to leave but froze when Callista added, "I particularly noticed how dull it has become this morning when I saw you in the catacombs."

Samara's heart drummed rapidly against her rib cage as though trying to break out. Her legs refused to move, and a chill ran down her spine. Callista's tone sounded bland and factual, throwing Samara off, making her unsure how to react.

CHAPTER SEVEN

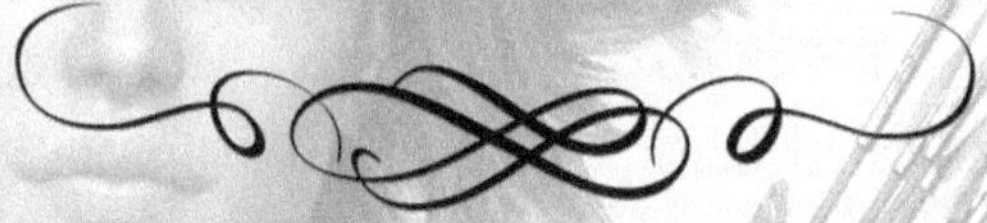

S amara nodded, not daring to look at the head sorceress before forcing her legs to march her quickly out the door.

Ulrieg raced behind. *Dragon moon! We've been busted. Well, you definitely have. I don't know about me.*

Wow! Thanks for your encouraging words, Ulrieg. You're really making me feel better.

Am I? He sounded surprised.

No! She yelled down their bond.

Then I just want to say that you responded with finesse. She wouldn't suspect a thing. He paused. *Other than you're completely guilty.*

What would be the point in denying it when she knew it was me and clearly saw my hair, and her only correction was that it should be brighter? Samara ran her fingers over the strands of her hair, infusing them with magic and brightening the pink as Callista had requested. She knew it was a mark of distinction and superiority for the Sacred Flame coterie, but it wasn't practical. If anything, it placed a mark on them, making it easier for the enemy to track them during a battle and exposing them and making it difficult to hide in the forest—or, in her case, the dark catacombs.

I know you're not really the one to ask, but I'm confused. What do you think it means that Callista didn't react to me being in the catacombs? Does that mean she isn't worried I was somewhere I wasn't supposed to be? Or that she will keep an extra-close eye on me and I'm already in trouble but don't know it?

Ulrieg's wings pushed air over Samara as he flew above her. *You know I can't give you an unbiased answer to that. And I recommend you stop making your hair pinker, or you will stand out from across the other side of the realm.*

Is it that bright?

Yes. How are you supposed to hide if you need to escape the coterie?

Maybe that's the point. Samara's shoulders sagged. Brighter hair would make it harder to sneak around, looking for Byzarid, and to stay hidden while checking the cave for more captives.

Maybe you should get Paxton to do more of the

sneaking around.

Samara shook her head. *Paxton's hair is less conspicuous, except every time he helps us, he's placed in more danger. I don't want to do that.* Samara reached the bottom of the stairs and paused, groaning. *Wingless flight!*

What? Ulrieg's talons tapped on the stair railings.

I've just remembered what lesson I'm supposed to be going to. I've been so lost in thought that I'd forgotten.

And what lesson is it?

Samara sighed. *It's weapons training with Zofia. Her tactics were harsh enough, but now, I know she's also part of the group that tortures and kills dragons and dragon elves.* She climbed the stairs. *I must grab my cloak to hide my hair. I can only hope the lesson will be over by the time I arrive.*

Maybe you can skip it and check the strange door in the catacombs. If Zofia asks you, you could say you were held up with Callista for the whole lesson.

And then all she has to do to check is ask Callista. Yeah. I don't think that's a great idea. Besides, if we find anyone in the room, it's not like we can sneak them out in daylight. Anybody could see me sneaking in the hole.

You forget, the bush covering the hole will hide you from prying eyes.

Samara reached her door. *We'll see when we get outside. I need my cloak anyway.* After entering, she lifted Gray onto his perch and fetched her cloak. On her way out the door, she eyed Gray. She knew that she would possibly be asked questions about where her familiar was, but it was much easier to leave the owl in her room to sleep than pretend he was her familiar all the time. She decided to leave him and descended the stairs to the common room, remaining on full alert. The building seemed empty as they made their way to the front door. *I wonder if Kaine and Mist have left yet.*

Probably. They rushed out of the meeting with Callista, so I don't think the sorcerers wanted to waste time.

As they traveled down the outside stairs, it felt like they were the only ones around, even though Samara knew Callista and Mystique were still inside the building, and other instructors would be around somewhere. She decided to move closer to the bush that led into the catacombs. *What do you think? Are we safe?*

I can check the windows on this side and have a quick scout around the edges of the forest. I'll let you know if I see anyone.

Trying to remain inconspicuous, Samara pulled a

few arrows out of her quiver and enchanted them with different magic spells, including a couple with the opening spell, and hooked them against her thigh. If anyone saw her doing this, they would think she was preparing for the lesson with Zofia. Above her, dark clouds caught her eye. A storm was brewing. Rain would make for a very unpleasant lesson with Zofia.

Several moments passed before she heard the beat of Ulrieg's wings rustling the wildflowers as he approached. *All looks good. I can't see anyone near the windows on this side of the building, and the forest edge is clear.* The ground thumped as he landed next to her.

Then I guess I'll risk it. We'll have to hurry if we want to beat the storm. The stairs have proven to be extremely slippery when it rains. Samara crouched behind the bush and entered the hole leading to the catacombs. Her boots drummed softly down the stairs, followed by the clack of Ulrieg's talons. She grabbed the torch off the wall and headed to the door of the room Ulrieg was keen to investigate.

Then the dragon stopped her. *Wait!*

Samara paused and looked down at Ulrieg's visible form, difficult to see in the dark corridor even with the torchlight. *What's wrong?*

The sensation I was getting from the door has changed.

Is it better?

Ulrieg sat still, his back straight, and lines formed on his forehead. *I don't know. I'm confused. I get a sensation of relief but also of terror.*

There's only one way to find out. Samara reached for the handle. It wouldn't turn. She tried the unlocking spell. *"Aperti."* Nothing. She tried again. The handle still wouldn't move. They hadn't found a spot for the coven's emblem, which left only one last option.

Pulling the bow off her back, Samara nocked one of the charmed arrows from her leg and shot it into the door. Slowly, the hole opened, and she climbed through, shining the torch into the darkness of the room. Something caught her eye, and when she saw what it was, her heart thumped wildly, screaming in her ears. She turned to find Ulrieg halfway through the hole and hurried over to him. *I think you should stay out there for this one.*

Ulrieg's red eyes filled with disbelief, but before he could answer her, she shoved him back through the hole, and he fell to the ground. At the same time, she yanked the arrow out of the door, a sure way to ensure Ulrieg didn't attempt to climb through again. The hole disappeared between them. *Samara. What are you doing? Let me in.*

I'm sorry, Ulrieg. It's not a good idea. Heart heavy,

she turned away from the door and sucked in a deep breath, holding the torch high. She had spotted something distressing in that room, and it was a sight Ulrieg wasn't ready to see.

CHAPTER EIGHT

Samara, *let me in.* Ulrieg's voice burned with frustration.

Sorry. I can't do that. I'll let you know how I go.

Flames lapped under the door.

Samara groaned. *You'll only call attention to us if you burn the door down. It's not the best idea when it could land us both in danger.*

A growl sounded through their bond. *Your going in alone is the stupidest thing you could do.*

Nice try, but I'm not changing my mind. Besides, you calling things "stupid" is getting old. Blocking out further insults, Samara held the torch high, illuminating the small room's area, which looked like a tiny space made of stone, possibly a cave.

She approached the crumpled figure in the corner of the room with hesitant steps. The room smelled of feces and what Samara was beginning to think might be rotting flesh. She hoped she was wrong, but that hope faded a little more with each step.

The light of the flame flickered over the figure, distinguishing it as a dragon as she got closer. What was worse, it was a brown dragon about Ulrieg's size. She hoped the tainted-flesh smell was because of infected wounds, but the figure in the corner didn't move.

The words formed on her lips, and she didn't know how they exited her mouth. "Byzarid, is that you? Are you all right?" Only a soft echo in the room confirmed she had indeed spoken them.

Something crunched under her boot, and she glanced down to see a dismembered talon on the floor. Bile rose in her throat, yet she pressed on, stepping around the talon. The light flickered harder against the walls as her arm trembled. "Byzarid?" She wasn't sure, but the dragon looked like him from what she could see.

She reached the dragon's side and listened for signs of life. None came. The dragon's back pressed against the floor and wall, and his jaw rested on his chest. Carefully, she lifted the unmoving dragon's head by the chin, looking for any reaction, only to spot a large gaping hole in the middle of his chest.

Crying out, she dropped the head and retracted as it flopped over to the side, leaving the hole exposed.

What is it? Ulrieg called impatiently.

I'm all right. She ignored the real question he wanted her to answer. She wet her lips just before her stomach bounced, emptying its contents against the wall. As much as she didn't want to, she would have to tell Ulrieg. She retched again, thinking, *It's going to devastate him.* They had tried so hard to keep Byzarid safe. Paxton's efforts to heal him had been undone.

When her stomach settled, Samara steeled her nerves and had a closer inspection. He had been tortured far worse than the dragons they had discovered the previous night, and even worse, Byzarid had been killed during it. She didn't understand what the senior sorcerers' reasonings were for doing this. She wondered if they knew the dragons could speak if they wanted to and were persecuting them to find out information. She hoped this wasn't the case, or all the dragons in Wraeyanor would be in danger.

What a waste of a wonderful creature. His body was still slightly warm, so he couldn't have been dead for long. If only they hadn't been spotted this morning, maybe he could have been saved.

Squatting down, she gently lifted Byzarid's chin again and studied the damage he had suffered. The rotting smell wasn't from him. Perhaps it was something else. Maybe it was in the room before. Heart heavy with grief, she lowered his head and quickly inspected the room. A door on the other side probably led to the official entrance for this little cave. She needed to be quick. If someone came through that door, she couldn't explain her presence.

The torchlight scanned over something in the corner, and she approached it only to see Kaida's tiny form crumpled in the corner, the cause of the potent smell.

Daena would be devastated to know how her bonded dragon had been treated. It might be best if she never found out.

Samara had seen enough. It was time to leave and face Ulrieg. She placed the torch on the floor and refired her arrow into the door, quickly picking it up after the satisfying *thunk*. She scurried to the hole, only to see her black dragon dive through the hole and into the room.

No, Ulrieg! Helpless, she held out her hand as if that would stop him, hurrying toward him to block the sight of Byzarid.

She was too late. Ulrieg scurried around her

directly to his cousin's still form. A heart-stopping keening echoed through their bond.

Samara's shoulders caved. There was nothing she could do to protect him from his cousin's fate now. She approached him slowly, wanting to throw her arms around him, hoping to comfort him. Instead, she might end up with one of his horns jabbed into her flesh. Crouching by him, she gently placed a hand on his side, hoping her touch would be a comfort. She'd wanted to gently break the news to him, not have him see his cousin like this. *Ulrieg, I'm so sorry.*

He wailed again.

Her ears thrummed with his devastation, one she felt in the depths of her heart. She was already grieving the dragon she had known briefly and had fought to protect, but now, her grief mingled with Ulrieg's misery. This was going to take some healing. Warm, wet trails formed down her cheeks, and her nose swelled, blocking her ability to breathe.

A noise outside the opposite door grabbed her attention, and panic quickly pushed aside her grief. *Ulrieg, we must go. Someone may be coming.*

He didn't move.

Samara pressed closer, gently nudging him, avoiding his horns. *I'm sorry. We can't risk it.*

His sides rocked with silent wails, yet he still didn't shift to leave. The door handle rattled.

Samara grabbed one of his front talons and pulled. *Come on. I know you can turn invisible, but I need to get you out. I must seal the door, or they will know we've been here.*

Left without options, she charged for the door, unable to see Ulrieg anywhere. *I've got to pull the arrow out.* Yanking out the arrow, she waited for the sounds of Ulrieg's talons scraping on the stones in the corridor as the hole sealed behind her. None came. Fear wracked her body. *Ulrieg. Where are you? Please tell me you're on this side.*

Then I would be lying. I'm not going to lie to you.

She froze, not knowing what to do. The grief in his voice was enough to cripple her, but knowing he was in danger would destroy her.

Go. I'll be fine. I'll find you later.

Head shaking, she stared at the closed door. There was nothing she could do. *Please stay out of trouble, and don't do anything that can get you killed.*

I can't promise I won't fatally injure the person responsible.

Ulrieg, she called.

He didn't respond. She hoped he wasn't answering purely to ignore her and not because he was in danger. Returning the torch to the sconce, she slowly climbed the stairs, slipping on the water trickling into the catacombs. She braced against the stone wall and gazed over the side at the drop. It wasn't too far a fall but still far enough to hurt herself. She pressed on, reaching the top and pushing aside the bush covering the hole. Drops from the leaves doused her head, then it was topped with heavy rain as she moved out of the bush's protection.

The rest of her class was probably training in the rain. She should join them, but there was no way she could think clearly enough for one of Zofia's classes right now. She pulled the hood of her cloak over her head and hoped no one would spot her sudden appearance from behind the bush.

Within moments, she was soaked, her cloak drooping around her body in a sodden mess and clinging to her fighting leathers as she ran into the building. She darted up the stairs, stripped the drenched cloak off when she entered, and carried it over her arm as she charged up to her room.

Peeling off her bow and quiver, she hung all three over the hook near her door, slumped on the wooden desk chair, and stared out the window at the bleak sky.

Time passed—slow or fast, she didn't know—as her stomach sickened with each moment. A knock pulled her out of her waiting stupor, and she hoped it wasn't one of the instructors looking for her.

Her feet heavy, she plodded to the door and opened it to find Paxton with Jojo sitting on his shoulder. He smiled. "You changed your hair."

She blinked. "Callista told me to." She backed up to let him in.

Surveying her, his expression dulled. "I missed you at weapons class today." Gently, he placed a hand on her damp shoulder as he entered. "You're saturated."

Samara grunted.

His brow furrowed. "What happened? Are you all right? How'd you get so wet when you didn't make it to training?"

She closed the door behind him. "Ulrieg and I went to investigate that room we were planning to open earlier."

After a quick look around the room, he asked, "Is he all right? You seem very distressed. Where is he?"

Wringing her hands, she looked out the window. "He's still down there." She collapsed on the chair in front of her desk. "We found Byzarid."

Paxton squatted before her and took her hands in his, the warmth gradually radiating to her bones. His brown eyes darkened but never left hers. "What happened?"

Tears ran down her face, retracing the lines left from the ones she cried earlier. Paxton wiped them away with his thumbs and returned to holding her hands.

"He's... he's dead," she choked.

The color leeched from Paxton's face. "Who?"

"Byzarid," she blubbered. "He was in the room with his heart cut out and fresh torture marks. They even left Kaida's lifeless and decaying body with him." She wiped fresh tears from her face with her sleeve, her hands still in Paxton's. "I tried to stop Ulrieg from seeing him like that, but he snuck past me."

Her eyes stung, and she was struggling to breathe again. She knew she would look a mess. "Then someone was coming, and we had to leave before we were caught, but Ulrieg stayed in there." She bent her head, trying to hide her shame.

Paxton stood and paced across her room. When he returned, he wrapped a towel around her shoulders, pulled her up, then guided her to the bed before sitting with her, tugging her into his lap and wrapping his arms around her. His large hands stroked her hair as he rocked gently, listening to her sobs. "Ulrieg is clever. He knows how to keep out of sight."

She wiped her eyes and rested her head on his

shoulder. "But he was so emotional. I'm not sure how he will act or if he will place himself in danger because he wants revenge."

He continued rocking her but didn't speak, as though acknowledging she had a point without wanting to cause more grief.

The sodden sky began to darken as a tap sounded at the door.

CHAPTER NINE

S amara glanced at the door, unsure she was willing to answer it. She and Paxton had skipped their afternoon class, and seeing they weren't in the infirmary, the instructors could be looking for them.

She glanced at Paxton. His face was so close, and she realized she was still sitting in his lap. Embarrassment warmed her cheeks. "I'm sorry." She shifted to stand only to find his arms still wrapped around her middle.

"Don't be sorry. You were upset and for a good reason." His brown eyes stayed steady on hers.

She wrapped her arms loosely around his neck before pressing her cheek to his. "Thank you."

He gently clasped her arms. "You don't need to thank me. I'm here whenever you need me."

The tapping sounded at the door again. *Samara. It's me.*

Ulrieg? Samara spun to stare at the door.

No, it's the evil sorcerer, the dragon quipped. *Can you let me in before someone steps on me by accident?*

In a few quick steps, she was at the door and opening it wide enough for her invisible dragon to fit through. When the sound of his talons clicking on the floor entered the room, she shut it, and he turned visible.

Ulrieg's back was rounded, his red eyes forlorn.

Samara squatted and cupped his chin, avoiding the horn at the end of his jaw. "I'm glad to see you safe. I was so worried about you. I didn't want to leave, but it would've made things worse if I had stayed. Plus, I can't turn invisible like you."

Ulrieg snorted. *I was more worried about Byzarid. But there's nothing we can do.* His red eyes met hers. *I want to rip all their throats open while they sleep.*

"I know, Ulrieg, I know. But I still hope that not everyone here is guilty."

We really must get to the bottom of this dragon capture and mistreatment. We need to find Dragoria and somehow release the realm so that the dragon elves and guardian dragons can rule over these kingdoms again. What they are doing to my kind is heartbreaking.

"We agree." Paxton sat on the floor next to

Samara, and Jojo croaked. "We are learning as much as we can while we are here. If we're to go against strong sorcerers, we will also need strong magic. Otherwise, we won't get very far."

Learn quickly. I don't know how much longer I can stay here without taking revenge. Ulrieg curled up next to Samara, and she rested a hand on his head.

"Who entered the room in the catacombs? I didn't get to see."

It was Zofia. No secret there. Your weapons class must have been finished.

Samara looked at the ceiling. "That leaves Zofia, Vexx, and Kellam as definite enemies. The rest have to be assessed properly." Her stomach growled, and she remembered the last things she had eaten were Paxton's snacks that morning.

Paxton placed a hand on her knee. "It must be dinnertime. I'll grab you some food and bring it back."

She nodded. "Thanks."

After Paxton closed the door behind him, Ulrieg focused his red eyes on Samara. *I know you don't like me saying this, but I'm going to anyway. I'm worried about our safety. I think we may have been found out, and they're biding their time before taking action. It's weird how Callista knew you were in the catacombs yet isn't mad at you. Don't you think that's strange?*

When Samara didn't answer, he continued, *The head sorceress sees you in a forbidden area and doesn't punish you. I think that screams a warning.*

"Maybe she is on our side, and that is her way of letting me know."

Ulrieg shook his head. *You worry me when you insist on believing no one is guilty until proven. By this point, you should be treating everyone as guilty until they prove themselves innocent.*

"But then I would go around feeling as though I should hate everyone, and I don't want to feel like that."

Ulrieg grumbled. *You need to start hardening up. Your actions seem soft and could get more of us killed.*

"I'll do everything I can to stop that from happening." Samara leaned back and looked out into the darkness. Rain pelted the window, hard and urgent, as the storm intensified, adding to her worry. She nudged Ulrieg and coaxed him to the bed, sitting beside him. She noticed that she hadn't changed yet, although her clothes were no longer soaked, having dried over the hours and with the help of the towel Paxton had wrapped around her earlier.

Thinking about how he had sat with her as she let out her grief and worry sent a mixture of emotions through her. She would have been embarrassed to act like that with Kaine, yet she only felt warmth and understanding from Paxton. Her abdomen warmed. He had made her feel important in the most giving way.

A knock sounded at the door, and Samara rose as Ulrieg turned invisible. She didn't think Paxton had been gone very long. Perhaps he'd decided to eat his meal in her room as well. Keenness washed through her, and she flung the door wide. "That was quic—"

Forgrac stood in the doorway, his dwarven arms loaded with food, while Paxton towered behind him. "'Allo, love. Do ya mind if I come in? I brought ya an' ya familiar some food." He peered down the corridor as if looking for eavesdroppers before turning back to her. "An' I 'eard ya both had a tough day."

Seeing the cuts of rabbit on Forgrac's tray, Gray hooted and flapped his wings.

"Sure." Samara stepped back to let them in, closing the door behind them.

After placing the trays on her bench, the dwarf handed Gray a few cuts of meat as Ulrieg turned visible. "Ah, there you are." He held up half a rabbit. "This is for ya. Though I think it's best if ya get off Samara's bed to eat it."

Ulrieg climbed to the floor, taking the rabbit, his movements as slow as if he were in a daze.

Stretching up and rocking on his tiptoes, Forgrac

grabbed the tray from under the food on the bench. "Hang on. I think it best if you eat over this." He placed the tray in front of Ulrieg, the dragon shrugging before sitting beside the tray and putting the food in the center.

The dwarf eyed Ulrieg's sluggish reaction then grunted. "I 'oped it would cheer ya up a li'l, but I understand if ya don't eat it."

My appetite is dulled. Although it was very thoughtful of you to bring me something.

Forgrac stood beside him, placing a hand on his side. "I know ya torn up inside, but ya need to eat to keep ya strength up. I'd hate to think ya couldn't escape a difficult situation 'cause ya were too weak. I imagine it's more vital that ya keep up ya strength to combat any danger ya may face."

Ulrieg eyed him with his red eyes and snorted a short plume of steam before slowly tearing off a piece of meat.

Samara grabbed a plate off the bench, sat on her bed, and dug into the roasted pheasant and sides of herbed carrot, turnips, cabbage, and beans.

Paxton joined her. "You're a fantastic cook, Forgrac. How do you know just how much seasoning to use?"

"It comes with practice an' taste testin'." He rubbed his slightly protruding belly.

"There's hardly a belly there." Samara noticed he wasn't eating. "Did you bring some food for you, or did you need some of ours?"

Forgrac shook his head. "Don't worry 'bout me. I've already eaten." He gazed out the window, looking lost in thought. "Ya lot are really concernin' me."

Samara paused her eating and gazed at the dwarf. "What do you mean?"

"I think ya stirred up a hornet's nest by rescuing the dragons. Please tell me that none of the instructors know ya been in the catacombs."

Gazing down at her plate, Samara pushed a bean around with her fork.

Forgrac pulled his gaze from out the window and observed the three with his eyebrow raised. "Samara, love. What is it?"

She swallowed. "Callista saw me in the catacombs this morning."

"Oh, 'at's not good." The dwarf tossed his head to the side.

Sitting straight, Samara leaned on her hands. "I don't know that it's that bad. She purposefully told me by bringing up my fading hair color. It wasn't said like I was in trouble. I thought you trusted Callista."

"I never said I trusted her, although I'm 'oping

she's goin' to keep her word and let me pass over the borders to see me family after me service time is up." The dwarf crossed his arms over his chest before leaning forward and frowning. "I wish me time servin' the coterie was done. I've still got over a year and a half. I don't know if you lot are goin' to be safe for that long."

Paxton gazed at Samara with confusion.

"Forgrac has offered to let me join him when he leaves to act in his traveling stage show." Samara rubbed her arm. "That way, I could earn money to support my family if I left the coterie."

"Ya'd be a good addition as well." Forgrac slapped Paxton on the shoulder. "I'm sure Samara would appreciate ya company."

Paxton looked embarrassed. "I'm not sure how I'd go on a stage. I'd prefer to have my face shoved in a book."

"If ya can't act, I'm sure I'll find other things for ya to do." The dwarf shrugged. "Anythin' to keep ya lot safe, although Callista could be on the dragons' side an' may stand up for ya an' turn things around. If she does, then there won't be a need for ya to escape. I don't know if dragons 'ave always been tortured under the coterie or if it's a recent thing. None of the apprentices have talked to me before."

Maybe Callista is on our side, Ulrieg said. *Even if*

she's not, I have the overwhelming pull to end a specific instructor's life.

Forgrac blinked in disbelief. "I understand how ya feel, but I'm not sure that'll be the best for all of ya. It could make things more dangerous."

Ulrieg leveled his gaze at the dwarf, his red eyes eerily determined. *Pretty much every way we turn now is another step toward danger. It's a chance I'm willing to take in order to get some revenge.*

CHAPTER TEN

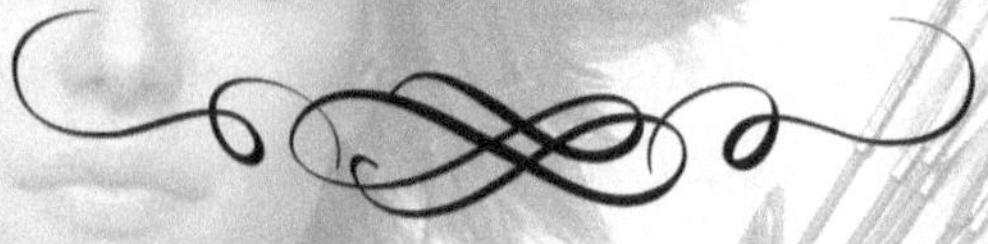

Samara couldn't shake the uneasiness that swamped her as she entered the room where Luna, Peadar, and Paxton stood, ready for their next lesson with Devi. She should have felt more relaxed, knowing that the overbearing presences of Kaine and Mist would be absent while they trained at the borders. Ulrieg hadn't gotten over his grief from Byzarid's death, and it also ladened her heart, making it more difficult to think clearly.

Paxton shifted next to her, and Jojo croaked a greeting, instantly taking away some of her tension. At least the lesson was with Devi, although she wasn't sure how to deal with Luna. As they waited for the lesson, Peadar scratched Ziggy behind the ears, and Luna picked up Coco, stroking her head and back.

Devi joined them in the middle of the room, her light-copper wolf familiar, Zion, always lurking near her. "Today's class is outside."

The apprentices filed out the door, following Devi and Zion. The wolf wasn't as intimidating to Samara as Jet, Mystique, Vexx's snake, or Kellam's monkey. She didn't know why. The wolf was as much a ferocious creature as any of the others. It made Samara wonder if Ulrieg was onto something when he said the familiar represented the sorcerer that it bonded with. She eyed the back of Devi's short salmon hair before gazing at Zion and working her bottom lip. *Or perhaps it's just the kind of treatment the animal experiences with its bonded,* she thought.

Devi stopped in the common room and faced them. "Samara, you must get Gray and probably your bow and arrow for this class. We'll be going a fair distance from the building, and you'll need your familiar close so you can use your bond to strengthen you."

Keeping up the pretense, Samara did as instructed, despite knowing that Ulrieg was following them in his invisible form, and quickly rejoined the others.

Along with their familiars, the tiny group entered the small clearing where Samara had planted a mulberry tree to help attract a familiar. To her surprise, the tree still bore fruit, keeping the wildlife fed. Gray flew to the tallest tree nearby and snuggled his head under his wing. Samara huffed. He wasn't even trying to look interested, but she couldn't blame him.

Devi stopped in the middle and faced the apprentices, her long brown gown tapered at the waist, billowing around her ankles. "Callista has told me that you were acquainted with your stronger magical powers during her brief individual instruction. Today, we're going to focus on those outside. I think it's the fairest place for everyone to practice." She waved her arms, indicating the open space with one lonely mulberry tree. "I want you to use them against your fellow apprentices."

Samara blinked in disbelief. "But mine isn't really something to use against people or beings."

Amusement flashed over Devi's face. "You'd be surprised what can and can't be used against living beings. At least if you hurt someone, you know we can fix them quickly. Just don't try to kill them."

Samara gazed around at the apprentices. She didn't know what Peadar's gift was, but Luna and Paxton had impressive powers that made hers look amateur, and theirs had nothing to do with the impressiveness of their familiars. In her opinion, a dragon was a much more spectacular animal than a rabbit, raccoon, or frog. Although she knew she was biased.

Without the presence of Mist, the apprentices showed little enthusiasm for attacking each other.

Devi hooked her hands together in front of her. "All right. Since you seem reluctant, I'll get this started. Luna, I want you to use your power on someone."

"Oh." Luna chuckled nervously. "Who?"

The instructor shrugged. "Anyone. If you need more confidence, start on the one you think would be easiest to use your power against."

Quickly, Luna assessed each of the apprentices, pulled back her shoulders, and let out a long breath before sucking in another deeply. Her eyes focused on Peadar, and surprisingly, she started to sing. Her voice was like an angel's, and it was the sweetest song Samara had ever heard. She had no idea that Luna could sing.

Samara listened closely but didn't recognize the words. They seemed to blend into the tune, but she felt it making her shoulders relax and all her worries disappear. She wondered if the spell was working on her, too, even though Luna was focused on Peadar.

The male shifted then walked, one foot in front of the other, heading toward the beautiful elf. His eyes glazed over by the second, almost as though he had lost control of his body the longer the song continued. At that moment, she knew she wasn't under the direct spell. Peadar's eyes were fixed on Luna as he started to circle around the tall elf in a slow, purposeful gait. Ziggy constantly chatted to Peadar as he kept up with his bonded's pace.

Devi turned to Paxton and Samara. "Any time one of you wishes to join in and stop Luna with your magic, go right ahead."

Samara grabbed an arrow from her quiver, looked at it dubiously, and muttered, "I wish I had another kind of magic I could use. If I use my so-called enhanced gift, I have no idea what it would do to a living thing other than shoot an arrow into them. I hate hurting people, even the ones I know despise me."

Just hurt her. When she didn't react, Ulrieg added, *I'll do it if you want. I'm still looking for someone to sink my talons into.*

I understand, but I don't think that's such a great idea. It would be too difficult to explain who the invisible attacker was.

He grumbled. *Then you do it. I'm certain she would hurt you without thinking about it.*

Samara frowned. *You're probably right, Ulrieg. But I still wish I didn't have to.*

Paxton eyed her arrow. "I'll give this one a shot." He waved his arms in a circular motion in front of him, closed his eyes, and tilted his face to the sky while twisting clawed hands by his sides, palm up. He paused. A moment passed, and his fingers twitched then seized as he slowly raised his hands.

At first, nothing seemed to happen as Peadar pressed forward toward Luna's song. Then tree roots moved in rapidly from the sides and back, catching Luna by surprise. They wrapped around her waist and then aimed for her mouth despite the shock already silencing her. Within a few moments, the roots continued to grow, lifting the young elf into the air, legs flailing beneath her as she rose higher.

Samara enchanted two arrows before firing them at two of the roots, creating a void on one side. Luna slid from the roots' grasp, dropping several stories.

Having come back to himself only a few moments prior, Peadar dived toward the falling apprentice, tossing his hand as if to catch Luna, but he was too far away. It looked like Luna was going to hit the ground, until Luna bounced backside first on an invisible barrier several feet above the ground. She was slowly lowered to the ground as Peadar lowered his hand until she could safely climb off.

Eyes lit with encouragement, Devi clasped her

hands in front of her chest. "That was wonderful. Now, try to use your powers in different ways." Zion stalked around the students, his eyes focused on their every move as though taking in things Devi might miss.

Luna's eyes connected with Paxton's, and she sang again, her sweet, angelic voice rippling over the apprentices. The melody was simultaneously enticing and commanding, momentarily taking hold of Samara. Despite Luna's eyes unwavering, the mesmerizing music didn't have a grasp on Paxton. Instead, he called to the trees and their roots with his magic, preparing an attack. Confusion covered Luna's face before she redirected her voice toward Samara.

Instantly, Samara felt the pull, and her brain turned numb. She was vaguely aware of her hands working swiftly, enchanting an arrow and nocking it before aiming at Paxton. The fear on Paxton's face registered somewhere in her mind, but there was nothing she could do. She couldn't fight what she was doing despite her heart wanting to do so.

Paxton turned his palms up by his sides, calling for roots as he shifted out of Samara's sights, only for her arrow tip to follow him. Samara's fingers released the bowstring before the tree roots could catch her, sending her arrow flying straight at Paxton's chest.

Paxton, move! Samara, what've you done? You should've aimed for somewhere less deadly! Ulrieg cried. *Argh! I should have intervened. Why am I holding back?*

Samara's heart cried for the arrow to stop, but her mind was still blank then distracted by the roots of a tree wrapping around her legs.

In the same instant, Peadar threw out his hand toward her arrow, cheering when his invisible barrier halted it in midair. Paxton's roots wrapped around Samara's torso a second later, securing her arms by her sides. Luna stopped singing, her task accomplished, and Paxton released his hold on the roots, setting Samara free.

Samara blinked, then her eyes widened as she gazed at Paxton. "I'm so sorry. I don't know what came over me. It's like I knew what was happening, but I could do nothing about it. I would never fire an arrow at your heart."

"Luna, you shouldn't have had her aim the arrow at his heart," Devi called from the side. "A heart shot would kill him, even if it was enchanted to do other things."

Mock gasping, Luna slapped a hand over her

bottom lip and put on her sweetest voice. "I didn't think her aim would be that good."

The instructor ran a hand through the side of her short, salmon-colored hair, scorn marring her face. "That is an excuse that you cannot use. You know Samara is highly trained with the bow and arrow. It's well known through the coterie along with her unique gift of enchanting her arrows for specific purposes." Devi faced the rest of the apprentices. "It's good to see you pairing and working together against a threat. Have another go with a different scenario." She leveled her gaze at Luna. "And no one is to try to kill anyone, or you will face my wrath. Do you understand?"

Luna's mouth pressed into a thin line, but she nodded before facing the other three apprentices. She sang, her gaze holding all three of them. Samara's body shook as her hand involuntarily grabbed an arrow from the quiver and spelled it. At the same time, Peadar turned to Paxton and thrust out his hands, pushing Paxton out from between them, sending him backward toward the forest, and holding him in sight at a perfect distance for an arrow.

Paxton's palms faced out by his sides as he called for the many tree roots in the ground and sent them toward Luna, Samara, and Peadar.

Samara raised her nocked arrow before the roots could reach them, aiming for Paxton's middle. She tried to fight it. She summoned all her inner strength, trying to work against the siren's song. Instead, she watched as her fingers twitched, ready to release the arrow into Paxton's stomach. She could see the roots hurrying to stop her, and she silently cheered them on. All her effort to resist Luna's call was proving fruitless. Perhaps Paxton could save himself, but a sinking feeling filled her stomach as she realized the roots were moving too slowly.

She could hear Ulrieg calling her to check if she was under control and aiming at a non–life-threatening body part, but she couldn't find the strength to answer him. The bowstring flicked over her fingertips, setting the arrow free, straight toward Paxton's stomach, and there was no one to stop the fatal shot.

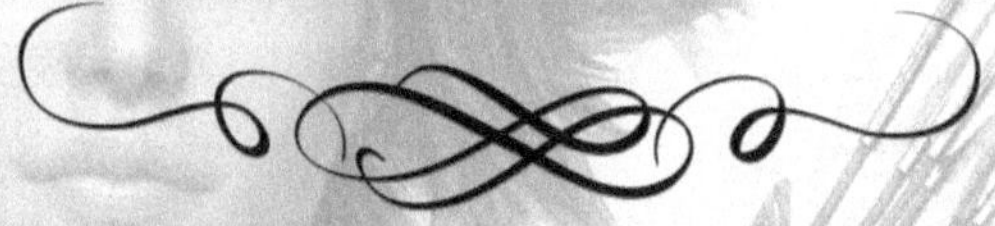

CHAPTER ELEVEN

Samara's heart screamed. She wouldn't be able to live with herself if the arrow killed Paxton.

Something flashed in from the side, racing into Samara's vision and colliding with the arrow, knocking it off course and into a tree trunk. Samara released her breath, happy to see her shot failed.

Devi hit Luna with a spell an instant later, breaking her siren's call. Peadar withdrew his barrier, holding Paxton in a compromised place, and Paxton dropped his control of the tree roots.

Large welts blistered on Luna's skin like hives, and she clawed at her marred face. "That's not fair!" she screamed at Devi.

The instructor shook her head. "What's unfair is you going for another potential kill shot when you were warned not to."

"You could've healed him." She scratched her arms before reaching down to her legs, groaning with frustration.

Devi lifted her chin, peering down her nose at Luna. "For a shot like that, I'd rather not risk it. Especially when Samara's spell would have made that part of him disappear until the arrow was removed. Depending on where it hit, he could've bled out quickly."

After scratching her skin roughly, Luna growled in frustration again and moved closer to Devi, feigning remorse and innocence. "Oh, clearly, I didn't understand the assignment. My mistake. Aren't you going to heal me or remove the spell?"

Devi shook her head, her mouth turned down. "No. I think you need to learn your lesson. I don't tolerate serious violent behavior in my classes. That's Zofia's specialization."

"Well, that's confusing." Luna chortled, the rash on her face growing more prominent. "Since you often teach us to attack each other with spells that can hurt us."

"As this is a lesson for defensive arts, yes, sometimes you'll get hurt on purpose for a limited time. However, Luna, despite this front of being friendly and naive, your actions had an underlying malice attached to them, and you caused Samara to strike with an actual weapon that could kill in moments if it hits a vital area." The instructor turned to face the other apprentices. "It's time for someone else to initiate the attack."

Samara drew an arrow and enchanted it with the same spell before nocking it. "With pleasure." Before Luna could start singing, Samara released the arrow into her arm.

Luna's arm disappeared, and she winced in pain as she stared at the void, eyes wide. "I can't feel my arm at all, and it won't scratch the areas I need to scratch."

Seeing Luna reaching for the arrow with her other arm, Samara repeated the process on the other side, smirking when that arm also disappeared.

Luna glared at her, a strange look from the bubbly apprentice. Samara wondered if there was more to Luna's behavior than what was happening within the lesson. She wouldn't be surprised if Kaine had influenced Luna's actions lately.

With what looked like a glimmer of approval, Devi turned toward the males. "Aren't you two sorcerers going to defend Luna?"

Paxton called for the roots, and Peadar prepared a barrier as Luna opened her mouth to sing, moments after Samara had let loose another enchanted arrow, this time into one of Luna's legs.

The young sorceress wobbled, barely regaining enough balance to stop her from toppling to the ground.

Paxton continued to work with the roots, one grabbing Samara from behind, the other curling around Luna's body, its thin tip coiling around one of the arrow shafts before yanking it out of Luna's arm. Almost immediately, her arm turned visible. Teeth clenched, Luna set to work pulling out the other arrows and stopping the bleeding with a mild healing spell. Then her song rippled through the air directly at Samara.

As much as Samara tried to fight it, she felt like a spectator as her hands grabbed another arrow from her quiver and nocked it, aiming it at her own foot.

The song paused, and Luna chuckled as the arrow shot straight through Samara's leather boot and into the middle of her foot.

Crying in pain, Samara sucked in a deep breath before grasping the shaft, ready to pull it out, when the song started again, causing her to ignore the pain and grab another arrow, this time aiming for the other foot. When her fingers released the string, she watched it pierce the boot and foot, but the pain didn't register until Luna's song stopped controlling her.

Samara yowled. Her legs felt numb, yet at the

same time, they screamed that they were in pain. It was an odd feeling. She wanted to pull the arrows out, but roots were wrapped around her upper torso, inhibiting her from bending over. She looked at Paxton, pleading, "Release me."

Paxton's face was torn, but he glanced at Devi before shaking his head, his eyes filled with sadness.

"It doesn't matter how good of friends you are outside this lesson. You must leave that all behind before you step into this training. The rest of you must devise a way to release Samara from Paxton's roots."

Samara squirmed, trying to wriggle her way out, each movement resulting in more pain from the arrows in her feet and up her legs. The roots weren't so tight as to cause her harm, and it wouldn't surprise her if Paxton did this on purpose, but he wasn't allowed to pull them away from her, either. The roots were too close to shoot arrows into them to open a void for her to push through. She tried to push the roots away, but they were unwavering, stiff, as though they had been growing for years.

Samara eyed both Peadar and Luna, weighing up their talents. If Peadar had brought his machete, he could try to cut through them—although knowing how clumsy he was, it was a relief he didn't have it.

He would probably slice off one of Samara's arms in the process.

Sweat trickled from her brow. Not finding anything useful from Peadar, she concentrated on Luna, unable to come up with a solution.

Ulrieg, do you have any suggestions? I'm stuck, and my feet are causing my brain to fail.

Do you mean besides ripping at Luna with my talons for making you hurt yourself?

Yes. I've already told you that this would be too difficult to explain.

All right then. He snorted. *You could try and convince Luna to sing to the roots.*

Would her magic work on plants?

I don't know. You're the first magic wielder I've been around. But it might. A tree is a living thing.

"Luna, please try your siren magic on these roots."

Momentarily taking a break from scratching, Luna lifted her chin, amusement flashing across her face. "After what you did to me, I don't think I should."

"Luna!" Devi chided. "You're supposed to be trying to help your colleagues, no matter what. We only survive if we work together."

Luna shrugged. "I don't even know if it would work."

Devi indicated the roots wrapped around Samara. "And this is one way to find out."

Luna resumed her scratching, giving off the impression that she wasn't going to comply. When Devi paced toward her, Luna chuckled, and the sweet, angelic sound drifted into the air. Samara felt in control of her body again, and when she observed Paxton, Peadar, then Devi, they, too, were acting like themselves, showing no signs of Luna's control.

Several moments passed, and nothing happened.

"Are you aiming for the roots?" Samara asked.

Luna lightheartedly flailed her arms. "Of course I am."

Samara closed her eyes, sucking in a breath to ease the pain. "Just asking, because it doesn't seem to be working." Something pressed up against her pants and stayed there. Glancing to the ground, she saw nothing had changed, and the arrows remained in her feet, causing her pain to worsen.

At least you know that Luna's magic only controls beings and not nature as well, or else she might be able to do what Paxton does. That could be dangerous.

But it still doesn't get me out of this trap, Samara whined. *And these arrows hurt.*

Ulrieg grunted. *Try the enchanted arrows without the bow.*

Her brow pinched. She didn't like her chances,

but it was worth a go. She enchanted the arrow and then clenched her fist around its shaft before digging it into one layer of the root. Nothing happened. *Now what?*

Luna and Peadar were trying all kinds of magic spells to get the roots to release without success.

Call Gray down.

Holding up her hand, Samara called to her pretend familiar. He didn't move. Instead, the owl tucked his head farther under his wing.

"Wingless flight!" *He's refusing to move.*

Give me a moment. The branches next to Gray bobbed heavily, low enough to indicate a dragon's weight, and the owl began flapping profusely as though trying to escape. Instead, he looked to be in awkward flight to Samara's shoulder, as Ulrieg was dragging him there.

Gray squawked and fluffed his feathers before grumpily settling on her shoulder, allowing Ulrieg to let go.

Huh! The owl's feeling stubborn today. Talons dug slightly into her back as Ulrieg climbed down the roots to the ground, then he slid a front claw onto some bare skin on the small of her back. *Try to charm the arrow again and shove it into the root without the bow.*

This time, when the tip lodged into the root, that

chunk of root disappeared. Heart pounding, she tried again for the second binding root, cheering outwardly when it also stuck, vanishing the last barrier between her and freedom. She yanked the arrows out of her feet and stepped through the gap, removing them from the root to expose its stiff, empty coils.

Devi cried in delight. "Fantastic effort, Samara!" She placed a hand on Luna. "Since you tried to help Samara, I'll remove these festered blisters for you." Her eyes passed over the three apprentices. "Maybe if Luna had used the power of her familiar, she could have controlled the root, as it's a living thing, but if Paxton's familiar was touching him, the roots still might not be able to be controlled. You need to work on these things to find your strengths and accentuate your magic. Besides being with you, there are other ways your familiar can make you stronger."

CHAPTER TWELVE

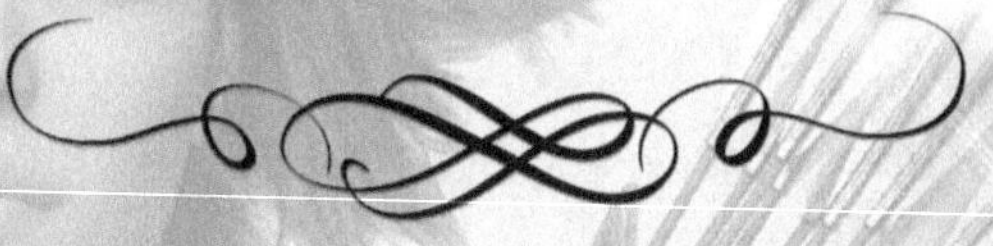

T he sconce's light flickered shadows over Samara's bedroom's stone walls. Because she was exhausted from her efforts in Devi's defense lesson earlier and still dealing with what happened to Byzarid, the bed beckoned to her, a temptation too strong to resist. She had bathed, dressed in her night shift, and was ready to curl up on her soft mattress. Then knuckles rapped on the door.

Gray hooted, and she scratched him on the back of his neck. Ulrieg turned invisible as her shift swished against her calves on her way to the door. She cracked it open, surprised to find Paxton dressed as though ready to go hunting, Jojo sitting on his shoulder.

He glanced over her attire. "I guess you're not wanting to go for a wander in the woods."

She shook her head and fiddled with the handle. "I'm exhausted. I was planning a night away from the underground. Another visit tonight would probably get us in more hot water. I just hope no dragons were captured today, especially since Vexx and Kellam are gone." She stepped back, widening the gap to give him access to her room. "Did you want to come in?"

He slipped past her, and Jojo slid under the cover of his tunic. "For a little while, if that's all right?"

She closed the door and nodded, indicating the edge of her bed not far from where Ulrieg had turned visible, his red eyes surveying Paxton affectionately. Paxton sat while nodding his acknowledgment to Ulrieg. Samara stood before him, and he caught her hands in his, causing her cheeks to heat.

His brown eyes gazed into hers, and he tightened his grip. "I wanted to make sure you knew I didn't want to attack you in defense class today."

Samara looked away. "I know. As I would never want to attack you. It was part of our lesson, and it's good to practice."

He let out a breath. "Good. Because it's important to me that you know that."

Tingles rushed up her arms as Paxton rubbed his thumbs over the backs of her hands. She nodded and glanced back at his face, still pale in the candlelight against the dark-green hair that fell down his back in a low ponytail. Gently, he pulled her to sit next to him on her bed.

Ulrieg grumbled, tugging at the flail strapped to Paxton's back. *Why don't you take this off? It can't be comfortable having this on. Here, let me help.* He grabbed the strap as Paxton threaded it off his shoulders and back, allowing the dragon to rest it on the floor against the wall.

Ulrieg then climbed to the window and wedged it open a little. *I'm going out for a bit. I've got a few things I want to do tonight, including catching a good meal. I'll leave this open for Gray and bring him back later if he doesn't come.*

Before Samara could say anything, Ulrieg had flown out the window, followed by Gray, taking the opportunity to spread his wings in the night sky. She suddenly realized that she was left alone with Paxton —aside from Jojo, still tucked away in Paxton's pocket. She shifted, uneasy.

Paxton wrapped her hands between his and smiled. Despite his being an avid scholar and at home in nature, his large hands were strong and easily enveloped Samara's. "I wanted to make sure you know I'm not like Kaine. I won't turn against you."

She squeezed his hand with her fingers. "I know.

It's also something Ulrieg has been telling me from the start. He would never leave me alone with Kaine, as much as Kaine made him gag."

Paxton frowned. "What do you mean?"

She huffed out a laugh. "Every time Kaine used to kiss me, Ulrieg would retch."

Paxton leaned back, laughing, the sound rich and sincere, filling her with warmth. In that one moment, she had never seen a more attractive male. By the time his brown eyes connected with hers again, she was mesmerized.

Paxton's eyes softened. "How are you both holding up? Are you coping all right after finding Byzarid?"

Samara nodded. "Ulrieg is very bitter at the coterie and Zofia."

"That's understandable."

"It is. It's disgusting what they're doing—whoever is doing it. We don't know if Zofia was the one who killed him, but she was the one Ulrieg saw in the room with Byzarid's body. I'm worried he might act out and put us in danger. He wanted to tear into Luna today at the practice, and she's only an apprentice."

"I'm sure Ulrieg will refrain from doing anything stupid in public. Despite his sarcasm and short temper, he's intelligent, and I imagine he'd think through what he would do." Paxton cupped the side of her face.

"I hope you're right." She leaned into his touch, her insides warming. This felt completely different from her times with Kaine. She didn't feel forced to participate, and her mind stayed her own. Closing her eyes, she inhaled deeply, soaking in Paxton's comforting touch. It felt so right.

Samara cupped her hand over his and was pleasantly surprised when Paxton's warm lips met hers, gently urging them open. She reciprocated, yielding readily, her lips tenderly massaging his, and she shifted closer as his other hand traced over her shoulder and onto her back, drawing her closer.

As his arms wrapped around her, she melted into him. With each caress, her hunger grew, wanting more. She shuffled closer, closing the distance separating them on the bed, and he slid his hand up her back and threaded his fingers through her hair.

Groaning, she arched her back and pressed herself into his chest—then pulled back when something wriggled against her breast. "Jojo! I'm sorry. I forgot you were there."

The frog peered out of Paxton's pocket, and Paxton laughed, glancing to the side before giving her an amused look. "Um. Jojo has requested I leave him in the pocket but drape my tunic over your desk chair, so he has some protection in case Gray comes back." Paxton looked embarrassed. "I just wanted you to know that it was his idea in case you think I'm being too forward."

Samara's cheeks heated, and she shook her head. "That's all right. I don't mind."

Paxton raised an eyebrow. "I can leave my tunic on if it makes you uncomfortable."

Her toes curled. "You can take your tunic off."

Carefully, Paxton pulled the tunic over his head and placed it on the chair as Jojo had requested. Samara couldn't pull her eyes away from the surprising number of defined muscles in the scholar's chest and torso. She was suddenly aware that she was only wearing her white night shift.

He moved toward her with no sign of ego or expectation from her and as though he was completely unaware of the way his muscles rippled in the sconce's light. His lack of overhyped selfregard and the respect he showed her filled her with confidence and desire.

Springing to her feet, she pressed against Paxton, wrapping her arms around his neck and her fingers into his hair, then stretched up on tiptoes, determined to get another taste of his lips. He ran his hands over the small of her back, moving her backward and catching her when her feet stumbled over themselves. The backs of her legs pressed against her bed, bending at the knee and lowering her and Paxton onto the blankets.

As she lay on her back, Paxton lined her side, one leg draped over her lower half. Her fingers dug into his bare back as he caressed her neck and face with his lips, her skin burning under his touch. As his fingers fiddled with the strings lacing her shift together at the neckline, she wrapped her legs around him.

CHIRPING birds pulled Samara out of her sleep, and she stretched then paused, feeling the warmth of another body in her small bed. Her eyes struggled against the brilliance of the sunlight, taking a moment to focus on the face before her.

Paxton's brown eyes watched her, warmth radiating from them, and the feeling of his bare chest against hers caused her body heat to rise. "You are so beautiful," he whispered, kissing her forehead and tucking hair behind one ear. "I could lie here all day and watch you."

Her cheeks burned, and she kissed him before resting her head against his chest, listening to the steady beat of his heart. "I'm sure I don't look great first thing in the morning."

Scratching pulled Samara's attention to the window. Ulrieg entered the room, his eyes shining. *Well, it looks like you've finally come to your senses.*

Samara turned toward the dragon, and Paxton draped his arm around her waist. "Are you only just getting back?" She checked Gray's stand to find the owl snuggled into his wing. Quickly, she peered over at Paxton's tunic to see Jojo's eyes looking at them over the lip of the pocket. Her shoulders relaxed.

Ulrieg stopped on the bench. *Like I was going to disturb you when you're finally proving me right?*

"What have you been doing all night?"

A sly look passed over his face. *Let's just say I visited a particular instructor. Now I feel so much better.*

Samara's breath caught in her throat. "What did you do?"

He tilted his head to one side and showed his teeth. *Nothing that they didn't deserve. But I suggest getting up and getting ready for your day. The last thing you should do today is be late and draw attention to you both.*

CHAPTER THIRTEEN

Wild orange hair surrounded potions instructor Artemise Snow's aged face, illuminated by the fire burning under her large cauldron. Deep lines cutting out from the edges of her eyes filled in with shadows as the sorceress squinted into the room of apprentices.

"Today, we are making healing potions. I think it's about time you all learned this potion, so you can prepare it for any coterie members who need healing if you can't heal them with your magic."

She scrutinized each of the apprentices and their familiars before spotting Ziggy, charging up to him and grabbing his paw. The raccoon chattered his protest while tugging at his leg, trying to reclaim it, but the elderly instructor wouldn't release him from her tight grip. Instead, she inspected his claws then released his paw before assessing the other familiars again. "Do any of you have new familiars?" She continued stirring her potion, her eyes narrow.

When she was answered with a unified murmuring of "no," her eyes turned to Samara. "Where's your owl?"

Samara stiffened. "He's in my room, sleeping, like he often does during the day. He was out hunting last night."

Artemise cocked a hip and dropped the stirring stick. "Bring him down here and keep him with you all day."

Samara frowned. "Why's that?"

"Don't question your instructors—just do as you're told," the potions sorceress barked.

Samara nodded, suddenly apprehensive. "I'll go and get him."

As expected, Gray was sleeping on his perch. Samara coaxed him onto her hand and carried him to the potions room. The owl's head rotated expansively as he took in his surroundings.

When Samara was back in the room, Artemise dropped the ladle and grabbed Gray's claw. The owl squawked, attempting to yank it back. The instructor didn't let go, inspecting it closely, her mouth bunching at one side. "Hmm. Possibly."

"Possibly what?" Heat burned at the back of

Samara's neck, and her fingernails dug into her palms.

Artemise raised one eyebrow. "We shall see. Just make sure you take him to all your lessons today."

Frowning, Samara placed Gray on her shoulder as Artemise stepped behind the cauldron and resumed her stirring. Samara whispered to Paxton, "Do you know what's going on?"

Paxton shook his head and kept his voice soft, "But if my guess is right, I think Ulrieg might."

She clenched her teeth. *Ulrieg, what did you do last night?*

There was no answer.

Ulrieg, I know you're here somewhere.

He still didn't answer, causing the torrent in her stomach to grow.

I hope you didn't do anything that could get us killed or kicked out.

His silence didn't bring her the reassurance she needed.

"Did he answer?" Paxton murmured into her ear.

Samara shook her head as nausea rose.

Paxton squeezed her arm. "We'll work it out. Don't worry."

She wondered how he could be so calm when they both knew better. Ulrieg could've done something that would endanger them and their families.

Artemise narrowed her gaze on them. "Are you two going to listen, or do you think you know it all already, Mr. Vigil?"

Paxton looked at the instructor. "I apologize. Please, go ahead. We'll pay more attention."

The instructor nodded. "If you don't, I'll have you sampling one of my disfiguring potions."

Samara cringed. She wouldn't put it past Artemise to follow through on that threat. She faced the front, catching a side glare from Luna that was quickly replaced with a toothy smile and a finger-wiggling wave.

Confusion washed through her. Although Luna had never been as hostile as Kaine and Mist had been before they left, something seemed to be lying beneath her usual cheerfulness.

I wouldn't worry about her, Ulrieg put in. *She's just missing her lover.*

Samara rolled her eyes. *Oh, so now you talk to me.*

I don't know what you mean. Samara could hear the feigned sincerity in Ulrieg's voice.

Hmm!

"Miss Wren! This is your last warning." Artemise's voice cut through her thoughts, bringing her attention back to the instructor.

"Sorry, Ms. Snow." Samara forced her eyes to focus on the instructor, although she couldn't help noticing that Luna wasn't reprimanded in the same way.

Artemise tapped the stirring stick against the large cauldron while muttering curse words under her breath. "I'm not in any mood for you to disrespect me today. It's appalling that someone or their familiar has attacked one of our esteemed coterie leaders." She leveled the ladle at the apprentices. "Mark my words. If it was one of you, we will find out. You will be punished."

Gasps echoed through the room, a rumble of chatter breaking out among the apprentices. Samara felt the blood drain from her face. Ulrieg had said he gave someone what they deserved. To get a reaction like this, it must be bad.

Artemise held up a hand. "Silence!" With narrowed eyes, she scrutinized the apprentices. "Now is not the time for talking. As far as I know, you could be conjuring up some story to cover your tracks."

"Ms. Snow, what makes you so sure it was one of us?" Rehan asked, his face pale as he stood next to Peadar, Ziggy hiding behind his bonded's legs.

Artemise glowered at him, the lines on her face deepening. "Because whoever did it knew that their familiar was out of their room so they could attack the instructor when they slept. And you all know that no one can enter this building unless you are magically allowed to, either by selection or by bonding with a being accepted into this coterie."

She grabbed a bottle that sat next to where Tabatha lay and eyed it longingly. "If it were up to me, I'd make you all drink this truth serum until the real story came out." She then snatched a bottle off the far side of her bench. "And then I'd make the guilty party drink this poison as their punishment." She smirked as she fingered the small bottle then returned it roughly to the bench. "But no. Callista said we are to give the person the opportunity to come forward, and they will be dealt with accordingly."

Licking her legs, Tabatha eyed her bonded as Artemise paced along the bench where the cat reclined. Then Tabatha stretched and pushed a bunch of vibrant pink, red, and orange flowers toward the instructor with her back feet.

Artemise grabbed them. "Yes, yes. I get your point," she snapped at the cat then set to ripping the flowers off the stems and throwing them into the cauldron. "Echinacea flowers are an essential part of this potion with its fast-healing capability." She grabbed some kind of root vegetable, dropped it in a mortar, and ground it with a pestle before adding it to the potion. "And so is turmeric."

Glaring up from her mixture, she swatted one arm at the apprentices. "Why are you all just standing there? You're supposed to make these potions so we have plenty to go around. Thus far, you've done nothing!"

The apprentices scurried to the tables at the back of the room, all set up with ten smaller cauldrons and several ingredients lined up behind the individual pots, and they set to work replicating the method written on the wall, ripping off the heads of the echinacea flowers and grinding the turmeric.

Shoulders bent, Eliphas wandered into the room with a large pot filled with different plants. Slowly, the herbology instructor made his way to the front, seemingly oblivious that the room was filled with apprentices.

"Ah, Eliphas. About time you brought the rest of the ingredients." Artemise weaved her way around the large cauldron, grabbing the pot from him and placing it on the table, narrowly missing Tabatha's tail. Her familiar glared at her only to be ignored as Artemise sorted the plants.

Without looking up, Eliphas turned to leave.

"Where do you think you're going?" Artemise glared over her shoulder at him. "Since you brought these in so late, you can help distribute them."

Phobae swayed over the top of Eliphas's green

ponytail, her front legs raised as though she was ready to box the rude sorceress. The way Artemise was acting today, Samara didn't think anyone would object to the stick insect's threat. Yet Eliphas set to work, silently executing Artemise's demand.

Samara watched the herbology instructor as he shifted through the apprentices, handing out different ingredients. She nudged Paxton. "I can't see anything wrong with Eliphas, can you?"

Looking up from his almost-completed potion, Paxton shook his head. "No. He looks uninjured. Although if I know Ulrieg well enough, he has nothing against Eliphas, if that's what you mean."

She nodded. "True. In a sad way, I wish it was someone as timid as Eliphas. Then there might not be any retaliation. I'm worried Ulrieg's anger has led to something much more sinister."

"I still stand by my earlier assumption. He's usually levelheaded and wise enough to make a sensible decision?"

She sighed. "Usually, but his cousin's death really took a toll. I'm afraid he's not thinking straight, and I'm more worried because he won't tell me who it was. By now, his temper has probably dampened. It may be that he's realized he's done something detrimental to our safety."

Paxton stirred the mixture in the cauldron, looking lost in thought. "I think this is fin—"

A magical pulse vibrated through the room, and the apprentices dropped what they were doing.

Samara's and Paxton's eyes connected.

"That's not Callista's call," Samara said.

Paxton shook his head. "I think we're about to find out."

CHAPTER FOURTEEN

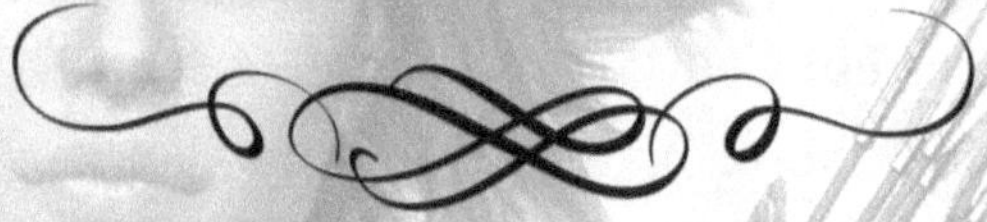

After coaxing Gray down from the rafters, Samara dragged her feet as she followed the apprentices out of the potions room and into the hall, Paxton beside her. She didn't know where Ulrieg was, although she assumed he would be lurking close by in his invisible form.

Confusion covered the younger apprentices' faces as they wandered down the corridor after the strange lesson with Artemise.

The sight of Zofia at the end of the hall, dressed in her usual warrior leathers, sent chills through Samara's bones. The sorceress had deep scratches marring her face, robbing her of some of her toned beauty. They looked clean but open and raw. It was surprising that they hadn't been healed magically by either Zofia herself or the other senior instructors.

Zofia's bright-purple hair hung loosely over the edges of her face, and she tied it back, accentuating the damage on her neck and hands. There was no mistaking the claw marks.

Samara's heart thumped against her rib cage. *Ulrieg, what did you do?*

She deserved it. She's most likely the one who killed Byzarid. I could've done a lot worse. A puff of hot air wafted over Samara as Ulrieg passed overhead and released a plume of steam.

Bewildered, she met Paxton's gaze to find it reflected her own.

He mouthed, "Ulrieg?"

She nodded. *I understand you're upset, Ulrieg, but how will we explain this? Zofia isn't one to be messed with.*

Well, neither am I. In fact, I should've done worse. I showed an enormous amount of restraint.

Clenching her teeth, Gray on her shoulder, Samara followed Paxton to some seats in the middle row, hoping it would hide them from the glowering weapons instructor's eyes. She was wrong. Zofia's unwavering stare followed them. Samara pulled back her shoulders, feigning innocence, and returned Zofia's gaze. Yet her stomach roiled, and a sour taste filled her mouth.

Paxton squeezed her hand, reminding her she

wasn't alone, but that only intensified her worry. He could also be in danger because of Ulrieg's actions. Samara attempted to swallow the lump in her throat without success.

Zofia's tiny form towered over the seated apprentices, causing even the innocent to squirm away from her intimidating glare. Unnecessarily, she pointed to her marked face. "As you can see, I was attacked in my sleep last night. Jet was on duty, guarding certain areas of the building while I was sleeping, and one of your familiars, unprovoked, cold-heartedly attacked me. I didn't identify this cowardly attacker, as it was too dark for my eyes to see."

Zofia clasped her hands behind her back and paced purposefully, her eyes rarely leaving her audience. "Even though there are only a few familiars among you apprentices that can leave these kinds of marks, I've called you all here to demonstrate what can happen if you go against the senior members of the coterie."

Rehan raised his hand, and all eyes turned to him. Zofia nodded, and he stood, appearing reluctant. "How do you know it was one of the apprentices' familiars? Other familiars have claws, like Tabatha."

A level voice called from the back of the room. "I can guarantee it wasn't Tabatha. She would never attack Zofia like that." Artemise stormed down the short aisle, her beige gown swaying as she twisted to squint accusingly at the apprentices. Her amber eyes fixed on Rehan as the tabby cat prowled closer and flicked her tail.

The young apprentice's face paled. "I didn't mean it was Tabatha. I was only using her to reference other animals with claws."

Pausing, Artemise bent awkwardly and placed a hand on her familiar's head. "We know that, don't we, Tabatha?"

The cat licked her lips then yawned as though showing off her vast array of pointed teeth before turning up her nose and following Artemise to the front of the room.

The sorceress's faded eyes turned sharp, and her crow's feet deepened. "When you rule out Tabatha, the only other instructor's familiar with claws is Mystique. Is anyone here accusing the head sorceress's familiar?"

Everyone in the room shook their head.

The elderly sorceress raised her chin. "Then that only leaves the ones bonded with the apprentices." She waved a hand toward Zofia's face. "It's why we haven't healed her marks, so we can compare them to the claws of familiars here. Earlier, before my class, we discussed what we should do." She faced the apprentices, her puffy orange hair giving her a look of insanity and adding uneasiness to the room's tension. "Out of the apprentices, only three with familiars have claws. One of them isn't here, as she is spending time learning on the borders, so that leaves two."

Samara's stomach pitched in a raging torrent as she waited for her name to be called.

Artemise sat on the armrest of Callista's throne-like chair made of branches and stroked Tabatha's head.

Zofia straightened her shoulders and called, "Peadar, come forward, and bring your familiar."

Sitting at the front right, Peadar's face paled, and his eyes widened as he reached down and picked up Ziggy, the raccoon kicking his legs against the movement. Peadar stumbled the last few steps but stopped before Zofia, trying to calm his writhing familiar.

A sadistic amusement passed over the weapons master's face, and she dragged Peadar and Ziggy in front of Artemise, catching one of the racoon's flailing legs and forcing its claws to splay wide by pushing into the middle of his paw.

The potions master leaned forward and compared the claw to the marks on Zofia's face. Her lips thinned, ironing out the wrinkles, before she shook her head. "I don't think it's the right kind of claws to make the mark. You may take your familiar and sit, Peadar."

Samara's blood chilled as Zofia focused on her then Gray.

The weapons master's eyes turned cold. "Samara, bring your owl to the front."

Samara fought to keep her face devoid of all emotion as she gently pushed past Paxton with Gray on her shoulder. Her legs trembled, making it difficult to make her steps seem sure, and she was glad she wore a pinafore today instead of her usual tight pants.

When she reached the front, Gray's head turned one hundred and eighty degrees, assessing the room behind them, until Zofia grabbed his claw and pulled it close to her scratches. Gray squawked and flapped his wings in protest, accidentally marking the weapons master's face with a fresh scratch.

Samara gasped, slapping a hand over her mouth. Although she tried, it was impossible to try and calm the owl, especially since he wasn't her true familiar.

Artemise's eyes narrowed as Zofia showed her the new mark. "The mark is like the others."

Zofia raised her hand to Gray, and Samara blocked the attack and yelled, "How could it be him?

He couldn't have gotten into your room. He can't open doors. And the mark isn't as deep."

The weapons master glowered. "I sleep with my window open. You let him out at night to hunt, don't you?"

Samara thought back to the previous evening and what she'd done with Gray, and her arms lost feeling. Ulrieg had left the window open for him to fly, feed, and roam freely for the night.

"I'll teach you for attacking me in the night!" Zofia struck the owl, and he lashed out again, breaking his leg free of her grasp. Her face distorted with anger, and she sent a spell in the owl's direction, but Gray swerved at the last second, and the spell missed.

Zofia sent another one after him, striking the tip of his left wing. Twirling, he careened to the floor in a squawking mess, landing in the aisle near Peadar. The owl flipped to his feet and ran awkwardly in the opposite direction, heading for the door, while Zofia sent another spell after him. Gray pushed off the ground, narrowly missing it, but his wings struggled to get any air.

Samara reached for her bow and quiver, hoping to create a hole for Gray to escape, but her weapons weren't there. When Zofia raised her hand, ready to strike again, Samara cried, "Stop! He didn't do it!"

She tried to grab the sorceress's arm to throw off the spell, but the weapons master easily dodged her attempt, flinging one arm at the owl.

Peadar shifted into the aisle, Ziggy in one arm, and blocked the spell, giving Gray time to struggle out the hall's door and away from the attacking sorceress.

"How dare you interfere with my punishment!" Zofia hurled a spell at the apprentice.

Peadar blocked the attack, his face pained. "I don't believe animals should be treated like that, whether they're familiars or not."

When Peadar checked over his shoulder to see if Gray had escaped the room, Zofia attacked again. He didn't have time to concoct another barrier to protect himself and fell to the floor, writhing.

The room was silent, and Samara glanced around in shock. None of them or their familiars had been treated this way before. It was almost impossible to believe.

Something scurried near her, and she realized too late that Zofia had aimed another attack at Peadar. Samara followed the spell's direction, expecting Peadar's pain to increase, but a figure stood in the way.

Arm outstretched with her palm facing forward, Devi shifted in front of the writhing male, blocking

Zofia's next attack. "What are you doing?" Her normally gentle face twisted in confusion as her top lip curled. "Why are you torturing this sweet soul?" Devi looked at Artemise then Zofia.

"He was disrupting my punishment of a familiar." Zofia sneered.

Devi leveled her gaze at the sorceress. "Are you the reason that poor owl struggled to leave this room in a hurry?"

Zofia must have nodded, for Devi continued, "What on earth would cause you to do such a thing?"

Zofia pointed to her face. "The owl attacked me in the night."

The defense instructor's head tilted to one side. "I thought you said you didn't see the animal because it was too dark."

"It had to be the owl! No other creatures have those kinds of claws, and Artemise matched the fresh claw mark to the ones already on my face." Zofia pointed to her latest injury as if to make a point.

Devi's mouth thinned. "You aren't known for being the most approachable instructor to the familiars or the apprentices. You know, there are times that rats or other creatures manage to find their way into this hidden building despite the magic ward keeping it invisible. Perhaps it was even Artemise's cat. Have you thought of that?"

The potions master glowered at Devi. "How dare you!"

Devi inclined her head. "I'm merely making a point. I think you both acted too quickly to judge the situation properly." She bent down, inserted a releasing spell into Peadar, and then helped him up. "This meeting is dismissed."

Holding him up by the arm, she led Peadar out the door, leaving behind a room full of perplexed apprentices and two disgruntled sorceresses following her with hardened eyes.

CHAPTER FIFTEEN

Samara and Paxton followed the others out of the room. There was no sign of Gray. Samara didn't know if he would come back after being so brutally treated.

With only a quick glance at Zofia and Artemise, the young apprentices charged down the corridor. Although their actions were quick, their hunched shoulders and fearful glances portrayed their lack of confidence. They probably just had their lives turned upside down. Most of the younger ones had been kept from the harshness of the coterie and their expectations. Now, their safe haven had been shattered in moments.

Samara checked the balustrades and any open beams in the building, but there were no signs of her owl. She then checked behind the potted plants,

Paxton helping. After a bit of searching, she realized she hadn't heard from her familiar, either. *Ulrieg, have you seen Gray?*

When he didn't answer, her stomach twisted into knots. She hoped Gray was all right. She wasn't far from the hall, but she wasn't sure of the distance her bond speak would travel. They continued to look for Gray. "I don't think he can get out of the building. I haven't seen any open windows, and the doors are closed."

There you are.

Ulrieg's voice boomed in her head, making her jump slightly. Samara twisted to peer around the room, not knowing where to look for her dragon. *I've been searching for you and Gray. Have you seen him?*

Yes. I let him outside. I felt sorry for the poor guy. He was squawking on the floor near the front door, so I let him out and ensured he got up one of the big trees.

I didn't know you could open the door.

I've learned a few new tricks since I've been here. You do realize I'm half your size and have large front talons, big enough to encircle a handle?

Of course I know you're half my size. I've had to carry you on my back many times. You're heavy. She indicated for Paxton to follow as she headed for the front door, leading them through it. *Can you show me where he is?*

Hang on. Hold the door open for me. I'm gliding toward you.

A breeze passed over her head as the invisible dragon exited the building, and she closed the door behind them, searching the treetops. *Where is he? I can't see him.*

Paxton touched her arm, drawing her attention to a bouncing branch at the top of a tree on the right. Gray perched in the center of the tree, hiding among the foliage. They descended the stairs and headed to the bottom of the tree.

Samara lightly grabbed his elbow. "Can you see him?"

Paxton shook his head. "Although more branches are moving up there. Perhaps Ulrieg is trying to capture him."

Samara's heart ached. Gray didn't ask for this life. He had been a loyal pet despite being dragged into her mess. *What's going on up there, Ulrieg?*

The dragon grunted. *Wait. Ow! He just bit me. He's never done that before.*

Samara winced. *He's probably hurting and scared. Be patient with him.*

Ha. Yeah, that's me. Full of patience. You couldn't get a more patient dragon. Ulrieg muttered something unintelligible. A few moments later, Gray was awkwardly lowered from the tree by the invisible dragon, moving from branch to branch but never getting his claws around them, wings flapping angrily. The feathers of his left wing were stained with blood.

Samara covered her mouth with a hand. "The poor thing. He's been bleeding."

Yeah. Well. That's what usually happens when a flying animal loses the end of a wing. That callous sorceress blew off the tip, including the bone.

Samara's face lost all feeling. "The poor thing! That's horrid."

"Bring him to me. I'll see what I can do." Paxton raised his arms, bracing to take Ulrieg and Gray's weight.

Instead, Ulrieg landed on the ground at Paxton's feet. Gray looked a mess. His feathers were in disarray, his eyes wide as he squawked protests.

Gently, Paxton cooed at the distressed owl. "Settle. I'm going to try to help you." Gray's chest worked hard as the owl took in panicked breaths then tried to bite Paxton, who pulled his hand away just in time. Paxton rubbed his hands together and closed his eyes before pushing out his palms. *"Childora."*

Gray instantly calmed, giving Paxton the freedom to properly inspect his wounds.

"Ulrieg wasn't exaggerating. Zofia has blasted off the top of Gray's wing bone." Gently, Paxton turned Gray, observing the different sides of the wing and the extent of the damage. "I'm not sure if I can regrow the bone. Not too much has been taken off, but the feathers have been destroyed along with it. I'll see what I can do." He cupped his hands around the wounded wing tip and closed his eyes.

The dried leaves around Gray shifted as the invisible Ulrieg circled the owl. *I'm sorry, my little friend. I didn't want you to get hurt.*

The empathy in Ulrieg's voice touched Samara. The dragon pretended to be distant and often uncaring, covering his feelings with snide comments, but when it came to someone he cared about, he proved he had a soft heart. She wondered if he felt more guilt because Gray had suffered for his actions. "Perhaps you can find Gray some comfort food while Paxton works on him."

I can do that. The dried leaves scattered as the dragon leapt into the air.

Samara sat quietly, constantly checking to ensure they weren't followed in case Ulrieg or Paxton's healing abilities were discovered. She hadn't felt anyone following them, but after the strange happenings of the last couple of days, it was best to be on the safe side.

Helplessness swamped her as she waited. Her mind spun with what had taken place in the hall. She wanted to discuss everything with Paxton but didn't want to disturb him from concentrating on Gray. The owl lay on the ground, more relaxed under Paxton's spell, yet confusion still filled his dulled eyes. Gently, she stroked the owl's head. "You poor thing. You didn't deserve that. You have been a wonderful companion and fake familiar."

A branch snapped a couple of feet away from her. She turned to find a dead rabbit on the ground, its colors precisely like those of Luna's familiar. *Please tell me this is a wild rabbit and not Coco.*

What do you think I am? I'm not a familiar killer, and I only hunt animals for food, not for torture! Thanks to Gray, I no longer kill owls. Ulrieg snorted. *My food selection is growing smaller by the day. Although I must admit, I took out some of my frustration on this poor rabbit.*

Samara glanced at the lifeless animal and noticed many deep scratches in its fur. *Ulrieg!*

Relax. I didn't do it until after the animal passed. I'm not cruel.

She expelled her relief in a long breath. *You had me worried for a bit.*

I would never treat an animal as badly as the sorceresses in your coterie.

Just the sorceress you are accusing of Byzarid's death. Samara's mouth thinned.

Exactly! You can't tell me she didn't deserve it.

No, I can't say that. But your actions did cause more trouble for us, and Gray took the blame because his claws were the closest to yours. Actually, that's not fair. His claws were too small, but he still got blamed by Zofia and Artemise. Hot rage fired through her veins. It wasn't right that they blamed her owl. Gray was an innocent bystander. His claw marks might look similar to Ulrieg's talons, but their size and spacing was very different.

Paxton released Gray and flopped onto his backside, his face pale with dark circles shadowing his eyes. "I've done as much as I can for now."

Gray shuffled to his feet and spotted the rabbit. His eyes were tame again, no longer wild with fright and pain, and Ulrieg's remorseful offering had won his attention. Gray tore into the rabbit. His feathers were still matted with blood, but he tucked the injured wing tightly by his side as though it no longer hurt.

Relief flooded Samara, and she placed a hand on Paxton's arm. "Are you all right?"

He nodded. "Healing always takes it out of me,

more than when I command tree roots or help plants grow. It's almost like it takes some of my health to heal others." He chuckled. "It's good that I'm healthy, so my energy eventually recovers. Otherwise, I probably wouldn't be able to heal anyone."

"You've done well. Thank you." She watched the owl as he tore deeper into the rabbit's flesh. "Do you think he'll be able to fly well again?"

He leaned back and propped himself up on his arms, palms digging into the dried leaves behind him. "It's too early to tell, but he may have slightly less flying ability on the injured side."

Samara watched Gray shuffle around the rabbit. "I'm sure whatever you have done has helped him. He certainly seems less distressed." Her gaze traveled around them, trying to figure out where Ulrieg was. "Although I don't think I can force him to be my fake familiar anymore. If he wants to leave us, I don't blame him and won't make him stay."

Ulrieg's voice spoke to both of them. *No. I'm not going to force him, either. He's already suffered enough because of our bond.*

They waited until Gray had finished eating, the owl's eyes drooping as they sat around him, giving him protection.

"Ulrieg, can you please see that he rests safely away from predators for the night?"

I think the safest spot will be in your room until he's confident enough to fly. You can leave the window open for him to leave any time he wants.

Samara sighed. "If I leave the window open, will you behave and not attack anyone?"

I've attacked the one person I wanted. I don't plan on attacking anyone else.

She rubbed her arm. "If no one can get in my room, I guess it's the safest place until he heals completely, but I won't take him to my lessons again, no matter what the instructors say."

CHAPTER SIXTEEN

After a few days, Gray could fly several yards, but the ability to fly in a straight line had been taken from him. Every night, Samara left the bedroom window open for him. If the owl decided to leave for good, they would just have to deal with it.

Ulrieg came in that morning with a rat for Gray and placed it on his perch before climbing the wooden desk chair. The sun peeked over the treetops as it lit the pale-blue morning sky with vibrant hues of orange and yellow.

Lifting herself into a seated position, Samara stretched her arms high then rubbed the sleep out of her eyes. With no urgency to check the catacombs or look after beings in the forest, she had caught up on some sleep.

She eyed Ulrieg. "Have you been out all night?"

Most of it. Ulrieg scratched behind his head with a rear leg.

"Did you see anything suspicious while you were out there?"

The dragon jumped onto the table and curled on top, his head resting on his front talons. *No. It's been quiet out there since Vexx and Kellam have gone.*

Samara crossed her legs on the bed. "That's strange, since Zofia is still here."

I guess Zofia only gets involved when the dragons are already captured. I don't see her leaving the building often. I haven't even seen her go out to find more ogres for her apprentices to fight.

"Maybe Callista has told her to stop after the trip that got Blade killed."

Ulrieg grunted. *We can only hope. You must admit, though, an eerie silence has fallen over the coterie.*

"What do you mean?"

He fixed his red eyes on her. *The apprentices don't seem as settled as they used to be. There's a lot more whispering and sidelong glances.*

She frowned. "I haven't noticed. But I wouldn't be surprised after what Zofia did to Gray and Peadar. A lot of the younger apprentices are probably dealing with shock. It's not like Callista's been here to reassure them that everything will be all right."

A rapid knock on the door took her by surprise. She rose and opened the door a crack, and her heart fell to the floor when she discovered Mist on the other side, her sword strapped by her side and Okak on one shoulder. A light tan colored Mist's skin, but the time in the fresh air of the border hadn't softened her features, judging by the scowl that deepened the lines on her face.

"Mist, you're back." Samara couldn't help letting the disappointment leak through her voice.

Arms crossed, Mist straightened her back. "I'm just as excited to see you too. Callista wants to see you. Bring your familiar."

Samara's jaw dropped. "I didn't know she was back." She glanced over her shoulder at Gray, and the bird tossed aside the remains of his rat and flew out the window in a lopsided flight to the nearest tree. The sudden action made her wonder if Ulrieg had chased him out. Either way, she wasn't going to chase him.

Samara turned back to Mist, acting like her pretend familiar hadn't just left. "I'll get dressed and go. Is she in her office?"

Mist nodded then turned to leave.

Closing the door, Samara hurried to get dressed. "Did you chase Gray out the window?"

Please! Like I'd do that. Ulrieg became visible and stood under Gray's perch, leaning against the stand, his teeth viciously displayed in what was supposed to be a cheeky smile.

Samara shook her head. She couldn't blame Ulrieg. The owl had been through enough. However, what it did to their future and safety was yet to be seen. "I wonder if this means that Kaine is back, too, or if Callista has brought Mist back after a visit." Her insides churned. It didn't feel like a good thing that the head sorceress wanted to see her so quickly after returning—and she would have to see Callista without Gray. Considering Callista asked for her familiar to be brought along, she appeared to be openly going against the head sorceress's wishes.

Samara slid on a plain, long-sleeved top followed by a brown pinafore, releasing the fabric and letting it drape to the floor. The clothing reminded her of her days on the farm, in some ways making her feel her family's warmth and surrounding her with comfort. The thoughts of them gave her strength to press forward for their good fortune and safety, even if her own security slipped away. As much as she missed them, she had come here to provide for her parents and six siblings.

She walked onto the balcony overlooking the common room, and the smells of hot food wafted to her. Her stomach growled. She badly wanted to grab breakfast, but that would have to wait. There was no point in aggravating Callista. They might need her help in the future.

An occasional breeze brushed over her as she made her way to Callista's office, as though Ulrieg was passing over her several times to remind her that he was there despite being unable to give her visual confirmation.

Samara felt the yellow eyes of Mystique well before she saw the black jaguar sitting upright in a dark corner near Callista's office door. The large cat's intimidating gaze followed Samara's approach, and she twitched, fiddling with the straps of her pinafore, trying not to let the scrutinizing slitted pupils set her further on edge than she already was.

"Hello, Mystique. Welcome back." Samara tried to sound confident and sincere despite the shiver that traveled through her body from those yellow eyes.

The large cat yawned and gave off the air that Samara's presence was as welcome as that of a pestering insect.

Coming in!

Samara braced herself for Ulrieg's weight, gritting her teeth and cursing through their bond as his talons pricked through the thin material and into her skin. *I should've worn my leather protector straps, but that would look strange, considering I didn't bring Gray.*

I'm sorry. Ulrieg settled down. *I'll try to not dig them into you, but it's only until we get through the door.*

Whatever you do, don't let them pierce my skin. I don't know how I'll explain away patches of blood from under my clothes.

The door to Callista's office opened, and the head sorceress's slight frame filled the entrance. She wore a beige leaf-patterned dress, her face unreadable as always. "Ah, Samara. Mystique told me you were here. Where's your familiar?" Her eyes searched the ceiling and walls before she stood to the side, indicating for Samara to enter.

Samara walked in, keeping her distance so Ulrieg wouldn't accidentally knock into the head sorceress. "I'm afraid Gray couldn't make it. I don't know if you know, but he suffered quite a beating from Zofia the other day, and although he's healed as much as possible, he's lost trust in people. I'm not sure if he'll return to normal."

Callista closed the door behind her then clasped her bracelet. "It's highly unusual for Zofia to treat animals harshly. It would be distressing to wake in the middle of the night while being attacked by a clawed creature yet unable to see it to defend your-self. It's almost as though the creature was invisible." She stroked one of the crystals in the corner of the room, letting out a soft murmur.

Ulrieg used that moment to climb off Samara's back, hopefully ensuring Callista didn't notice Samara swaying under his shifting weight.

Callista turned to face Samara. "How odd. An invisible creature."

Dumbfounded, Samara nodded shakily, unsure where to look. "Yes. Very odd."

The high sorceress studied Samara as she saun-tered to another corner, running a hand over the crystal on the pedestal. "I have heard of a particular animal that can turn invisible."

"Oh." Samara frowned as her stomach cramped.

"There is a kind of animal species known as the dragon. Have you heard of them?" Although the sorceress's face bore no emotions, her words played with Samara's nerves, especially when she kept toying with her bracelet. The tone of Callista's voice made it difficult to tell if she was digging for infor-mation from Samara or if she knew that Samara had a dragon for a familiar.

"I have come across them in a book in the library." She left out the part where Paxton had found them in a book after becoming curious about the Sacred Flame coterie's history. "In the book, there seemed to be many different kinds of dragons. Are there any around here? It doesn't seem to be an animal that people talk about."

Callista approached the next corner past the lounge chair, and Samara noticed indents moving in the chair's padding as Ulrieg evaded the sorceress's reach. "There aren't many in Wraeyanor. Probably because the coterie members don't put up with their superior attitude. Dragons are also not an animal we talk about here. They aren't normally animals that will volunteer to be a familiar. They are often too arrogant and aggressive to bond with a magic wielder and always think they are in the right."

Samara thought out her words carefully, knowing there was a fine border here that she couldn't cross. "How do you know this if they don't bond? Can't animals only communicate with their bonded partner?"

One of Callista's lilac eyebrows rose. "Dragons are magical creatures. Not only is one of their breeds able to turn invisible, but the race also can communicate with other beings. I have met a few in my lifetime, and all of them have been aggressive. If one of them had found our building, it could easily have done the damage to Zofia."

Samara wasn't sure what to say that wouldn't incriminate her. It sounded like even if Callista wasn't the evil magic wielder that hid the realm of Dragoria, she still wouldn't welcome a dragon as a familiar. It made Samara wonder what Kaine had told her before he left for the border. "I thought that no one could see this building, including the animals, unless you have invited them to."

Callista rubbed her chin. "True, but besides being magical, dragons are also intelligent creatures. Perhaps they found a way around my invisibility ward. Perhaps an invisible dragon could see past an invisibility spell."

Samara froze, her mind whirling, trying to find an answer for the comment. Finally, she chortled nervously. "It's all sounding too complicated for this apprentice witch."

Casting her a side glance, Callista made her way to the empty pedestal, fiddling with the stone in her bracelet as she walked. "Don't sell your intelligence short. You may not be a dedicated scholar, but you are intelligent." She placed one hand on the pedestal. "In any case, I have a new task for you, and I need you to take your familiar. Can you do this?"

"I'll try and bring Gray. He may insist on staying in the trees."

A rare flash of emotion crossed Callista's face,

but it was gone too quickly for Samara to decipher its meaning. "You are due to go to the border for your training. Leaving your familiar behind isn't an option. I'll take you to the border of Slosiaran and have you trained to patrol the crossings to and from the realm of the humans. Kellam will oversee your training."

Samara's cheeks turned clammy. Being trained by either of the senior sorcerers was one of her nightmares. Both seemed evil to the core, and neither seemed to like Samara. "Are any other apprentices coming with us?"

Callista shook her head. "That's not my plan. This is the one part of training that is to be completed individually. Kellam and Vexx are determined to know the apprentice fully and test their loyalties." She paused. "If you don't pass this next part, you will need to reconsider your future in the coterie."

The thought of being alone with one of the two senior coterie members made Samara's toes curl. "But I don't know that much magic yet. Don't I need further training before I go through the testing of the senior sorcerers?"

"You already have the basics. Most of the rest is practice and using your head to discover what you can develop in execution." Callista ran her hand over the top of the pillar. "I'll be traveling into the human realm while I'm there. I've heard rumors that the last crystal for my collection is there. It has evaded me for hundreds of years. It's time to find it."

"Then you should take at least one other apprentice to be trained. We can take turns learning from you." The thought gave Samara hope and lightened her mood. Another apprentice to take the attention away from her would help.

Callista pushed her mouth to one side. "I'll think about it. Go and pack for a few nights away, then meet me in front of the building."

CHAPTER SEVENTEEN

Whatever happens, she can't get her hands on that last crystal. When they entered Samara's bedroom, Ulrieg turned visible and climbed onto her bed.

"I don't know how we're going to stop her. What does she need the other crystal for, anyway?"

If she gets it, she'll be stronger. More difficult for anyone to go against. He rested his head on his front talon. *Lately, they have been killing many dragons. I don't know if this is something they have done for a while, or maybe they are finding more dragons, and she's part of the antidragon group—like I've always said,* he sniped. *And thinks she needs the extra power. She's probably worried after they found a guardian dragon and a dragon elf. They may think there's more.* He exposed his teeth in a sneer.

Samara tapped her lips with a finger. "I'm not sure, although I do know we have enough problems of our own. Our biggest priority is for you to stay alive and safe." Samara leaned against the door, letting her head fall back to rest against it. She studied the large wooden planks used for the ceiling. "I'm worried about us, Ulrieg. And my family and anyone helping us."

And so we should be. I don't know what she was playing at in there, but I don't like it. Then again, maybe it's good that we're going to the border while she's planning to search for the crystal. Perhaps we can hinder her. I might have the chance to warn any dragons I see to stay away.

Samara pushed off the door and grabbed her bag, placing a few essential items in it. "I better pack. She wants us to leave soon. I also want to grab some food from the kitchen." She placed a few essential items in the bag then paused to face Ulrieg. "Can you please check to see if Gray will come with us? If he won't get close, then don't make him. If he does come, he can stay in the trees in the distance if he wants to. I hope we can get him to come." Her frown deepened. "Actually, I kind of don't want him to come, to be honest. It would only be more convenient for us if he does."

I'll see what I can do. Ulrieg left through the window.

~

FORGRAC PUT TOGETHER a special package for Samara, Ulrieg, and Gray, and after saying goodbye to the dwarf and Paxton, she returned to her room with a heavy heart. She was going to miss them. Aside from Ulrieg, they were the only ones she could confide in.

She found Ulrieg sitting on her bench before the window, his shoulders curved. "What's wrong, Ulrieg?"

Gray's gone. He flew in the opposite direction when he saw me.

Samara expelled a breath. "I can't blame him. It leaves us in a tricky situation, but we'll work it out. We don't have a choice. If they know he's taken off, they'll expect me to have weaker magic—unless they already know about you."

Can you tell them he's in the trees and refusing to come down?

"I can tell them that, but whether or not they believe it is another thing. It'll help if there's an owl like him around to point to."

I'll see what I can do as we go along. But I'm not keen on capturing another owl after what they did to Gray.

"I agree." After packing the last of her clothes, Samara looped the bag over her shoulder. "I guess it's time to go."

Ulrieg climbed onto her shoulders, leveraging most of his weight on the backpack and quiver to protect Samara from his talons, turning invisible as she reached for the handle. When she pulled the door open, she was shocked to find Mystique sitting outside her door, the jaguar's yellow eyes an eerily contrast to her dark fur. Her nostrils flared as though sniffing the air.

Samara held a hand over her heart. "Mystique! I didn't expect you to be outside my door."

The jaguar's eyes constricted before she raised her chin then led them down the stairs, her tail up and twitching.

A few younger apprentices approached the dining hall, oblivious to Mystique leading Samara and Ulrieg through the common room and out the front door to what felt like impending doom.

At the bottom of the stairs, Callista sat astride a white horse, her beige dress draped on either side, holding the reins of a beautiful brown horse also saddled and ready to go.

"You remember how to ride a horse, don't you?"

Callista's steel-blue eyes observed Samara's every movement as she descended the stairs.

Samara nodded. "It's been a while, but I'm sure I'll be fine."

The head sorceress nodded once. "And your familiar? Where is he?"

Fighting to remain steady as Ulrieg pushed off her back, Samara was keenly aware that her every movement was being assessed. The treetops closest to them rustled, thanks to Ulrieg in his invisible form, and she pointed to the spot even though she knew it was Ulrieg. "He said he will travel at a safe distance and most likely stay in the trees."

Mystique yawned and made a slight meow that felt to Samara like she disagreed. It was difficult to tell if Callista was displeased or indifferent, but the head sorceress didn't demand a different arrangement or more information.

Heart pounding with anticipation, Samara introduced herself to the brown horse, letting him sniff her hand, before she levered herself onto his back. Once she was seated, a noise behind her caused her to start. She spun around and was confronted with the sight of Luna riding a pale-brown horse, her golden hair radiant in the morning sunlight, the strands barely covering her ample cleavage, which was accentuated by the low neckline on her blue pinafore and white undershirt.

Luna smiled, Coco snuggled on her lap. "You didn't think I'd let you have all the fun, did you?"

Luna sounded cheerful enough, and Samara was about to answer when someone followed behind Luna. It was Henriette, riding a speckled-brown horse, her pale face wearing a grin.

Samara's eyes widened. "What are you doing here?"

"Come on, apprentices. We must go." Callista nudged her horse and led them away.

Samara waited for Henriette to catch up before she fell into line, following the head sorceress. The young human apprentice pulled back the hood of her cloak, revealing her long hair and a panda-hued ferret that peeked from behind the turquoise strands. "I finally bonded with my familiar. This is Pixie."

Samara smiled. She was excited that Henriette had found her familiar and happy to have her company, yet at the same time, she was worried for the younger apprentice's safety. "That's great! But I thought you had to discover your special talent after you bond with your familiar before you can go to the border."

"Already done." Henriette beamed.

Samara's jaw dropped. "What do you mean?"

The younger apprentice's grin widened. "Did you know ferrets are known for causing trouble?"

Samara shook her head.

"They're a perfect bond for someone like me, don't you think?" Henriette waved her hand at the ferret, muttering something under her breath, and the ferret vanished.

Blinking, Samara attempted to find it in Henriette's hair, but to no avail. "Where did she go?"

"She's here." The younger apprentice waved her hand again toward where the ferret was, and Pixie reappeared.

Samara cocked an eyebrow. "That's a very interesting gift you have."

"I know. Think of all the mischief I can get up to with this one."

Samara smiled and shook her head. "No doubt. Can you hide yourself as well?"

Henriette shook her head. "I haven't been able to do that. Hopefully, one day, I'll work it out."

"I hope you do too." Hiding her worry from the younger apprentice, she hurried her horse to catch up with the white one in the lead. "Callista, doesn't Kellam hate humans?"

The head sorceress nodded. "Indeed."

"Then is it a good idea to take Henriette to his border? Won't he make her life miserable?"

Callista fixed her blue eyes on Samara. "They both need to learn to deal with it. If it gets out of hand, I will step in. Henriette is young and naive and needs to learn quickly to grow in our coterie, just like you did."

Samara clenched her teeth. Henriette was mischievous but had been mostly kept from the darker side of the coterie, although she had seen plenty during the lesson during which they fought ogres when her friend Blade was killed while protecting her. She had only recently recouped her humor.

"Besides, you should be happy," Callista continued. "I listened to your suggestion and brought along some more apprentices. Like you said, I could probably use their help."

Mixed feelings whirled through Samara. It sounded like Callista would still leave Samara with Kellam while she traveled through Slosiaran, which concerned her, but she didn't want Henriette left under his scrutiny, either.

With Mystique keeping pace with Callista's horse, Samara followed them, and Luna and Henriette trailed behind.

They traveled through the forest near where they had hidden Daena and Byzarid not so long ago.

What is she doing? Ulrieg sounded as nervous as Samara felt. *Is this a hint that Callista knows where we hid them, or are we passing this area by coincidence?*

I'm not sure. It's not like I can just ask her. Samara swallowed, trying to calm her nerves, then turned to Callista. "How long will you be staying at the border?" Samara wasn't sure if she wanted Callista to stay by her side. The head sorceress had stopped Vexx and Kellam from mistreating the apprentices before, but Samara didn't know if that was a once-off or something that would be repeated.

Callista considered this. "I don't know if I'll be staying there long. I may have to travel far into the land of Slosiaran to find the fourth crystal. I guess it depends on how long those trips take." Her body rocked with the horse's motion, and her posture bordered on regal, especially with the golden diadem adorning her forehead and her long lilac hair cascading down her back.

This was Samara's second year at the coterie, and it had been challenging to get to know the head sorceress. Although she seemed approachable enough, her aloofness was often puzzling.

As if he was in touch with her thoughts, Ulrieg mused, *I wonder if Callista has any close friends.*

Samara glanced up to the spot where the top of the trees swayed dramatically like something heavy had landed in them. *That's an odd question. Why's that?*

Just a thought. She doesn't seem the sort. It's like she's always got a rod stuck up her butt. I think it would hurt her to show any emotion.

Samara stifled a laugh. *Ulrieg! That's terrible!*

True, though!

The trees thinned, showing the sun a third of the way across the sky. The late-morning rays warmed Samara's skin after spending so much time in the shade of the trees. A steady breeze from the west blew strands of her pink hair over her eyes, and she brushed it away, hooking it behind her ear, her fingers brushing over the small point there. If she had to train with Kellam, at least she wasn't a straight human, although she wasn't confident that would make being stuck with him less of a nightmare.

It was odd that he was the one patrolling the border for the human realm if they were trying to keep peace between the realms. After they'd all witnessed his hatred for the humans, it no longer made sense that Callista would put him in charge of that border. True peacekeepers shouldn't hold such a bias against certain races.

Despite her apprehension, Samara enjoyed the

change of scenery. She hadn't seen much of Wraeyanor other than traveling from her home village, aside from the lesson fighting ogres and the time she and Kaine were made to battle trolls.

The quickening of a horse's hooves sounded behind her, slowing as Henriette caught up and matched her pace. "I can't believe we're going to see another realm."

"Me either."

"This is going to be exciting. I've never seen any others, and seeing the human realm first is even better." Henriette's pale-blue eyes shone with excitement.

Trying not to dampen the younger apprentice's spirits with her worries, Samara turned away, taking in the mesmerizing landscape framing them along their journey. Either Henriette hadn't experienced Kellam's hatred of humans, or somehow, she had forgotten how he acted while at the coterie building.

Samara stretched forward, trying to relieve some pressure on specific muscles. Her interest in the scenery began to dampen, her backside already feeling numb from the morning's ride. Knowing she might have a chance to enter the realm spurred her on despite her discomfort.

Eventually, even Henriette's enthusiasm waned, leaving them to travel almost silently. Samara wasn't one to need constant conversation to feel secure, but the silence Callista exuded bordered on awkwardness. Or perhaps it was Samara's nerves causing this. She couldn't quite tell. She cleared her throat. "How long does the trip to the Slosiaran border take?"

Callista turned to her and swept her long hair over the opposite shoulder and met her gaze. "If we keep a good pace, we should be there just after dark."

Samara raised her eyebrows. "Really?"

The high sorceress nodded once. "Wraeyanor isn't a large realm. Maybe that is why it holds the most powerful magic wielders."

Straightening her back and raising her chin, Samara attempted to peer as far as possible into the distance. "If Wraeyanor isn't that big, then where are all the villages? I haven't seen a village since we left."

The head sorceress's mouth flattened into a thin line. "Most of the villages we have are spread out. This is why the residents don't often travel far."

"Which way is my family's village?"

Callista gazed quickly at the sun's position, working out her bearings, before pointing to the left. "Your old village is over a few hills that way. It sounds close, but the hills and valleys are quite large."

Wistfully, Samara squinted, trying to see as far as possible, wishing she could visit her family to see if they were all right. She didn't know the directions to her village and had no idea how she would go there if she ever had to leave the coterie and travel alone. She wasn't keen to find out.

They crossed a long green valley filled with wild-flowers of all colors, a cool wind chasing them from behind. Goose bumps rose on Samara's uncovered arms. She wished she had Ulrieg's heat on her back to warm her against the breeze and realized she hadn't seen him for a while. Medium-sized trees were scattered through the valley, but none of their branches moved other than a gentle sway from the force of the wind. *Ulrieg, where are you?*

I'm in the trees in the distance on your right.

The top branches of a tree in that direction began to dramatically rise and fall.

I see you. It's been such a quiet trip. I'm glad to know you're still here.

Ulrieg's tone sharpened. *You could always spice up your trip and ask if she's been torturing dragons.*

Gee, thanks for the suggestion. I think I'll pass. It's been awkward enough.

CHAPTER EIGHTEEN

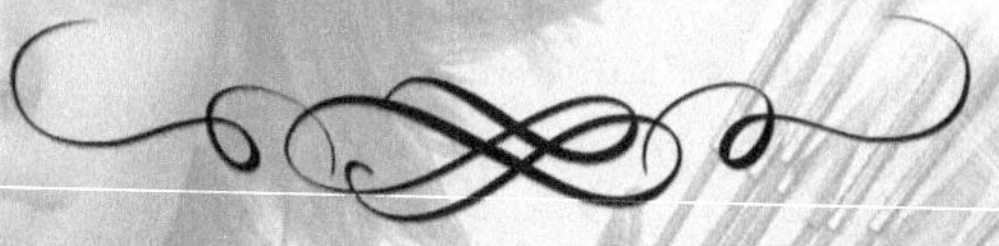

When the sun peaked in the sky, they followed a trail into a village on the lower edge of a mountain. About thirty cottages clustered in the middle, shadowed by various others with progressing sparseness until the mountain's edge. Many vegetable gardens grew in the village backyards, and the cottages on larger land often included sheep, oxen, and horses.

Callista slowed, allowing Samara to catch up with her. "Did you bring your cloak?"

A cloak was the last thing Samara figured she needed right now. If it wasn't for the breeze, she would likely be too hot. "Yes. Why?"

"You better cover your ears." Turning, Callista called over her shoulder, "You, too, Henriette. Grab your cloak." She nodded toward the village. "This village has a thing against humans and half-breeds."

"Oh." Samara tugged at her hair, pulling it down over her ears, and collected the black cloak from the bag hanging on the side of her saddle. She heard rustling material behind her.

Henriette did the same, perching Pixie on her shoulder and ensuring the hood covered her ears once she slid it on. "Is that better?"

Callista checked both apprentices and nodded. "Because you're with me and part of the coterie, you may be all right, but it's best to stay safe."

Samara's knuckles turned white as she gripped the reins with one hand and got Henriette's attention with a wave from the other. "Stay safe."

Somehow, Henriette's pale face turned lighter, and she hurried to catch up with Samara and Callista. "How many places are there like this in Wraeyanor?"

Callista casually eyed the village, her body in tune with the horse's motion. "Not too many. I think this one has been tainted by Kellam." She eyed Samara. "You know what he thinks about humans, and these elves are like zealots, wanting to impress him and punish half-breeds."

"Why, when he only hates humans?" Samara asked.

"He also hates half-breeds, but mostly, it's humans." Callista held her reins high as her horse passed over uneven ground.

Samara swallowed the lump in her throat. She'd thought he had a hatred toward her, not all half-breeds. This was going to be a difficult trip for her and Henriette. But she didn't want to go to Vexx for training, either. *Ulrieg, I'm not feeling confident about this.*

Me either. But it may be worth it if we can work out how to help the dragons and others against the coterie. If it becomes dangerous, I won't just stand back and watch.

She noticed a tree near the first cottage dipping in a different direction than the breeze and focused on it. *I hope you're right. We're also going to have to help protect Henriette when we can.*

I knew you'd say that. Of course, I'll do what I can, although she should be stronger now that she has a familiar.

I hope so. Samara worried at her lower lip. *I don't want to expose you, either.*

With Mystique leading the way, the distance to the village passed quickly. Samara's stomach was churning by the time they reached the first group of cottages. She kept her chin down, doing her best to keep her ears covered and encouraging Henriette to do the same. A twinge of jealousy passed over her when she spotted Luna riding proudly with a bare head and exposed ears. Especially when they went by several residents who had gathered at the front of their abodes to watch the newcomers pass through. Several people recognized Callista and called out to the sorceress as she passed, looks of awe crossing their faces as she nodded in greeting.

It almost seems as though they worship her. Ulrieg didn't hide the sneer in his voice.

The farther they went into the village, the more people came to greet Callista and follow the apprentices with curious eyes, undecided on how to treat the great sorceress's hooded companions. Several women handed the sorceress fruit, loaves of bread, and nuts, their children tagging behind or cradled in their arms.

Samara squirmed in the saddle. *Maybe they do.*

Something tugged at the back of Samara's cloak, causing the hood to fall from her head. Samara's limbs went numb as a gust of breeze hit her face, blowing her hair away from her ears.

Several women gasped, and a man in a dirty beige tunic tied at the waist over long brown pants ran toward her with a garden fork, the tines pointing straight at Samara. "She's a half-breed!" he called, and several angry cries echoed through the crowd.

Samara flinched, unsure what to do. She didn't

want to hurt any citizens, but it didn't look like they had the same inkling. She didn't have Peadar's ability to block attacks with a barrier. Her fingers itched to grab her bow and arrow, but she knew that to the untrained eye, it would look like a move to kill them, not hit them with unusual spells.

Henriette buried her worried face deeper into her hood, doing her best to avoid anyone who approached her, with Pixie sitting inside the front of her hood, holding it securely on her bonded's head.

Luna started to hum a tune, her magic unfolding onto the crowd, but Luna's siren song was cut off when Callista raised her hands threateningly toward the man.

Mystique crouched, ready to pounce, and Samara jumped as Callista's powerful voice boomed. The head sorceress sat tall on her horse, her arms spread wide. "Do not harm my apprentice. Surely you see her brilliant-colored hair and know she is with me."

"You would never have a half-breed as your apprentice," the man with the fork cried. "They are far beneath you, only worthy to be your slave."

Callista's eyes narrowed. "Only those wielders with powerful magic running through their veins can carry the true mark of the Sacred Flame coterie. None other can have hair with the brilliant color of distinction and prestige of our rank."

The man shook his head. "Even a simple magic wielder can concoct a potion that can change their hair to such a brilliant color." He charged toward Samara before halting, fork still raised but body shaking violently. His face distorted in pain.

Samara glanced at Callista. The sorceress's arms stretched toward the man, her fingers hooked into claws. Her back stayed straight, her face filled with determination and concentration. Mystique paced around the shaking man and hissed at his immobile form as Callista intoned, "I have said it before, and I'll say it again. You will not threaten my apprentices, no matter their race."

She continued her attack on the man as others of the village backed away from him and inclined their heads toward Callista. Clearly, the man was in great pain, yet she wasn't releasing him from her hold.

Henriette quietly gasped, her pale-blue eyes wide as she watched the man writhe in pain.

A shiver ran down Samara's spine. She leaned toward Callista and whispered loud enough for her to hear. "It's fine. You can release him. I'm sure he's learned his lesson and won't do it again."

Eyes hard, Callista glanced at Samara. "I'm not sure about that. These people never seem to learn."

Samara studied the other villagers and could feel their dread of Callista bordering on reverence.

"Please, release him. Give him a chance to redeem himself."

The sorceress released an exaggerated sigh and relaxed. The man immediately lowered his fork and inclined his head to her. "Forgive me, high sorceress. I was so carried away by my hatred that I didn't heed your warnings."

Although he was submissive to Callista, Samara didn't miss the animosity that radiated from his eyes as they fell on her. She gritted her teeth, bracing for any aggressive actions against her. Instead, the people parted, leaving them clear access to the path through the village.

They seem like lovely people, Ulrieg quipped.

Don't they? Samara watched every movement from the others who approached them. *Make sure you remind me to avoid visiting this village if I travel to the Slosiaran border.*

Sure will.

Mystique wandered past and took her position at the front of the group, easily creating a path through straying villagers blocking their way. The word about Callista's protection of Samara must have traveled fast. Although no others attacked her, she could feel the hostility aimed her way.

Callista pulled some of the food offerings from

their bags and handed them to the apprentices. "You'll need this later."

"Thank you." Samara placed it in the bag hanging from the saddle along with the food Forgrac had packed.

Look at the bright side, Ulrieg said. *At least you know it's not poisoned, as they intended it for Callista. And they seem to worship her.*

Samara huffed. Ulrieg had a point. She was glad when the cottages and the people thinned out, although she couldn't understand why Callista passed through that village if she knew they would utterly hate Samara and Henriette. It didn't seem wise, even if she did it for their food offerings.

They passed several more cottages, the last few people calling their greetings to Callista until only a few abodes occasionally appeared along the path.

When they reached the last cottage at the edge of the mountain, Callista tied her horse to one of the posts out in front before indicating for the apprentices to dismount. "We're visiting this house." Several sheep flocked around the back.

A young boy charged around the side of the cottage before seeing them and racing inside the front door. "Ma!" he yelled. "The sorceress is here!"

Soon, a thin elven woman with dark eyes and shoulder-length dark-brown hair stood in the doorway, wiping her hands with her blue pinafore. "Go and get your father."

The boy headed out the front door and disappeared behind the cottage.

"Great sorceress, we are blessed with your presence?" Although the woman's tone reflected her words, apprehension haunted her eyes.

Hurried footsteps sounded from around the side of the cottage, and a tall man with a homely face approached. Samara caught herself gaping at his rounded human ears. She pulled her eyes away and looked closely at the young boy trailing him.

Callista walked to the door, addressing them both. "Don't worry. Paxton is fine and doing well." Although her tone was formal, their shoulders visibly relaxed.

"That's fantastic." The woman stood to the side of the door. "Please, come in."

Callista held up a hand as she entered the house, beckoning the apprentices to follow, and the man joined them with his small son.

There was a distinct, potent aroma in the house that confused Samara until she spotted a spinning wheel and a large basket piled with sheep's wool. She also saw large bowls filled with wool soaking in some kind of liquid.

"Can I offer you something?" the woman asked Callista.

"No, thank you. I was only checking in to see how you are doing and if the villagers are leaving your family alone."

Samara gaped from the woman to the man and the boy while taking in the tiny, cramped space of the small cottage. She wasn't sure if she understood.

Callista touched her arm. "Samara. This is Paxton's family." She then turned to the family and indicated to her. "This is Samara, one of Paxton's close friends."

Samara felt the heat rise in her cheeks. She didn't realize that Callista knew about their friendship.

Well, now we know why we're here.

Samara didn't know where Ulrieg was, but he was close enough to hear the conversation. Paxton hadn't been exaggerating about his situation. *I can see why his family needed help against the villagers. But why would Callista single me out?*

I don't know. Just be calm and try not to show too much emotion until we determine what she's up to. Maybe she's just introducing you to your future in-laws.

Against her will, her cheeks heated even more, and she tilted her head to hide the redness that covered her face. *Honestly, Ulrieg. Settle yourself down. Just because we've gone past the friendship barrier doesn't mean we'll be spending the rest of our lives together.*

We'll see.

She pulled her thoughts back to what was happening in the cottage. All eyes were on her.

The head sorceress indicated Samara's ears. "As you can see, Samara is also half elf and half human. She dealt with some grief on our way to your place, but being of both types of blood isn't frowned upon in our coterie. Wouldn't you agree, Samara?"

Samara nodded. "For the majority of members."

Callista raised an eyebrow at her. "Ah, yes. A few of our members struggle with accepting it, but this stems from their background and isn't as obvious as it is in the villagers of Tradedale." She turned her attention back to Paxton's parents. "Have the people of your village become more accepting since I stopped in?"

Paxton's mother fiddled with her fingers. Several knuckles were crooked from what Samara imagined must be endless hours of spinning. "They have been better but not welcoming to my husband. We don't send our younger son into the village. It's like they will leave the purebloods alone as long as we don't remind them of our marriage. But even though he's young, it's not a welcoming place for our youngest."

"They haven't tried to kill him lately, at least.

They simply don't acknowledge or communicate with him other than threatening glares," Paxton's father added. "It's an improvement but not a situation to instill confidence. At least they buy our products now, helping us earn money for food and necessities."

"That's good, but I'm afraid I can't change their hearts. Do feel free to tell me when I need to step in," Callista said. "Even Kellam will have to defend you if he wishes to hold his place in the Sacred Flame coterie."

Ulrieg, can you see their faces?

No, I can't. Why?

Samara studied them. *Although they seemed relieved, they also seemed apprehensive about something. I wonder if my family is the same. Do you think they know something about the Sacred Flame coterie we didn't when we volunteered to save our families?*

It's difficult to say. I didn't communicate with nondragons before I met you, so I don't know what the beings of the realm of Wraeyanor know. You could always ask your family next time you see them.

Whenever that will be. Samara clenched her jaw.

They left Paxton's family not long after and headed around the mountainside, away from Tradedale. Although it was interesting meeting Paxton's parents, and she was glad she could tell him they were well when she returned to the coterie building, she was glad to leave the hateful place.

Callista slowed her horse to ride beside Samara, her blue eyes stern. "Do you see why it's important that Paxton follows the rules and stays with the coterie?"

Samara nodded, trying to hide her confusion over the pointed question. "I can imagine that their lives would have been in danger from those villagers, and it sounds like they also couldn't earn enough to cover their basic needs because the people refused to buy from them."

The head sorceress held her reins firmly and looked back to Luna and Henriette, who rode several lengths behind them. "Good. Then I'm sure you'll do anything to ensure that his life and his family's lives aren't in danger."

Swallowing the bile that rose in her throat, Samara looked at Callista. "Of course."

"Wonderful! Because they are in a worse position than your family." Callista nudged the horse's sides and trotted ahead, closer to Mystique.

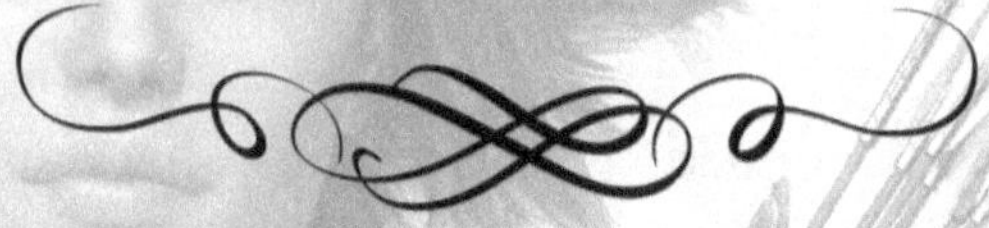

CHAPTER NINETEEN

The group had yet to reach its destination when the sun lowered behind the distant treetops, the sky impressive with its brilliant orange, red, and deep-blue hues.

Samara shifted in the saddle, trying to get comfortable. *Can you see the border, Ulrieg?*

Not yet. Would you like me to fly ahead?

No. It's all right. I'm just getting impatient. My back-side hurts so much I almost would prefer to be with Kellam.

It must be bad, then.

Samara hurried her horse to walk beside Callista, pain jolting up her spine from the jerky movements. "How much farther?"

"Not too far. We're going to be a little later than we thought. Our stop in the village took more time than expected." Callista raised her head and assessed the area, her golden diadem catching the last rays of sunlight. "I estimate we will be there just after dark."

Samara studied their surroundings, storing the scene in her memory in case she needed the reference for future travel in the area. A tall mountain range had framed their south side for most of their trip. "What's behind those mountains?"

Callista followed her line of sight, and Samara thought she caught a flash of emotion, but it left the sorceress's face too quickly to be deciphered. Callista's chin lifted as her posture remained rigid. "As far as I know, no one has found anything behind that mountain range. I believe several wild ogres and possibly trolls live near them."

"What do you mean by 'wild'?" Henriette had quickened her horse to come up to Samara's side.

The sorceress shifted in her saddle. "They hate other beings and will attack anyone who goes there. Not many live to tell the tale."

All the apprentices gawked at the mountains. Samara hadn't realized that there were large groups of trolls and ogres. If that were the case, the few they'd had to fight in the past must be nothing.

Shivers ran down Samara's spine when she remembered her battles with only a few of the giant creatures. Mystique turned to face them. Her yellow eyes sent Samara back to the day she and Kaine were left fighting the trolls alone. Life at the coterie hadn't been the same since.

Lost in her thoughts, Samara was surprised to hear shouting coming from ahead, followed by a response from Callista, who called, "It is I, Callista. And I have brought some of my apprentices."

Samara blinked. The sun had disappeared entirely, replaced by a quarter moon, the darkness obscuring the voice's owner in the distance. She must have been lost in her own world for quite some time.

Callista turned to her. "Has your familiar kept up with us, Samara?"

As if in answer, a loud rustling sound came from bouncing branches in the nearest large tree.

Samara pointed to it. "Yes. He's up there. But he said he still wants to keep his distance. He doesn't especially like Kellam and Vexx or their familiars."

Samara could see the twitching edges of Callista's mouth, and uncertainty filled her. *Ulrieg, I'm not sure Callista doesn't know about you.*

Let's deal with that when we have to. Just remain alert and ready in case that is dangerous for us.

Oh, I'm alert, all right. As for ready, we'll see when the time comes.

A large figure moved closer to them, barely

visible through the darkness. Samara jumped, reaching for her bow and arrow as Henriette gasped.

"Relax!" Callista held out her arm, her palm down. "The ogre is with Kellam's group. You're not under threat if you're with me."

Lowering her arm, Samara's nerves still twitched as she studied the hideous, enormous being in his loincloth. Muscles tense, she swallowed the lump in her throat.

"It's going to be interesting working with ogres rather than attacking them," Henriette whispered through her teeth. "I'm not sure I can relax after what they did to Blade."

Samara squeezed the younger apprentice's hand, whispering in return, "My thoughts exactly. Just remain alert and do your best."

The ogre stood tall and thumped his chest once. "Great sorceress. Kellam not expect you."

Callista touched the side of her diadem, her posture regal. "I thought I'd surprise him with a new apprentice to spend time with."

Samara's stomach churned as the ogre studied her then the others. She still didn't like the thought of being close to Kellam and his monkey familiar. She didn't think she'd be able to work with and learn from someone she didn't trust.

The ogre turned. "Come. Glikag take you to Kellam." His large back was slightly curved with shoulders bent forward, and a large club swung from his left hand. His butt cheeks were partly visible under his loincloth, causing the apprentices to look away. Luna's nose turned up in disgust.

Samara looked for the fence that marked the border, but there was none—unless they weren't quite at the border yet and the wall that split the kingdoms was farther ahead. The ogre led them between two clusters of trees. A large building sat behind one copse on the left. Barely visible on the right were a few tents that reminded Samara of the ogre camp the senior apprentices had invaded to prove themselves to Zofia.

She turned to Callista. "Is the border close by?"

Callista seemed to indicate the spot in line with the buildings. "We are at the border."

Henriette sparked with enthusiasm as she realized how close she was to the realm of her race. "Am I looking at Slosiaran?"

The head sorceress nodded once. "It's the start of their border."

The younger apprentice clapped softly, her face beaming, and Pixie circled her neck.

Luna squinted. "Where is the wall or fence?"

Callista looked amused. "There isn't a physical

fence or wall. It's all patrolled by an invisible magic barrier. This is the only spot between the realms that doesn't have a barrier. Instead, it's patrolled by our sorcerers. It's the same for the border of Clialarion. No one can cross through to Slosiaran or Clialarion without permission."

Samara cringed. The coterie said that this was for the goodness and safety of the kingdoms, but after how she'd seen Kellam and Vexx act, it could be used in the opposite way to stop anyone trying to help the dragons and travel freely to make the kingdoms better places to live.

Henriette's enthusiasm appeared to wane, and she whistled. "That seems excessive."

Callista fixed her with a stern gaze. "This ensures that any unwanted traveler can't move between our realms."

Samara cringed at the look Henriette had received from the sorceress, and she tried to soften Callista's scrutiny. "Are there really people out there who are that bad?"

The iciness on the sorceress's face melted as she answered Samara. "Worse than you can imagine, especially people or beings against us keeping the peace."

Or destruction, Ulrieg sniped.

Samara held her tongue, although several things

that had happened at the coterie building lately tended to make her agree with him, and the hairs on her neck stood on end. The idea of controlling the borders wasn't new to her, but she didn't realize it was as strict as this. She had thought perhaps Forgrac was a rare case, or maybe it was something in place for the dwarves. However, now she also knew it was to stop dragons from escaping. *Are the dragons in all the realms hunted as much as the dragons here? Or is it only dangerous for the dragons in Wraeyanor?*

I've only been to Wraeyanor, but I imagine it would be the same for the dragons in all the kingdoms when the Sacred Flame coterie is around.

Really? You've only been to Wraeyanor even though you can turn invisible?

Way to make a dragon seem stupid, he grumbled.

That's not what I meant. I just assumed you would test the rules with your ability.

You know I do. I just didn't think to use it to cross the borders. All the family I know of are in this realm, and I didn't see the need. Although if I knew where Dragoria was, I would've tried to go there.

Glikag led them to a large bonfire surrounded by a few ogres who occasionally stirred large pots of stew bubbling over the heat. "Glikag beg sorceresses to stay here, and Glikag will find master Kellam." He motioned roughly at the ogres around the fire. "Other ogres will feed you." He grunted at the ogres, then without waiting for a response, he stomped toward the building.

Callista dismounted and led her horse to the nearest tree, tying the reins securely around the trunk. The apprentices followed her lead, and they made their way to the ogres. Samara sat beside Henriette on a log near the fire, with Pixie balancing on the other side. Mystique lay beside the log Callista occupied, and Luna sat with Coco on another. Without uttering a word, the ogres shoved bowls of stew and a large knob of bread at them.

After blowing on the spoonful of stew, Samara placed it in her mouth and was surprised at how delicious it tasted. Not as good as Forgrac's, but considering she didn't know ogres could cook foods suitable to their palate, she was pleasantly surprised.

Discreetly, Samara watched the ogres as they set about their work. Their faces were grumpy, as though they hated their jobs, but having little experience with ogres, she wondered if it was their usual manner. The mound of their eyebrows was prominent and their lips pouty and thick. None of them attempted to talk to the sorceresses. Thinking of Zofia's ogre-fighting lesson, she wondered if this was because they were classed as below the coterie members and treated as slaves. She wanted to confirm this with Callista, but asking in front of the ogres seemed rude.

As conversation was lacking, the crackling fire filled the silence, and nervousness emanated from the apprentices until loud footsteps sounded behind them. Samara spun to find the source of the noise and cringed when she spotted Kellam and his snub-nosed monkey heading their way.

Kellam's orange hair glowed in the firelight, making it seem like his hair had caught fire from his hatred. He stopped a few feet from the head sorcer-ess, and when Callista turned, he inclined his head. "Callista, this is unexpected. What brings you here so soon?"

Elegantly, the sorceress rested her half-finished bowl on the log beside her. "I have come in search of the last crystal. I've heard it's in Slosiaran, and I'm here to follow up on that rumor." She pushed her long lilac hair over one shoulder.

"You're always welcome here, high sorceress." Kellam's gaze landed on Henriette then Samara, and his eyes constricted. "And what are the apprentices for?"

Henriette's breath quickened, her face ghostly white even in the orange glow of the fire.

Behind their backs, Samara reached for her hand and squeezed it.

Curious about how Luna was handling the visit, Samara glanced at her. The beautiful elf didn't seem at all disturbed. Instead, confidence radiated from her as she silently watched the interaction between the sorcerer and Callista.

"They are ready for training on the borders, and since you don't have an apprentice at present, I brought Samara with me for you to train," Callista said. "The other two will accompany me while you work with her."

The sorcerer's eyes skimmed the area around Samara. "And where is her familiar? I cannot train anyone without a familiar."

His monkey circled her and Henriette, causing Pixie to cuddle closer to Henriette's neck. The hairs on Samara's back and arms rose as the monkey sniffed around her. She imagined he was looking for Ulrieg's scent.

After shooing Kellam's familiar away from the two apprentices, Callista waved her hand to a tree. "He is nearby. Zofia beat Samara's owl, and now he refuses to come close."

The monkey tilted his head to one side as he glanced from the tree to his bonded. Kellam raised his chin and glowered at Samara over his nose. "Then she isn't ready to be trained. She cannot conduct her duties properly if the familiar isn't close to her."

Callista raised her chin, and firmness filled her voice. "I assure you, her familiar is close by but keeping out of sight. She is more than ready to learn the borders and cannot progress any further in our coterie until she has completed her border-control training."

"Perhaps we can discuss this in private, great sorceress." Kellam inclined his head and turned to Glikag. "Show the apprentices to their room."

Callista nodded in acceptance, and the apprentices scarfed down the last of their stew and snatched up the last of their bread as the ogre stomped their way.

The snub-nosed monkey sniffed the air around Samara again, making it hard for her to chew the chunk of bread in her mouth, especially when he stared toward the tree where her dragon perched.

Swallowing roughly, Samara took a sip of water from her canteen. *Are you all right, Ulrieg?*

Sure. I can spend the night outside. I need to hunt anyway. It's been a long journey. But let me know if you have a room with an easily accessible window. I'll join you when I'm done.

As they followed Glikag, Samara hooked her arm

through Henriette's, hoping to offer the other apprentice a comfort she didn't feel. She wondered if the ogre would fit in the building to show them the way, but confusion filled her when he walked past the main door. She envisioned a disturbing image of them sleeping in the open, clearly visible to the ogres and other potential attackers.

However, he walked three-quarters down the side of the building on the Slosiaran side and pointed to a door on the lower level. "That is for elf."

Luna entered the room without acknowledging him, Coco hopping close behind her.

The ogre then stopped at one of the doors that lined the outside first level and pointed to a door on the second story, the entrance lined with a balcony. He fixed his gaze on Samara. "That is yours."

Feeling Henriette stiffen by her side, Samara squeezed her arm and whispered, "You'll be fine." She offered the human apprentice a grin. "Besides, you know where I'll be." Gently, she released Henriette and turned to the ogre. "Thank you."

Samara noticed stairs a few doors down that made a path to that level and climbed them, the strain on her muscles a welcome change from riding all day, but her backside still ached. Tossing a last smile at Henriette, she opened her door and found a room with a single bed. She closed the door behind her, threw down her bags in one corner of the room, and cracked the window enough for Ulrieg to lever it open. Then she flopped onto the bed. *Did you see where I went, Ulrieg?*

Sure did. I'll check on you after I catch my dinner.

Stay safe. She paused then added, *Can you take a quick look at Henriette before you come, please? She's beside herself.*

She heard his sigh through their bond. *I'm on it.*

Thank you.

You better have a nice comfy spot for me when I join you.

Samara chortled. *You know I'll always save you a spot on my bed.*

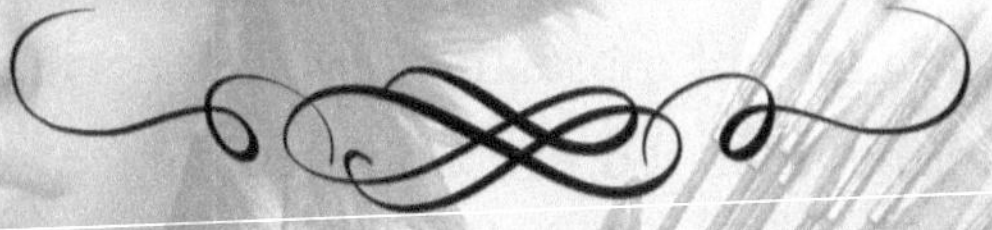

CHAPTER TWENTY

Her body shaking, Samara slowly roused from her sleep and opened her eyes to find Henriette and Pixie leaning over her. Soft light radiated from the sconce on the wall, framing Henriette's turquoise hair with a faint glow and dimly illuminating the bare room.

Samara pulled back, wiping the sleep out of her eyes. "What are you doing here?" she asked Henriette and Pixie. "I didn't think we would be allowed to wander around the area at night. Were you followed?" She sat up slowly, pressed her back against the wooden wall, and hugged her knees.

Henriette chuckled. "No, we didn't get followed. I made my cloak invisible and unlocked your door with a spell." She looked rather pleased with herself.

"I'm in the mood for a little adventure. I thought you might want to come with me."

Don't worry—I helped her get in, Ulrieg interjected. *Not that she knows that. Besides, I'd let you know if someone unwelcome tried to get in.*

Samara let out a breath. "I would, normally, but knowing my luck, I'd probably get caught. The last thing I need to do is further annoy Kellam or his monkey."

"I can make your cloak invisible also, silly." She nudged Samara's arm with her fist. "I don't want you to get caught, either. Where would be the fun in that?"

Samara brightened. "Sure. Obviously, I'd love to feel like I'm doing something Kellam wouldn't be happy with, without being caught." She grabbed her cloak and handed it to Henriette, and the young apprentice began spelling it.

"Are you going to bring Gray?"

"I'm sure he'll tag along in the distance just to keep an eye on me." Samara pulled on some pants and a tunic then looped her bow and quiver onto her back. She hated lying to Henriette, but the less the human knew about Ulrieg, the better.

Henriette wrapped Samara's cloak over the top of the weapons on her back and tugged up her hood. "There. That's better. We can both sneak out without being seen." She pulled her cloak back over herself, making her disappear before Samara's eyes.

"How are we going to see each other to know where we're going?" Samara asked.

"Good question." Henriette chuckled, nudging Pixie under her cloak. "Maybe we should hold hands until we know we're safe to take our hoods off."

"That may work. Where are you planning on going?" Samara reached for her hand.

"I thought we'd travel along the border, the opposite direction to the ogres. The border is transparent, and I'd like to see a little more of Slosiaran in the moonlight without Callista or Kellam breathing down our necks."

"Sounds good." Samara opened the door and led the way out, giving Ulrieg enough time to follow.

Slowly, they descended the stairs, avoiding any that looked like they would squeak. The moonlight was ample enough to see where they were going and some things in the distance but not bright enough to see the kingdom of Slosiaran clearly. However, Samara wouldn't be surprised if Henriette had simply wanted to do something mischievous.

Traveling in the opposite direction to the ogres was tricky, and dodging many twigs on the ground proved difficult with the low light.

When they had traveled far enough to suspect

they were out of earshot, Henriette whispered, "I wonder if you can feel the border, even though you can't see it."

Slowly, Henriette redirected them toward Slosiaran and let her arm extend past the shelter of her cloak, reaching for the border. She gasped. "You can feel it. There is definitely something there, restricting my arm from going past it."

Samara mimicked her actions, surprised to feel the smooth, invisible surface. She tried to force her arm through, only to find it blocking her like a solid wall. The response didn't surprise her, for after all, that was what a ward was supposed to do, yet she found it fascinating that one could be this vast—and on every border surrounding Wraeyanor.

They followed the border for quite some time, well away from the buildings at the opening until they could no longer see them.

Samara's fingers sprang to life as they ran over the leaves of a tree the ward ran through. "The power it must've taken to build these wards and hold them in place is phenomenal."

Henriette pulled her hood off, exposing her head. "Perhaps that's one of the reasons that Callista travels to the borders so often. She might have to reimbue it with additional energy."

The image of Callista almost worshiping the

crystals and doing something similar with the orb flashed through Samara's memory. Despite having access to additional magic power, Callista hadn't shown any supremacies that exceeded those of the other senior coterie members. Topping up the strength of the wards would use a lot of that excess power and advantage. "That must be exhausting."

"I'd imagine so." Henriette stopped on the other side of the tree, gazing longingly through the ward to Slosiaran soil, illuminated faintly by the moonlight. Trees scattered the land, some clustered like an orchard, casting shadows underneath them. "Do you think there's a way to make a hole through the ward? I'd long to sneak over and have a quick look around, maybe find out what kind of fruit is on those trees, without one of the senior coterie members watching my every move."

Pixie climbed out from under the cloak and chattered in her bonded's ear.

Henriette answered out loud. "I don't think my invisibility spell will make an invisible ward nonexistent. But I'll have a go." She placed her hand back on the ward and closed her eyes, her brows pushing together in concentration before she took a deep breath.

Several moments passed. A wild rabbit hopped casually in the opposite direction on the other side of the border, stopping to nibble some grass under orchard trees.

You're lucky I've already eaten, rabbit. Otherwise, you'd be the first thing on my menu if we could get through this ward.

The branches in the tree just above Samara dipped, the leaves rustling as they held Ulrieg's weight. The rabbit heard the noise, glanced behind it, caught sight of Samara and Henriette, and hopped in the opposite direction.

Henriette groaned and scratched Pixie under the chin. "It didn't work. The border is still in place, stopping us from passing through."

Pixie snuggled up to Henriette's hand, clearly enjoying her affection.

It's not surprising, really. It would be hard to make an invisible thing intangible, Ulrieg said wryly. *Why don't you try, Samara?*

Samara frowned up at Ulrieg, sitting invisibly in the tree. *I'm so glad she can't hear you. At least she tried something.*

Samara drew her bow from her back and an arrow from her quiver, waving her hand over the point and shaft, uttering, *"Aperti."* She backed away from the ward and closer to Ulrieg, feeling his invisible form press up against her leg, giving her his strength, then nocked and released the arrow at the ward about waist height. It stuck, and she caught her breath. "Did that just do what I wanted it to?"

Henriette stood motionless by the arrow, her eyes enlarged with wonder. Samara waved her arm toward the border in the gap beneath the arrow and smiled as it went through.

"It worked!" Henriette chuckled and swiped her hand through the gap after Samara pulled away. "That's amazing!" She jumped up and down. "Can I go through first?"

"Of course." Samara waved her hand. "Just make sure you leave the arrow in, or else it will close."

Feet first, eyes filled with wonder, Henriette stepped through the opening, which didn't quite reach the ground. A huge smile spread when she straightened on the other side. "That's a fantastic gift!"

Samara fiddled with the tip of her bow. "It's all right. The others have better gifts than mine. I think yours has more benefits." She stepped through, lightly tossing her bow onto the ground on the other side.

"I still think I could get up to a lot of mischief with your gift." Henriette's grin widened. "Look what you just did. You pierced a significant ward, going directly against what the coterie wants." She wandered over to the orchard, grabbing one of the fruits in her fingers before plucking it. "They're pomegranates. We even have a snack for our little trip."

After grabbing a couple of pomegranates and placing them in her quiver, Samara wrapped her arm over Henriette's shoulders. "So, what sort of mischief were you planning?"

Nudging the older apprentice in the ribs, Henriette giggled. "I think you've managed the mischief tonight. I honestly wanted to get some fresh air away from the senior members and their ogres. I hoped we'd find a hole in the border, but you did even better." Her gaze turned wistful as she scanned the land. "I always wondered what Slosiaran was like." She took in a deep breath. "The land of the humans."

As far as Samara could see, the land didn't look much different. "Can you see any difference?"

The younger apprentice shook her head and chuckled. "No, not really. The landscape looks the same this close to Wraeyanor. Hopefully, I'll get to see some humans on the trip. Maybe they are different than the citizens of Wraeyanor." She plucked a couple of pomegranate seeds and popped them into her mouth as they walked away from the border. "So, what's going on between you and Paxton? I saw your face redden when Callista introduced you to his parents as a 'good friend.'" She nudged Samara lightly with her elbow.

Samara felt her cheeks warm again, just thinking about how close she had become to Paxton. How he'd held and kissed her, made her feel safe and loved. She nudged a fallen pomegranate with the toe of her boot. "I guess you could say we're more than friends."

"Ha. Good for you. He's reticent, but he seems nice, like he really cares for people."

Samara rubbed her upper arm. "He is. It's surprising how nice he is after my brief relationship with Kaine."

The young apprentice screwed up her nose and threw more pomegranate seeds in her mouth. "Kaine's good-looking but very conceited and a little too flirty with all the girls, if you ask me."

Heavy footsteps sounded nearby, and the two ducked under the cover of low-lying branches, eyes scanning the area.

Ulrieg, can you see what made that noise? Some branches lifted quickly, bouncing until they *leveled.*

It's some kind of weird creature I haven't seen before, but judging by their weapons, they are experienced archers. Ulrieg paused. *They're coming your way. You need to get out of here.*

A creature experienced in archery. Seriously?

Yes. That's what it looks like. They look like they're on patrol.

"My familiar says it's an armed creature that looks to be on patrol," Samara whispered. "We need to get back to the other side."

Henriette nodded, her face looking ghostly in the dim moonlight.

Ulrieg, do we have a clear way back to the border?

For now, but you'll have to be quick and keep low.

Rising to a squat, Samara murmured to Henriette. "Come. We have a clear path for a little while."

"Did Gray confirm that?" Henriette rose to Samara's level and followed her, tiptoeing through the orchard toward the border.

"Yes." Samara half lied, guilt eating at her. She wanted to tell Henriette the truth. She believed the younger apprentice wouldn't tell anyone, but the last thing Samara wanted to do was put her in danger because of Ulrieg.

Quickly, they passed through the gap, and Samara reached for the arrow.

"Why don't you leave it?" Henriette asked.

Samara paused. "Why?"

Henriette shrugged. "We're the only ones who know about it, and the tree should block it from being seen easily. It might come in handy in the future. Are you able to replace the arrow?"

"Sure. That's just finding a perfect stick and fashioning it into an arrow." Hesitantly, Samara withdrew her hand.

Several noises sounded closer, and they quickly ducked behind the nearest bush, peeking through the leaves and wrapping their cloaks around their shoulders and hoods over their heads. Squinting, they tried to make out the creature as it neared. It didn't make typical footprints, and it passed through the orchard not far from where they were, the top half hidden behind the trees.

It looks like a horse from here, Samara told Ulrieg.

Very careful observation, Ulrieg retorted. *Although the top part is very different.*

Samara squatted, trying to see under the foliage. *I still can't see.*

Whatever you do, don't move. I wouldn't be surprised if it has excellent hearing.

The clopping of hooves continued past, the upper part of the body remaining hidden by the bushes.

Sighing deeply, Samara stood. "We should get back. That was close, and I'm not sure Callista and Kellam would be pleased that we're wandering around."

Henriette nodded, and they snuck back to their rooms.

CHAPTER TWENTY-ONE

When the sun peeked through the window, Samara stretched and sat up, grateful to feel the comfort of one of Ulrieg's invisible spikes digging into her leg. After the adventure through the border and the ambiance of this strange place ruled by Kellam and his monkey familiar, she'd had a fitful night's sleep. Knowing she was supposed to be training alone with him soon didn't help.

A noise sounded at the window, and she froze when she spotted the white face of the snub-nosed monkey staring into her room. He had climbed onto the thin windowsill and dug his fingers into the edges around the window.

Feeling her stiffen, Ulrieg groaned. *What is it?*

It's Kellam's monkey at the window. I'm glad you shut

it when you came in and remained invisible, or he would've seen you.

His tongue clicked against the roof of his mouth. *And that's precisely why I did those things and will probably remain invisible the entire time we are on this trip. I can't risk being caught. It'd be dangerous for both of us.*

The monkey's beady eyes fixed on Samara before examining the room, patches of condensation forming on the glass from his nose expelling warm breath. Samara glowered at him, wanting to shoo him away.

Throwing off her blanket, she padded to the window and drew the curtains shut in the monkey's face, saying out loud, "This is my private room while I'm here. I'm not having his monkey spying on me, even if it is blatantly obvious."

The monkey hissed and squawked outside her window, bringing a grin to her face. *Serves him right, the little snoop.*

Ulrieg turned visible and chuckled, his red eyes brimming with pride. *I really have rubbed off on you, haven't I? No more Miss Naivete. You're slowly becoming a young woman with your eyes open, realizing the coterie doesn't have your or your family's best interest in mind.*

Samara placed her hands on her hips. *It probably doesn't help that I don't feel relaxed around here. If I thought having Kellam and his monkey stay at the coterie building was bad, this is worse. It's like we're outnumbered in their territory. At least at the coterie building, there were others we could depend on.*

She dressed in her fighting leathers, unsure what the day would entail. *Are you ready for today? I'm not, but what choice do I have?*

Ulrieg grinned, *Hopefully, I'll have a chance to eat the monkey.* His exposed array of teeth looked vicious.

She caressed him under his chin, carefully avoiding the horn under his jaw. *Although the temptation is great, you know we're not supposed to harm other familiars.*

He huffed out steam. *It's not like the sorcerers and sorceresses of the coterie uphold that rule. Just look what they did to Gray, thinking he was your familiar. If they want us to follow, they should lead by example.*

She nodded. *True. But I think I'd feel better if you didn't eat the monkey.*

You'd change your mind pretty quickly if our lives end up in danger.

A thunderous knock sounded on the door, causing Samara to jump and Ulrieg to turn invisible. Samara straightened, strapped a knife to her waist, and marched to the door. When she flung it open, she was surprised to see just a giant fist reaching across the balcony, aiming at her door. Glikag stood on the ground, tall enough to peer straight into her room on the first level.

Samara balked, remaining near the doorframe. "Yes?"

The ogre cleared his throat. "Head sorceress and master Kellam wait in dining hall. You must eat breakfast with them."

A wave of guilt washed through Samara as she wondered if that was the reason the monkey had been staring in her window.

Push that thought away. There is no way you should feel sorry for that monkey, Ulrieg grumbled.

Samara frowned at the spot Ulrieg had been only moments before, wondering if she had accidentally spoken to him.

Don't give me that look. I can also connect to your emotions through the bond. You don't need to tell me everything for me to sense what's on your mind.

She turned back to the ogre. "Thank you. Can you direct me to the room?" As a coterie member, she had no idea how she was expected to address the ogre, so she resorted to respect and how she wished to be treated.

Confusion washed over his face as he nodded.

She turned toward Ulrieg. *Are you coming?*

I'm already out and in the trees.

Samara closed the door behind her and descended the stairs before following the ogre to the area where she was to meet with Callista and Kellam.

The ogre indicated the door. "In room."

In the daylight, the unadorned wooden building seemed basic, even a little hideous, as a higher lookout level shadowed the lower two stories, lining up with the balcony surrounding the first level. The two thin upper-level windows were pushed open, and two guards with bows and quivers on their backs peered down at her before returning to their survey of the surrounding area.

Sucking in a breath to calm her nerves, Samara opened the wooden door and entered the lower level. Her eyes struggled to adjust to the dimness, and her body tensed when her ears picked up the noises of others before she could see them. Her arms raised and ready to defend, she relaxed slightly when her eyes adjusted enough to see Callista's outline in front of her, only for the hairs on her neck to stand on end when Kellam and his monkey also took shape. The head sorceress sat at a dining table with Mystique by her side, while the sorcerer sat on the opposite side of the rectangular table.

Kellam leaned back in his chair and folded his arms over his chest, kicking his feet out in front of him and crossing them at the ankles. The senior sorcerer's mouth pressed into a thin line as he turned his disapproving gaze from Samara to Callista.

Ignoring him, Callista indicated a seat at the table between the two of them. "Come, sit. We have much to sort out."

Uneasy, Samara took the indicated chair, her back straight and her mind alert. "Where are Luna and Henriette?"

"They will join us later. We wanted to speak to you alone." Callista's voice was gentle and reassuring, but her words had the opposite effect on Samara's nerves.

A clang sounded from behind, and Samara jumped, spun in her chair, and spotted a dwarf through the door working in the kitchen. He climbed up and down stools, just as she had seen Forgrac do many times, in order to reach the benches designed for taller beings. Her brows pinched as she wondered if the coterie often used dwarves as servants. If they did, it was a sign that they would never treat all races fairly. Perhaps that was the reason the ogre had looked so confused when she thanked him.

"Samara, are you listening?" Callista's voice brought her mind back into the room, and she realized that words had been spoken, but she was too invested in her thoughts to hear. *Ulrieg, did you hear what they've been saying?*

I'm a little busy here. Haven't you seen what the monkey is doing? Although I think Kellam asked where your familiar is.

Samara looked around the room and spotted Kellam's monkey standing on his back legs in the corner behind her. His front paws grabbed the wooden beam halfway up the wall. She shook her head. "I'm sorry. I'm a little distracted." She pointed to the familiar. "What is the monkey doing?"

The golden snub-nosed monkey faced her and squawked. Kellam rested an ankle on one knee, his blue eyes critical. "He says he's picked up a strange scent that followed you in."

She chortled and sniffed under her arm. "What do you expect? I spent all yesterday traveling on a horse and haven't been offered a bath." Pretending to be embarrassed, she gazed back at the monkey. "Surely the smell hasn't wafted all the way over there."

The sorcerer's lips twisted to one side with a look of disapproval. "Never mind the monkey. I asked where your familiar is."

Samara looked from Kellam to Callista. "He's not coming close because of how he's been treated by some senior coterie members. He's remaining nearby in the tall trees. Callista knows this."

The sorcerer thumped his fist on the table, causing Samara to start. "This isn't acceptable! Your familiar is supposed to be by your side. He needs to toughen up. As pitiful as you are, you're training to be a sorceress in the most powerful coterie."

The dwarf brought out three bowls of porridge, serving Kellam and Callista before placing one in front of Samara. She was glad for the distraction, and she said a quiet "Thank you."

The dwarf's eyes widened before he backed away hastily and returned to the kitchen.

Kellam picked up his spoon, his frown landing on Callista. "Haven't you taught her how to treat these wretched creatures?"

A flash of annoyance passed through Callista's eyes, which were fixed on the sorcerer, and she whispered something too quiet to be understood before Kellam dropped his spoon and scratched furiously at his thighs and crotch.

The sorceress casually scooped up some porridge and blew on it. "I have been too busy with other matters and teaching them magic to worry about such trivial topics."

"But it's essential that they learn how to treat inferior beings, or we will lose all respect." After a moment, his body writhing, Kellam cried, "All right. I apologize. I overstepped."

With a flick of Callista's hand, Kellam relaxed, beads of sweat gathered around the edges of his orange hairline. He inclined his head toward the head sorceress. "Thank you. I sometimes forget my place after being in charge for so long."

Mystique's long black tail whipped back and forth as she circled the monkey. Wearing a shamed face, the monkey rejected his pursuit of Ulrieg and scooted back to Kellam's side.

Samara silently shoveled porridge into her mouth, glad the attention had been removed from her. Still, a new wariness washed over her. She'd been elated to see the uncaring sorcerer put in his place, although she had never seen Callista punish others while emotional before. It was disconcerting. The head sorceress was usually levelheaded. There seemed to be more between these two than she had witnessed in the last few minutes. Head down and shoulders tense, she shifted her gaze from one to the other.

Callista filled her spoon with porridge and elegantly raised it to her mouth with no sign she had just inflicted pain on one of her coterie members.

What have we gotten ourselves into? Samara asked Ulrieg.

Good question. We're going to be on our toes this whole trip.

After a few more spoonfuls, the head sorceress turned to Samara. "I'll be leaving today to follow up on the crystal's rumored location."

Samara's stomach tightened, and she poked her spoon through the rest of her porridge, dreading what was coming next.

Watching Samara's movements, Callista said, "After discussing it with Kellam, I have decided that it is best if you travel with me, where your familiar will be able to be close to you yet still distanced from the coterie members."

Filled with relief, Samara met her gaze. "Thank you. I was worried how this would affect what we're doing."

"We usually treat familiars respectfully, and I want yours to see that. Hopefully, that will reinforce his trust in us and bring him down to participate at a reasonable level."

Pfft. Like that's ever going to happen when I'm visible.

Spooning a small portion of porridge into her mouth, Samara nodded, keeping her eyes focused on her breakfast. She swallowed. "So, all three apprentices are traveling with you?"

Callista leveled her gaze at her. "No. Henriette will be staying behind to learn from Kellam."

A chill ran through Samara's stomach as she remembered how the sorcerer had treated Kaine, even though Kaine was on his side. "But she is so young and only just bonded with her familiar. Wouldn't Luna be better suited to train with Kellam?"

Callista's eyes hardened at the suggestion. "He has accepted her to stay."

Samara frowned and hissed softly, "But she's human. Won't she be in danger?" Quickly, she glanced at Kellam, only to be taken aback by his sneer.

"What? Are you jealous that I chose to educate a human over you, half-breed? Allowing her to surpass you in your training?" There was no effort to hide his loathing of her.

Samara straightened her back and shook her head, looking him directly in the eyes. "No. I'm honestly worried for her safety."

He smirked. "Then she'll have to learn to defend herself, won't she?"

With pleading eyes, Samara met Callista's gaze.

The senior sorceress shook her head. "It has been decided."

CHAPTER TWENTY-TWO

The moment Callista excused Samara, she didn't linger, happily leaving the room. The awkwardness of it stayed with her, only to have guilt replace it when she ran into Henriette, Pixie on her shoulder.

Luna shadowed her, followed closely by Coco. "You're up early. Did you eat all the food? I'm starved." She laid a hand where her pinafore tapered in to show off her thin abdomen. The pale blue blended with her eyes, the neck low cut.

"I believe there's plenty left. A dwarf is working hard in the kitchen."

"Fabulous. I need a good meal before we set off. Come on, Coco, let's see if they have something for you too."

The elf and her familiar entered the building,

leaving Samara with Henriette and Pixie. Henriette wore a deep-brown pinafore and a white short-sleeved tunic underneath. The girl was visibly shaking, and her ferret didn't seem any more confident, pressing hard against her neck.

Samara's heart melted. "Have you heard the news?"

Eyes wide, the younger apprentice nodded, and her bottom lip trembled.

Biting her own lip, Samara grabbed Henriette's upper arm and squeezed. "I tried to get them to leave Luna, but they wouldn't budge. I'm sorry. It seems they've made up their minds, and Kellam hates me more than humans."

"It's not your fault, but I don't know what's happening. I've only just bonded with Pixie. We haven't even had a chance to get to know each other." She rubbed her arm, her eyes darting to the ogres' camp. "It's just so hard to be around the ogres after what happened to Blade and what we went through in that lesson."

"I know, but I honestly don't think these ogres are allowed to hurt us. At least not without Kellam's instruction. Besides, I'm certain you're stronger than you think." Samara nudged her slightly with her elbow. "Also, don't forget you can turn invisible with a cloak. It's not just for pranks."

Henriette's eyes brightened, and a sly smile crossed her face. "What makes you think that would be helpful?"

Samara could hear the mischief returning to her voice, and she smiled. "Well, for one, you can hide if Kellam or anyone at the border gives you grief. An invisible cloak is a perfect way to get away from them to clear your head and settle your nerves."

Henriette's grin widened. "Great idea. That gives me some relief."

Samara hugged her. "Take care while we're gone. I guess I've got to change and dress more like Luna and Callista. Good luck in there, and never let your guard down. And remember, whenever possible, you can use Pixie to help build your strength, assess the situation, and watch out for you." She smiled at the ferret. "Now that you have a familiar, you'll find the sorcerers are tougher on you. To grow stronger, practice when you're alone together."

Henriette squeezed her shoulders, hugging her back. "We will." She released Samara and headed to the door.

Despite feeling slightly better about Henriette staying, a large knot of guilt still churned in Samara's stomach. *She seems so much younger than me, even though it's only two summers' difference.*

You've learned a lot since I joined you. I'm confident

Henriette will, too, and hopefully, she'll create havoc when she knows her strength.

Samara huffed, but the edge of her mouth turned up in a half smile. *Maybe. I just hope she has a chance to live a long and happy life.*

Ulrieg grunted. *Always so serious. I hope she causes endless mischief that rocks the coterie.*

AFTER CHANGING into a blue pinafore with long sleeves, Samara gathered her few things and descended the stairs, attaching them to her horse's saddle. She looped her bow and quiver over one shoulder and waited for her traveling party.

At least it was a beautiful day to travel, with barely a cloud in the sky and a soft breeze to cool any heat from the sun that had crept to the first quarter of its long daily journey.

Trolls sat by the border, occasionally glancing her way or at any movement between the opening. The border seemed quiet, as though people rarely attempted to cross it.

This sparked Samara's suspicions. *I wonder why there aren't many beings coming through the border.*

Probably because during the time the coterie has been in power, many have heard how difficult it is to be allowed to pass. I would say that not too many are granted access to other kingdoms.

Is that the true generalized belief or just the cynical Ulrieg speaking?

Ulrieg grunted. *I'll always be cynical about this coterie, but I think it's also the generalized belief.*

She heard claws tapping on the balcony and looked up, unable to see anything. *Ulrieg, is that you?*

Sure is.

She smiled.

"Oh, has your familiar abandoned you again?" Luna stood behind Samara, ample cleavage displayed for all to see. "Such a shame." She sounded sympathetic, but there seemed to be something else in her voice.

Flicking her golden hair over her shoulder, Luna picked up her familiar, which had been hopping beside her. "Coco would never do that to me. Would you, Coco?" She touched her nose to the rabbit's before stroking her head.

"My familiar hasn't abandoned me. He just informed me that he has me in his sights, even if I can't see him."

Luna gave her a pitying look. "I'm glad you believe him. That would be very reassuring for you, even though he isn't a strong animal as his form implies." Her beauty suddenly turned alluring, and

Samara's head went light and woozy as Luna's voice started to form a song. "You should force him to stay by your side, where he is always visible."

Samara felt herself nod absentmindedly, and she turned to face the balcony, ready to command her dragon to turn visible and remain by her side.

You have got to be kidding me! Samara, she's using her power on you. Can't you feel it?

The fog around her brain cleared slightly, but she still opened her mouth, ready to call him down.

Samara! Snap out of it! She is using her siren powers on you!

Her mind remained fuzzy, only pulling out of her stupor when something heavy landed on her back and sharp talons dug into her flesh.

Ouch! She lurched forward as Ulrieg pushed off her back.

"Are you all right?" Face filled with amusement, Luna hooked golden hair over one pointed ear and placed a hand on Samara's arm.

Samara nodded as she spotted Callista heading their way from the other side of the building. "It was just a sudden cramp."

Luna nodded, then, hips swaying, she went to her horse, attaching her bags to the saddle and shifting the bo staff on her back out of the way as she mounted her horse.

With Mystique by her side, tail twitching, Callista approached her white mare, assessing Samara with crystal-blue eyes. "Are you ready to go?"

"Yes. I'm sure it'll go away." She wanted to scowl at Ulrieg for making his interaction obvious, but she knew he was protecting her from Luna's power before she gave everything away. Uneasiness settled in her stomach. She wasn't comfortable with how quickly she kept falling under Luna's powers, especially since there wasn't an apparent reason the elf should use them on her. She placed her foot in the stirrup and levered herself onto her horse's back.

Nudging her horse's sides, Callista led the way, Mystique keeping pace only a few feet behind. The cat constantly scanned the area around them as though looking for danger.

After several yards of being semiblinded by Luna's hair glowing in the sunlight, Samara gazed over her shoulder to find Kellam standing on the other side of the opening from the ogres, an extremely pale Henriette a few feet away, nervously playing with her hands as she watched them go. *Poor Henriette. I hope she'll be all right.*

A hint of a breeze pushed down at her from above, and she knew it was Ulrieg, showing her he was close. *I hate to say it,* but you *can't be by her side* every time *she's placed in danger.*

She sighed and turned back around. *I know, but she feels like another little sister.*

The sway of the horses ahead lulled her into a false sense of security, and she had to remind herself to remain focused. She believed without a doubt that Luna's loyalty lay with Kaine, and she still didn't know what was going through the senior sorceress's head.

"Callista, are we going to a specific place in Slosiaran?" Samara asked. "Or are we wandering through the realm, hoping you will feel its power?"

With one lilac eyebrow arched high, Callista gazed back at her. "We have a location to investigate. Although I'm a crystal witch, I must be close to a large crystal to connect and feel its power."

Samara frowned. "You don't seem that close to the crystals in your office, while you seem to be soaking up their power." She moved her horse closer.

"Ah, yes. I have enchanted those crystals to feed me their power when I'm within their boundaries. I haven't seen this crystal, only heard of its beauty and existence."

"It's shocking the humans have hidden it from the rightful inheritor." Luna stroked Coco's head as the rabbit rested in her lap. "They should have handed it to you when you defeated the evil powers four hundred years ago."

Callista held her reins loosely. "Unfortunately, not everyone is on our side, even though we have made the kingdoms better by diminishing our enemies and keeping the peace between the realms."

After worrying her lip with her teeth, Samara asked, "Who exactly are our enemies?"

The high sorceress lifted her chin. "Why, everyone who isn't with us, of course."

Well, that's highly vague, Ulrieg said. *She could have just told us it was the dragons paired with dragon elves. She hinted at that in her office. And to think for a millisecond, I thought she might tell us the truth.*

Samara ignored Ulrieg's remark. "So, there's no particular race or trait we are fighting against?"

Callista shook her head. "Only if they are against us and try to disturb the peace we have brought to the land."

Ulrieg snorted. *She makes their cause sound so noble despite the fact that there are races out there, like the dragons they have suppressed and even hidden in our realm.*

Maybe she doesn't know that all dragons are suppressed, Samara argued. *Maybe Vexx and Kellam's ancestors, were the ones that hid the realm and killed the dragons, making the known dragon elves useless. We saw how clumsy Daena became and how bad her magic was after she lost Kaida.*

Ulrieg huffed.

"Who do you think has the crystal?" Luna asked.

"A royal family used to rule Slosiaran. It's believed that someone associated with that family has it hidden," Callista said.

"What happened to the royal family?" Samara asked, shocked at Callista's indifference to the absence of such an important family.

"Kellam's predecessor reported that they supported the evil power that ruled the realms before us. He gathered an army of ogres to make them surrender. They didn't, so the army destroyed them."

Dragon moon! Completely destroying a royal family. That's nasty!

CHAPTER TWENTY-THREE

The path from the border was isolated, with several damaged buildings strewn on either side and wild bushes flourishing within their crumpled walls. Evidence of battles from the distant past.

Why do you think they leave these buildings erect? Samara asked Ulrieg through their bond.

There could be a few reasons. Either they are too scared to remove them since they are so close to the border, or they leave them as a reminder of the past war and what happens if you go against the coterie.

Neither seems like a peaceful way to live.

Despite this being a so-called peaceful time, wars are still being fought. The only difference is that they are much smaller.

Something moved on her right between two ragged buildings, and Samara turned and gasped.

Without the slightest portrayal of self-consciousness or moving to hide, a shirtless man stood there, his long dark hair blowing in the breeze. His eyes stayed on the small traveling group of sorceresses as he moved closer. He looked like any other human man except that his torso was attached to a horse's body. A large bow looped over one shoulder, and another nine like him followed behind.

Samara's hands tightened around the reins. *Are these the same as the creature we saw last night?*

They sure are.

Then why didn't you say they had the torso of a man?

If I did, would you have known it was this that I saw?

No.

My point exactly!

Luna pulled up beside the head sorceress, a frown creasing her perfect face. "What are they, Callista?"

"Have none of you seen centaurs before?"

Both apprentices shook their heads.

"I don't know why you haven't been taught about them. It looks like we will have to introduce the subject of different species." Callista looked at the centaurs. "Do not worry. These centaurs are part of Kellam's army. They live along certain parts of the border close to the opening, and they train regularly to fight with their bows and other weapons if they must. They are very powerful for their size and get from one location to another quickly. These ones will be traveling with us to help enforce our actions if we face any opposition."

Hearing the serenity in Callista's voice, Samara relaxed a bit, yet the way the centaurs' eyes narrowed in on them kept some of her edginess close.

The first centaur stopped a few feet before Callista's horse, followed closely by the other nine, halting slightly behind the first.

"Meet Zoltos and his crew." Callista introduced them.

"At your service, great sorceress." The leader's voice was deep and rough. The muscles on the centaur's chest rippled as he inclined his head, and Samara gulped. Although they had the torsos of humans, their muscles were well defined and chests broader than any human or elf Samara had seen.

The head sorceress pushed forward, and the centaurs shifted to the side to let them through. Led by Zoltos, the centaurs fell in line behind them after they passed.

The part of the kingdom they traversed was green and luscious, with healthy trees scattered between plains filled with wildflowers and fields of beans, peas, corn, and turnips. Cottages sat on the farthest side of the fields, away from the border patrolled by Kellam and his ogres. In the distance on their left, a gap revealed a large patch of barren lands behind a cluster of mountains.

"What is wrong with that land over there?" Samara trotted her horse closer to Callista's and pointed to the area. She hadn't seen the likes of it before.

Callista's eyes narrowed on the spot. "That is what the locals call the Merciless Sanctuary. It's a desert wasteland. Rarely does it rain there, and the heat kills everything trying to grow."

"Ew. That doesn't sound like a very nice area to live." Luna screwed up her nose.

The head sorceress's mouth pressed into a thin line. "It's impossible to live there. There wouldn't be enough water to gather for one person, let alone more. And the heat is intense, causing bodies to lose more fluids than can be replenished."

Samara scratched behind her ear. "I thought mountains often drew rainclouds, especially mountains that high."

"That is true. They draw clouds to one side of the mountain, and the other side is often caught in shadow, meaning the mountain blocks the rain from falling on the other side." Callista shifted in her saddle. "I visited the area a long time ago. It was quite sad to see. So much wasted space."

The sorceress fixed stern eyes on Samara. "You haven't brightened your magical color enough. Your pink has faded, and I can see your dark roots in the sun. Are you not proud of being part of the coterie?"

Dropping her chin, Samara felt the color drain from her face. "Of course I'm proud of being part of the coterie. I just forget to cast the spell more regularly for the color to shine bright."

Callista's blue eyes were sharp. "You're lucky you can find difficult locations that potentially hide things, or I wouldn't be bringing you along."

The words were barely audible, as though Callista was purposely cutting Luna out of the conversation. Glancing up, Samara couldn't tell for sure from Callista's expressionless face, but she could have sworn that was a reference to when the high sorceress spotted her in the catacombs.

Callista continued, "You need to do it more regularly, at least once a week, if not more, to keep the sacred markings of our coterie."

Samara fiddled with the reins. "Of course. I'm sorry. I'll try and remember to do it more regularly. I don't look in the mirror often enough to remind myself."

Luna let out an exasperated breath. "Oh, I can tell. Your hair is always sticking out everywhere. It often looks more roughed up than brushed smoothly."

Samara frowned at Luna and reached for a clump of her own hair, ready to fulfill Callista's request.

Oh wow! I bet that made you feel ugly!

Thanks, Ulrieg. That's not helping.

It wasn't supposed to be an insult. Besides, you're not my type. I don't know what makes someone beautiful in their eyes. I just meant the way she said it sounded like it would knock anyone off their pedestal if they were on one in the first place.

Muttering the spell, Samara watched as the pink in the strands she could see deepened to the bright Sacred Flame coterie-accepted color before turning to see the following centaurs only a few paces behind her. She nudged her horse to speed up.

When the sun reached its apex in the sky, a cluster of buildings spread before them. Callista slowed, and the centaurs passed them, heading directly toward the remnants of a wall that used to protect the residents. A large building took up the majority of the back of the cluster. Made of stone, it was taller and grander than the other, more humble buildings.

Traveling along the main road, Samara thought something about the place didn't seem right. It looked as though it was supposed to be an affluent area, yet there were obvious signs of neglect and damage, and an air of depression radiated off the few people still wandering the street after the centaurs arrived. "What is this place?"

Wingless flight! It looks nasty. Just look at the destruction of that enormous building. And to think it was just left there like that.

"This is Paddosha Palace, where the royal family of Slosiaran used to live, and the immediate surrounding abodes." Back straight, Callista smoothed down her leaf-patterned gown and adjusted her diadem. "The palace is mostly destroyed but remains as a reminder not to cross the coterie." The buildings spread before it were made of stone and thatched roofs. "For many years, we allowed the royals to continue to rule the kingdom under our observation. However, a hundred years after we held the peace in the realms, there were rumors of the royal family building a rebellion, and Kellam's predecessor destroyed them."

Samara's mouth turned dry as she imagined the bloodshed that must have taken place.

"I know it doesn't look nice to keep the palace ruins left here, but the ruling sorcerers of the border have demanded that it remain as a reminder not to go against their rule." Callista's voice was monotone, making it hard to tell if she supported the decision. She nodded to Zoltos, and he turned to gallop down the street, followed by his warriors as though they had understood the unspoken instruction.

Mystique led the way for the three of them, her posture intimidating. They slowly followed the direction the centaurs took. With her usual unreadable face, Callista made eye contact with many of the people stopping to watch them pass.

"There are a couple of rooms still intact in the destroyed palace," the sorceress said. "We will be camping there for the night or perhaps longer. The centaurs will remain our guards while we are here, so they have gone ahead to make sure the palace doesn't have squatters."

The centaurs climbed up the broad stairway leading to the front of the palace and disappeared behind the ruined walls.

Huh! Interesting!

What is? In an attempt to look friendly, Samara smiled briefly at a couple of people watching her. It was a difficult task when she was aware that the behavior of the centaurs and Callista was most likely coming across as menacing. The whole experience made Samara uneasy, and she was the one with a powerful sorceress and centaurs to protect her.

I guess it pays to have a dragon's-eye view. I see a few

people discreetly disappearing from view of the centaurs and Callista.

That is interesting. Samara checked the gaps between the buildings, searching for some of the people disappearing into the shadows. A man with a bushy black beard who looked to be in his thirtieth summer ducked around the corner of one of the buildings, glancing back at her over his shoulder. He paused, faced the street, and leaned against the wall, arms and legs crossed as though he was casually waiting by the side of the house, shaded by the thatched roof.

They may have defeated the royals three hundred years ago, but it doesn't look like they killed their subjects' spirit, Ulrieg noted.

If that's the case, keeping the destroyed palace could also remind them of what they have lost and who took it from them, driving them to rebel.

I'm going to track as many as I can. Some of these may be the ones that know about the crystal.

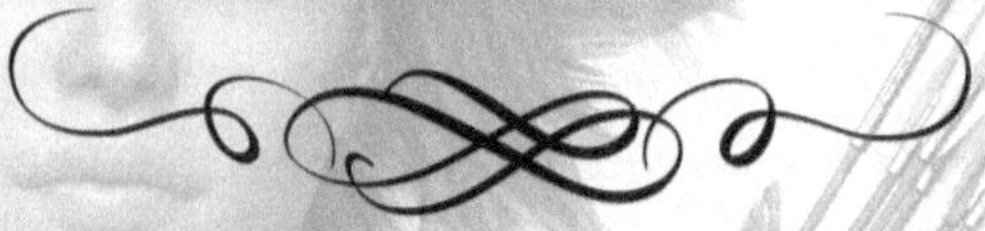

CHAPTER TWENTY-FOUR

Leaving their horses tied at the front of the building, the three sorceresses stood in the middle of one of the palace rooms, bland gray stone walls surrounding them and beams thrown on top as a makeshift roof. Samara had to admit this might be less comfortable than the troll dungeons where she and Kaine had been imprisoned. There wasn't even a thin layer of straw on the hard stone floor.

She fiddled with the straps of her bags, and her arrows rattled in the quiver. Her bag might make a suitable pillow if she took out all the hard items, yet even this didn't make the solid floor look enticing.

"Oh, my stars. This place looks so uninviting and drab." Luna screwed up her nose and covered her mouth with her hands. "Even Coco wants to sleep in the wild."

The clopping of hooves faded as the centaurs exited the remains.

Callista shook her head. "I know we look after you with comfort at our base, but being a member of our Sacred group doesn't mean you will always live in luxury. But don't worry. I've organized the centaurs to gather enough straw from the farmers for three beds."

"Don't the centaurs need some too?" Samara felt terrible thinking the centaurs might knock their joints on the hard floor while lying down.

The sorceress shook her head. "Centaurs don't like the indoors. They would rather find a copse of trees to sleep under or a grassy plain." She grabbed her bag off her shoulder and let it swing by her legs. "Place your things in here. This will be your room. I'll be in the one next door. After you've had some lunch, we'll search the citizens' homes and ask them questions. I've heard rumors that the person who knows the whereabouts of the crystal lives in this area. To cover the ground quickly, we'll separate. We don't want them to leave. Several centaurs circle the palace area and its citizens, ensuring no one leaves."

She leveled her eyes at each of them in turn. "If you have any suspicions that someone isn't telling the truth, and you think they might know something, I want you to report it to me immediately.

Then I will finish the questioning to deduce the truth."

Wanting to appear supportive, Samara imitated Luna after the elf nodded. "Will the people respond well to being questioned?"

A slightly smug look crossed the head sorceress's face. "The people here must respond to our questions or face the consequences. The coterie has a lot of power over the people. If they don't respond as requested, it will bring a lot of trouble to them and the people they love."

Callista looked deep into Luna's eyes then Samara's. "If you find the crystal, you must bring it to me. Once it is with the other crystals in my office, I'll be able to soak up the power from all of them, making me stronger to fight against the beings that want to destroy our peacekeeping efforts." She paused. "We had many crystals and other powerful trinkets when I led our coterie and armies against the evil ruling the lands. Over the four hundred years we have ruled, these have diminished or been stolen and need to be replicated."

Samara felt her cheeks turn clammy. *Ulrieg, are you hearing this?*

No. Honestly! My hearing's not that good. I'm still following some of these people that acted weirdly.

I can tell you later. You stay on those people. Like you said, we mustn't let Callista get her hands on that crystal.

Samara was jerked out of her conversation with Ulrieg when she realized Callista was still talking.

"Someone stole this crystal from me," the sorceress said. "I need to get it back and all the other trinkets to regain the power I once had to hold the peace. Only a few know that I no longer have these items. Any word that is spread about this is squashed by our coterie's loyal supporters."

Samara clapped her hands once and rubbed them together. "Let's eat so we can get started. We need peace in the kingdoms."

Luna fished in her bag, pulling out some bread freshly baked by the dwarf serving Kellam. "Is your familiar going to be joining you while you question everyone?" she asked Samara.

Samara shrugged. "He'll be nearby in the trees."

Brushing her long golden hair out of her face, Luna handed some bread to Callista then Samara, and her words turned into a tune. "Shouldn't he be near you in case you need to draw from his bonding power? This could be dangerous work."

Samara instantly felt a strangeness wash over her before she realized what had happened.

Samara! Ulrieg's voice cut through the fog. *I can*

feel an oddness coming from you. Talk to me. Are you still thinking straight?

Samara shook her head, dullness remaining in her frontal lobe, but her thoughts were again her own. *Thanks, Ulrieg. Shout at me anytime you feel that peculiarity. I think Luna just tried to use her siren magic on me.*

Samara glanced at Luna and Callista and thought she caught them casting a knowing look at each other, but she pretended she didn't see it. "I'm sure he'll come down if I need him." Nonchalantly, Samara took out some apples from the border and handed them out. Biting into her bread, she placed her bag against the wall, keeping her quiver and bow on her back. As she moved, she felt eyes on her, and when she turned, both sorceresses were watching her, filling her with unease.

Luna cuddled Coco to her chest then fed her a slice of her apple, and the silence was broken by the rabbit's soft clucking sounds.

How are you doing out there, Ulrieg? Have you found anyone you want me to talk to?

I think I have someone on the right side of the road we took to enter the community.

Callista gave them some dried meat before her eyes turned to the windows made with pale stained glass. "We had better eat quickly and head out. The longer we take, the person with the crystal may figure out what we have come here for and hide it before we can get to them."

Samara grabbed a piece of meat with the same hand holding the bread, and she made her way to the door. "I can eat as I walk. Do you want me to start questioning the right side of the community from where we came in?"

She thought she saw uncertainty flash over Callista's face, but before the head sorceress could respond, Luna said to Callista, "I'll catch up with her as soon as I finish this, if you like."

The head sorceress's strange flash of emotion vanished. "That's perfect. Thank you, Luna. I'll start on the left."

"I'll see you soon, Luna." Turning quickly, Samara left. *I hope you're right about this person, Ulrieg. We don't have much time on our own. Where exactly are you?*

If you follow the first street on your left, I'm in a house a few side streets down.

Taking another bite of the dried meat, Samara hurried down the alleyway, glancing over her shoulder to ensure she wasn't being followed. Footsteps thumped on the dirt path behind her, appearing to be coming from one of the streets. She quickened her pace, ducking into the first side street, and peered around the corner.

A young woman with long blond hair tied back in a braid hurriedly marched past, her beige pinafore flapping around her legs and eyebrows pushed together into a frown. She didn't look threatening, although her demeanor intrigued Samara. Purposefully, she angled her leather shoes to walk without making a sound and followed the woman from a few yards behind. It was a bonus that she seemed to be traveling in the direction Ulrieg had told her to go. Perhaps this young lady was working with the person Ulrieg pinpointed.

A cloud passed over the sun, darkening the area, and the young woman paused in front of a house and glanced around her and back the way she came, starting when she spotted Samara several feet behind her. Her cheeks paled before she turned abruptly as if to continue past the house.

Ulrieg, am I outside the correct house? Samara glanced up at the double-story building forged in gray stone. The upper level hung over the bottom story, giving the building a slightly misshapen look.

Just a moment. The dragon grunted softly as if he had to readjust to a difficult position. *Yes, it's that one. Who's the lady?*

Glancing back at the woman, Samara noticed she was increasing her footsteps. *I don't know, but she looks guilty over something.*

Hm. Then make sure you get her back here. She is probably working with this man over something.

"Hold up!" Samara called to the woman.

The lady paused and glanced over her shoulder, her expression neutral, yet her eyes seemed filled with hate.

Samara's confidence wavered until she reminded herself that the hate was probably aimed at the coterie. She climbed the next few steps. "Where are you going?"

The lines around the woman's eyes hardened despite her trying to keep her face neutral. "I'm going for a walk. Surely, there isn't a rule against doing that when the coterie members are around."

Samara paused. From the woman's words and actions, she wondered what the coterie had done to these people in the past. "Of course not. Although you looked like you were about to enter this building before seeing me. Is this your home?"

Neck stiff, the woman shook her head.

Raising an eyebrow, Samara motioned for her to follow her. "Let's have a look together anyway."

"But this house is in the middle of all the buildings. That's such a strange place to start a search," the woman protested.

Samara smirked, knowing that the woman couldn't refuse her without thinking there would be consequences from the coterie—even if Samara would never use this power unless someone was causing harm. "Let's just say I've got a hunch."

Reluctantly, the woman followed, her movements stiff and her legs heavy as though battling with every inch toward the door. Together, they entered the lower level. They were met with a small living area, a kitchen in the back corner, and a wide-eyed man standing in the middle of the living room, a large crystal propped between his hands. He quickly grabbed a nearby knitted blanket and tossed it over the crystal, placing it on the ground before shifting to stand before it. The crystal was so large it reached his knees. "Sela, what are you doing bringing someone here right now?" He glanced pointedly at Samara's pink hair.

The woman's eyes were jittery. "I didn't have a choice. The coterie member insisted we come inside."

Samara quickly closed the door. *Ulrieg, you didn't tell me he had the crystal.*

I didn't know he had it until you opened the door. He must have uncovered it when I looked to see if you were at the right house. He scoffed. *As if you didn't see him covering it up. Look at him. He thinks he pulled it off.*

Holding her hands in front of her, Samara

attempted to calm the couple. "Relax. I only want to talk."

"Said no coterie member ever," the man sniped and then roughly rubbed his bushy beard.

The invisible Ulrieg pulled the blanket off the crystal, letting it fall to the floor.

The man's eyes widened, and he moved in front of it again.

"Honestly, you can relax." Samara peered behind the man. "That's a big crystal. What're you planning to do with it?"

Chest deflating, the man stopped trying to hide the crystal and stepped aside. "I was merely moving it to another location."

She raised an eyebrow. "You seem awfully nervous for someone simply moving an item from one room to another."

He tried to cover up his panic with a grin. "Well, you see, it's an expensive item and not something you want strangers to know about. You never know who would steal it."

She eyed the crystal carefully, confirming its size to be about the same as the crystals in Callista's office. "I imagine so." She rubbed her chin. "Did you know that the reason for the high sorceress's visit is to find a particular crystal about that size?"

Both the man and the woman rapidly shook their

heads. The man's face looked oddly pale against his black, bushy beard. "No. Absolutely not. Or I would've given it to her."

"Aha. That's why you hid it from me when I walked in, even though I have the clear markings of a coterie sorceress." She tugged at her hair to emphasize the point.

"I swear, it's not the crystal she wants." The woman stood next to the man. "Loys's reactions were because of a stranger entering our home unexpectedly."

I think you need to level with them and tell them about me. Maybe if they realize you are working with a dragon, they'll believe you're not taking the crystal to Callista.

Are you sure? That's a big risk.

I think it's the best way to earn their trust.

Holding her hands out, Samara turned her palms up. "Look. I think we need to come clean with each other." She lowered her voice and moved closer to them. "I'm not here to take your crystal to the sorceress."

Both Loys and Sela frowned.

"Truth be told, my familiar has been following you since we arrived." Samara leveled her gaze at Loys. "He followed anyone who looked nervous, and you were one of the main people. You tried to cover it up by looking angry, but he followed you anyway."

Loys gazed around the room, looking for the familiar.

"You won't find him," she said. "He's an expert at hiding."

The man's eyes narrowed. "If you're not here to take it to the head sorceress, why did you follow me?"

"My familiar and I have a different agenda. Ulrieg, I think it's time to show yourself."

Ulrieg turned visible, standing only a few feet away from Samara.

"It's a dragon!" Loys's jaw dropped.

Oh great! Let's state the obvious. Ulrieg rolled his eyes.

The man's mouth pressed to one side, clearly unimpressed by the dragon's sarcastic comment.

Ulrieg! You're supposed to be nice to people when they first see you. It's the best way to get them to cooperate, remember? Samara chastised.

Steam shot out of the black dragon's nose. *Yeah, yeah. Let's get down to business. I'm sure we don't have long to get this sorted.*

CHAPTER TWENTY-FIVE

Grimacing at Ulrieg's abruptness, even to someone they were trying to get on their side, Samara moved closer to her dragon. "I apologize. He's often rude and abrupt, even to people he likes."

The couple were busy looking between Samara's brilliant-pink hair and the dragon tall enough to reach her waist.

Trying to ease the couple into trusting them, Samara lightheartedly continued, "Yes, he is a dragon, and despite his attitude, he cares a lot for anyone who supports the dragons."

Sela stuttered, "B-but we heard that the Sacred Flame coterie doesn't support the dragons. They are against them and will punish anyone who associates with them."

Giving her a half smile, Samara moved closer to Ulrieg. "And from what I've seen so far, I agree with you."

"But your familiar is a dragon." Loys apprehensively pointed to Ulrieg.

"And the coterie doesn't know that." Samara nodded. "He constantly remains invisible when we're around them. We used to have a pet owl, and I pretended he was my familiar. Believe it or not, that worked until recently." She rocked onto her toes. "So, now, we've trusted you with our big secret. Are you going to trust us with yours?"

The couple looked at each other before Sela slowly nodded. "We were taking the crystal to hide it. If the coterie wants this, we assume it somehow makes the magic wielder who defeated the dragons stronger. We hope that the dragons will grow stronger and Dragoria is found. If a few dragon elves and guardian dragons are left in the realm, they probably need all the help they can get."

And that is why we're here. I followed you to beat the others to getting the crystal, Ulrieg said.

Samara gaped at the people. "Wait! How did you know all of this?"

Not everyone lived a sheltered life like you. Ulrieg tilted his head to one side as he regarded the couple. *I assume that because you live so close to what remains of Paddosha Palace, the stories have been passed down through the generations after the coterie overthrew your royals.*

The man nodded. "Only a select few know the true story, and it's quietly passed on and drilled into us as children to guard this secret. My father's ancestors stole this crystal when the palace was destroyed. He sneaked it out of the servants' tunnels. I'm trying to keep it in our family until the lost royal heir is found."

Ulrieg's jaw dropped.

Samara froze. "Wait! There's still a royal somewhere?"

Loys nodded. "That's what my ancestors believed. They said the dwarven servants rescued the princess from the palace. They led her through the tunnel and had her raised somewhere else. If she had children, there's probably one, or many, circulating through the people of Slosiaran, and no one knows it except for a select few." He shrugged. "Probably not even the heir knows who they truly are. But I'm sure when the time is right and they are told their true ancestry, they'll be for the dragons like their forefathers were and want to reclaim their kingdom."

We just wanted to stop the coterie from getting the

crystal, but now there's even more reason, especially if the royals are willing to work with the dragons.

A stunned look passed over Loys's face. "Has Dragoria been found?"

"I'm afraid not," Samara said. "And the coterie is still killing and torturing dragons. Although we have met one dragon elf."

The couple's eyes lit with enthusiasm.

Samara raised a hand. "Unfortunately, her guardian dragon was killed by someone in the coterie. They had only been together for a few days. We rescued the dragon elf from them without the torturers knowing, but we were too late to save her guardian dragon. Still, it gives us hope there may be others."

We just need to find Dragoria. In your whisperings passed through your family, did they mention which direction it used to be?

Loys shook his head, his eyes meeting his wife's. She raised her hands in answer to the unspoken question.

Ulrieg's shoulders caved. *It was worth a try.*

"It appears as though the magic wielder who hid it also managed to influence everyone's memories of where it used to be," Sela added.

Samara sighed. "That's a problem for another

day. First, what were your plans for this crystal? Can we help?"

The man's eyes flashed to Sela, and she nodded.

"I was going to sneak it out of here and try to make my way to the underground servants' tunnels. There is an entrance a couple of houses down." Loys pointed in the direction behind him. "I've heard that it's not locked anymore, and they've removed the door on this side because there aren't any royals to protect."

He laced his fingers together. "I was going to take it as far as I could out of this area, but I saw the centaurs surrounding the palace grounds, so I was hoping to find the tunnel that the dwarves led the princess down all those years ago. It's grabbing at straws, but it was the only thing I could think to do in these circumstan—"

A loud, demanding banging sounded at their door, and the couple's expressions turned to panic. Loys looked from the crystal to Samara, then Ulrieg, and whispered, "We need to hide it."

Samara frowned and kept her voice low. "If it's the coterie, they may rummage through this place. Hiding it under something isn't going to be enough."

I have a thought. Ulrieg pointed to the nearest corner of the room not far from the table. *Clear that corner then put the crystal about a foot away from it, and*

I'll give something a go. Something Henriette does has given me an idea.

They did as instructed, then another knock sounded.

"Open up! We know you're in there!" Luna's voice bellowed from outside.

Ulrieg turned invisible, and Samara heard his talons lightly scraping the floor as he headed toward the crystal. *I haven't done this before, so here goes.* A few moments later, one side of the crystal disappeared behind a shape that looked like an invisible wing before the other side also disappeared, completely removing it from their sight. *Did it work?*

Yes! Samara didn't waste any time as she reached the door, pulled the latch across, and opened it. "Luna. You found me. How did you know I was here?"

A frown marked Luna's beautiful face, and she picked up Coco from behind her feet and swept her golden hair over one shoulder. Her fingers trailed through her familiar's fur. "Oh no. I didn't. Although while I was looking for you, I thought I'd do a little investigating on my own."

The elf edged her way inside. "I questioned a few people in the settlement. It's surprising how cooperative people can be with a little siren coaxing." Her voice was light and sweet as she swayed her hips and cuddled Coco closer. "A few said that they had suspicions that the people in this house were harboring the crystal."

Samara frowned. "Oh. I've been interviewing them and haven't retrieved any information of the sort."

The elf nodded toward the bow and quiver on Samara's back. "Did you shoot them with an arrow enchanted with a truth spell?"

Taken aback, Samara shook her head at the harshness creeping into the beautiful elf's voice. "No. There was no need to harm anyone."

Luna cocked her other hip. "Hm. I think you're wrong. It's very important that we find this crystal for Callista. But never mind. I'll ask them myself." She made eye contact with Loys, and the instant his eyes locked with hers, her words turned into a song. "Tell me where you have hidden the crystal."

He opened his mouth to speak.

Don't you dare fall for her siren powers. Ulrieg's voice reached him, blocking Luna out of the conversation. *Focus on something else and disengage from eye contact.*

The man's eyes didn't pull away, and he attempted to speak.

Sela, interrupt him, Ulrieg demanded. *Grab his face*

and make him look at you, but don't make it look too obvious.

The woman called to him. "Loys." When he didn't look at her, she reached up and shifted his chin to look at her. "We don't have any crystals, do we?" She shook her head, and a brief wave of relief washed over her face when recognition filled his eyes. "The rumors are stories made up by people our families have had arguments with in the past. It's all a local disagreement that the esteemed coterie members shouldn't worry themselves with. It would only lead them down the wrong track."

Loys sighed. "No. We haven't seen any crystals."

Luna's face hardened. "You must've. It would be very difficult to miss. They are big, about the length of a man's lower leg."

Keeping their eyes low, the couple shook their heads, and Sela answered for them. "No, we definitely haven't seen any crystals that size. It would be hard to miss."

Luna paced, examining the inside of their house. "I'm finding that very difficult to believe since several people from different locations have pointed to your house and said you have the crystal." She glared at them. "Samara, you need to stay by them and ensure they don't leave, and I'll search the house."

Samara nodded, hoping Luna wouldn't go near the corner where Ulrieg hid. Standing in the middle of the couple, she grabbed their arms and pulled them backward toward the corner, blocking Luna's way to what looked like an empty corner. "We'll just stand out of your way." She cast them apologetic glances. There was nothing she could do for them to get them out of this without raising suspicion.

Loys and Sela's expressions turned long, all color draining from their cheeks, as Luna tossed the lower level, disturbing everything before heading up the stairs. Dragging and banging sounds roared down through the floor above their heads. Sela jumped when a loud, isolated thump thundered above them before something shattered.

It sounded like she was destroying the rooms and pulling apart the walls.

"I'm so sorry," Samara whispered, quickly straightening when footsteps thumped down the stairs.

"I can't find it. You must have hidden it before we got to your house." Luna grabbed the man's arm.

"I promise you we don't have it," Sela almost begged Luna. "You're falling for untruths told about us. You must have run into the wrong people when you asked around."

Luna huffed and said, in a casual tone, "Tell that

to the great sorceress, Callista. Not only can she discern for herself, but she will know how to get it out of you." She led Loys out the front door and called over her shoulder, "Samara, you bring the lady."

Grudgingly, Samara followed her, footsteps dragging over the stones, eyes full of sympathy every time she looked at the couple. *Be careful, Ulrieg. Do what you can to hide it then get well away from the crystal.*

CHAPTER TWENTY-SIX

Sela tripped on a rock in the middle of the road, yanking hard on Samara's arm as she tried to balance before she fell.

Samara leaned over and helped her to her feet. "Are you all right?"

"Yes, I'm fine. I'm probably just nervous. Will he be all right?" She indicated the house with her head.

Samara nodded and kept her voice very low. "One thing for sure, I guarantee he has left already. Which means when you're asked, you won't be lying about not knowing where it is."

Sela's eyes brightened. "Indeed. That is one good thing." The woman brushed a strand of hair behind her ear.

Samara wanted to say more but was too afraid that the elven Luna might have some strong hearing abilities, even though she was several feet ahead. She directed Sela to follow Luna's footsteps.

Apprehension rose the closer they got to the destroyed palace. She was haunted by the expressions of fear from the people standing by, as though they believed the coterie and their laws were here to destroy rather than bring peace. The same fear had grown inside her since she met Ulrieg. A chill crept through her bones. She hoped he was all right and could hide the crystal from the coterie. If they were wrong and the coterie was genuinely trying to keep the peace, she would give the crystal to Callista.

They had rounded the last street corner heading to the palace when Samara spotted five of the centaurs lined up, with Callista standing on the palace stairs behind them. The head sorceress's usually unreadable face looked determined, her eyes compressed into a squint. It almost made her face unrecognizable, aside from the lilac hair and golden diadem glinting in the sun.

As Luna and Samara brought the couple closer, clouds blocked the sun, casting the area into a deep gloom. Sela trembled, the vibrations traveling up Samara's arm. She squeezed the woman's upper arm, trying to instill some reassurance that she didn't feel. There was something off with the way Callista was acting, and it was setting Samara on edge. She wondered if this was the real Callista starting to shine through.

Samara suddenly felt outnumbered and over-whelmed with a deep longing for Paxton and his support. She was extremely aware the support she was trying to offer the lady was beyond her own abilities. To make it worse, she knew that Ulrieg was busy hiding the crystal and was not near to help, but even if he had been nearby, she was sure she wasn't up to the challenge to go against Callista, who also had support from Mystique, Luna, Coco, and the centaurs.

Callista's gaze landed on the couple, and Samara's body went numb. She had never seen Callista like this, and worse, there seemed to be magic buzzing through the air.

They stopped a few feet from the head sorceress, and Callista raised her chin. Samara held her breath. There was no empathy in the coterie leader's gaze.

"Where is the crystal?" Callista asked as she cut through the lined centaurs with graceful and sure steps, approaching the couple.

Both Loys and Sela shook their heads.

"We don't know, great sorceress. It isn't in our possession."

The sincerity in Loys's voice was dismissed by a glare from Callista. "Do not lie to me."

Trembles transferred to Samara's arm from Sela as the woman attempted to defend her husband, somehow holding her voice steady. "He's telling the truth. We don't know where it is."

"Rubbish!" Callista's shrill voice sent chills down Samara's spine. "Several people of the palace's abode have confirmed that you are the crystal holders. There are too many to not believe."

"I'm afraid that they are mistaken, great sorceress," Loys protested. "I promise you, we don't have the crystal."

Callista waved her arm at a line of people in the audience that had grown since they had arrived. "Do you mean to tell me that all these people lied, when the people they accused of having the crystal were always you two?" The crowd was now several layers deep, and many people lowered their eyes to the ground when Loys turned to look at them.

"I think that perhaps they are mistaken," he said. "They may be going from a rumor set into motion years ago, saying that our ancestors were responsible for taking it from the palace." He shook his head and gazed at the ground. "I don't know if those rumors are true, but even if they are, the crystal is no longer with our families. Perhaps my ancestors got rid of it because they knew that it would bring us bad luck in the future." He shrugged. "They would've had a point. It's certainly bringing us bad fortune, and we don't even have it."

The faces in the crowd were filled with terror, and Samara wondered if what the man said was true. Perhaps the people of the village hadn't seen the crystal and were going by a past rumor. It was bad luck for the couple if this was their motivation. Her mind was jerked back to the current situation when Sela shifted, dragging Samara's arm with her.

"What he says is true." Sela straightened her shoulders. "Your sorceresses have searched our house, and the crystal wasn't found."

Callista raised her hands. "Silence!" Her cold stare sent chills through the air, throwing the crowd into stillness. "If these people have the crystal, they shouldn't have been able to remove it from the township surrounding the Paddosha Palace when we were here. The centaurs have surrounded the grounds, blocking all attempts to leave. No one has left. If the crystal isn't in their house, it must be in this area. Too many people have spoken and pointed out these two for there not to be any truth in their words. There is always some truth to rumors."

She turned to face the centaurs standing guard with her. "Centaurs, go and search their house. If it isn't there, then search the houses surrounding it. If necessary, you need to search the entire village. Go!"

After a quick nod from Zoltos, the centaurs galloped down the street, their long hair streaming behind them as the clopping of their hooves faded into the distance.

Uneasiness settled over the crowd, and Mystique sauntered in front of Callista, perching herself near her bonded, ready to defend if anyone came near.

The tension in Samara's neck tightened. An additional search of the property would put Ulrieg in danger. She hoped he was managing all right with the large crystal. She imagined it would be heavy for someone of his size. Not only that, but he also had to keep it hidden between his invisible wings to be able to move it without being seen.

The crashing of furniture being thrown around echoed down the street to where they stood. Sometimes, it sounded like furniture had been thrown out the window onto the street. She could only imagine the mess the centaurs were leaving inside and outside the house.

After several moments, Zoltos galloped down the street, standing at attention when he was within hearing distance. "There is no sign of the crystal in their house. We are widening the search."

Callista inclined her head. "Search the entire village."

A moan echoed through the crowd, quieting when Callista pinned them with her gaze.

A woman in the front, with a long dark braid, drummed up enough courage to speak. "Great sorceress. We are happy to have you search our properties to prove our innocence. However, could they please refrain from destroying our possessions? Since the palace's destruction, we are a humble village, barely surviving on what we have." She indicated the group of people around her. "We have cooperated with you and informed you who is rumored to have your crystal. Do we not deserve for our things to be cared for?"

Raising her chin, Callista turned back to Zoltos. "Have your warriors be gentler with the people's belongings."

The centaur inclined his head and galloped back to the others. The sounds of destruction lessened.

Callista turned to Luna. "Have you used your gift on them?"

"Yes, great sorceress. I didn't get anything out of them. I'm afraid I have failed you." Luna gazed at the ground.

Samara watched Luna. She was acting so formal in front of the people, speaking to Callista in a way that they didn't usually talk while at the coterie. Confusion washed over Samara. It was as though her two companions were utterly different from how they would typically be. She understood treating the head sorceress with respect, but the two of them also acted as though the humans living here were below them. It made her sick to her stomach.

"Do not wallow in your failures. Simply try again," Callista encouraged Luna.

Luna spun and faced Loys, instantly connecting with his eyes before he could look away. Her gaze held his, her voice filling with a sweet melody. "Tell me where the crystal is."

Loys didn't blink, and his words were slowed as though he was speaking in a trance. "I don't know."

Luna's siren questioning continued. "Did you have the crystal?"

"Yes." The man nodded.

Both Callista's and Luna's chests expanded with enthusiasm.

"I suggest you tell me where it is," Luna said.

"I don't know," Loys insisted, still in a trance-like state.

A deep frown soured Luna's beautiful face. "How is it you don't know?"

"It vanished from my sight before you came."

Samara's stomach twisted into a knot. This was becoming dangerous. It took all her effort not to react.

"What do you mean it vanished?" Annoyance tainted Luna's smooth voice.

"One minute, it was before my eyes. The next, it disappeared. I think someone from the coterie took it. How else could it disappear?"

Both Callista and Luna turned to Samara, breaking the man's trance. "Samara, did you see where it went?" the head sorceress asked.

Samara scrunched her toes. "No. If I knew where it was, I would've brought it to you." Her throat constricted tightly, barely letting out the lie. She kept her gaze set on Callista, avoiding Luna's eyes and trying to reinforce her innocence to the head sorceress.

Luna fiddled with her golden hair as she studied Samara.

Samara's heart thundered against her rib cage. She was surprised Luna couldn't hear it screaming how guilty she was.

Sela came to stand in front of Samara. "The crystal was gone before she came to our house. We honestly don't know where it is."

Luna connected eyes with the woman, her singsong voice filling Sela's ears. "Who took the crystal?"

Sela shook her head, eyes locked on Luna's. "I don't know. We didn't see. It simply vanished."

Samara wondered how the woman was getting away with such a blatant lie, then she thought about the moment the crystal disappeared. It was true. Ulrieg was invisible before he made the crystal disappear.

Callista stomped down the last of the stairs and approached the woman, her face set in steel. She placed one clawed hand on the woman's forehead. "I don't believe you." She then uttered an incantation too softly for Samara to hear.

Sela's knees buckled, and she took her head in her hands as she screamed.

Guilt rocked Samara. The woman had defended her, probably for no other reason than to protect the crystal, but now, she would pay the price. Sela's screams sent bile rising in her throat.

Sela's screaming cut through her soul. Samara couldn't take it any longer. Her ears were ring-ing, and the intensity seemed to be growing. She frowned. There was a deep undertone to Sela's screams. *No.* She was wrong. That wasn't only the woman screaming. Loys had joined her. She didn't know why until she looked at him and saw Callista with a hand closed over his forehead as well. He had joined his wife, both on their knees on the ground, mouths open and screaming in pain.

Sick rose into her throat, but she didn't let it out. Her eyes traveled from the couple to the people's horrified faces behind them. Out of fear, they had betrayed their townsfolk, but they didn't really have a choice. Samara wouldn't be surprised if Callista had threatened their entire village. It wouldn't be hard to believe after seeing what the coterie had done to their palace.

It's no wonder the people treated their families better after Callista became involved in their lives, she thought. The people were filled with fear over what the coterie and Callista would do to them. She didn't know why it had taken her so long to see it. She wondered if it was the same for her family. Did her parents know what Callista and her followers were like? If so, why didn't they tell her? Or had they found out after she was taken away, longing to get their daughter back but too scared that it would put the rest of their children in danger?

The whole scenario was a slap in the face. Ulrieg had been right this entire time. She mentally kicked herself for not believing him. The frustration of her naivete fueled her with determination, and she steeled her emotions. "Great sorceress."

Callista's hard, angry eyes turned to her.

Samara sucked in a breath. She was on her own. Ulrieg was busy, and no one else was here to help her defend the people. "I know you are determined to find the crystal, but I fail to see how it's beneficial to torture people who have not given you any more information under such pressure."

The head sorceress raised her chin. "I'm teaching these people a lesson. It's important that they see what the punishment is if they don't follow my rules and give me what I need."

"Yes, I understand." Samara's voice croaked as she fought against the bile threatening to rise.

"Do you?" Callista's eyes narrowed. "Sometimes, I wonder if some of my apprentices also need a lesson on how they should behave."

Samara flinched. This wasn't the Callista she had grown to know during her time in the coterie. There had to be a way around this without getting anyone else in trouble, including herself. She raised her hands in defense. "I'm merely suggesting that perhaps we could send the people to search for the crystal in their homes."

Samara pointed to the sun sinking low over the western side. "It'll be dark soon. You can get the people to search at night, and the first one to find the crystal will be rewarded." She glanced over her shoulder at the crowd behind her, their faces echoing her hope.

Turning back to Callista, she asked, "Doesn't that sound like an easier solution? You can lock these two up. Surely, the town has a cell." The people behind her nodded. "We'll see if the crystal turns up overnight. The centaurs can still monitor the village and make sure no one escapes."

Callista tore her hands away from Loys and Sela

and stood straight, readjusting her diadem and pressing the hidden crystals against her forehead. She readjusted her bracelet, holding her hand over the crystal, and took a deep breath, shaking her lilac hair down her back.

Just as Samara's tension was starting to melt away, Callista twisted her hands at the couple, and Loys and Sela collapsed to the ground, unmoving. A gasp of horror passed through the onlookers. "Let this be a warning. If I hear that you have come across the crystal and haven't informed me, whether now or in the future, this will be your end."

The people nodded, their faces pale in the setting sun.

Callista gestured at them. "Now go and find me the crystal. More of you will fall by my magic if you don't."

Samara removed the hand that had stifled her scream as she stared at the crumpled bodies, retreating footsteps from the villagers filling her ears.

"Come, you two," Callista called to Samara and Luna. "We will eat and rest to give us the energy to face tomorrow."

THE AWKWARDNESS in the palace was hard to deal with. Callista went to her room with Mystique while Luna and Coco shared the room with Samara. Never had Samara been so conscious of not having her familiar by her side, knowing he was risking his life to hide the crystal, while at the same time, she was left to face Luna and Callista on her own.

Noises constantly traveled in from the abodes around the palace as the people searched their own houses plus the homes of their neighbors. Whether they wanted to or not, the people had been forced to turn against one another to protect themselves and their families. Their neighbors whose houses they were tearing apart. More would die if they didn't find the crystal by morning.

Samara swallowed the last of her bread, the feel of it hard and stale to her stomach after the day she had and what she knew she would have to face tomorrow. She watched Luna cuddle her familiar, feeding Coco some of her apple, and a bitter taste filled her mouth. "I'm going to turn in early. We are going to need our magic at full power tomorrow." Samara fluffed her straw and lay down, feeling Luna's eyes watching her. She called over her shoulder, "Good night. I hope you sleep well."

"I sure will. I have Coco by my side and am confident in my role."

Samara heard Luna settle down on her own bed of straw and blow out the candle. She was glad for the darkness and being out of Luna's scrutiny, even though she knew Coco could report to Luna what Samara was up to. She closed her eyes, wishing she could sense if Ulrieg was safe. She missed her grumpy dragon, and it had only been a few hours.

A noise pulled her attention to the open door of the room, and she saw the gleam of yellow eyes cutting through the darkness. A sliver of light from the moon shone through the missing ceiling in the corridor, illuminating the dark, sizeable form of Mystique. Still to this day, those yellow eyes haunted her, reminding her of her and Kaine's first battle with the trolls. She returned the cat's stare before facing the wall once again. It was probably best if she pretended to be asleep. Maybe then, they would give up spying on her.

Oh, Ulrieg. I hope you're all right.

She heard fighting in the distance followed by the clomping of hooves as the centaurs barked orders to break it up. As the night wore on, it sounded like people were stirring themselves into a frenzy. This could only mean they were becoming more desperate about what the morning would bring. It was good news for the dragons and their supporters, as it meant that Ulrieg had hidden the crystal out of sight, but with it brought the devastation of knowing that Callista had threatened to kill more residents in the morning if the crystal wasn't presented to her.

Samara dug her fingernails into her palms. Today had been a disaster. It had turned her life upside down, and she couldn't even tell Ulrieg that it looked like he was right about Callista and the coterie. She didn't know what to do next. If she left, not only was her family in danger but so were Paxton, Forgrac, and all other good-souled apprentices like Henriette and Peadar, along with their families. Not to mention all the dragons the coterie might catch and torture under the building. She couldn't leave them there without help.

She placed her hand against the stones of the building and closed her eyes. Her mind whirled with images of the terror the palace staff and royals must have gone through the day they were brought down. Her heart ached for the little girl whisked away by the dwarves and hidden, along with her offspring, for all these years. She wondered where they could be now. Hopefully, some were still alive, strong, and passionate about winning their kingdom back.

She heard Mystique's soft paws as she sauntered away from the door of the room, followed not long after by the gentle, monotonous breaths of Luna as she slumbered into a deep sleep.

Ulrieg?

The silence was killing her. She shifted onto her back to stare at the ceiling, wishing for the dragon's familiar red eyes to glare down at her. Eventually, her eyes grew too sore to hold open any longer, and she let them close, her ears wishing she could tune out the ruckus of the villagers tearing each other's homes apart.

Her body rocked, pulling her out of a night terror.

Samara.

Her brain foggy, she nearly spoke out loud before she stopped herself. *Ulrieg?*

Of course. Who else would it be?

Eyes now wide, she searched the room only to realize he would still be invisible. *I would love to throw my arms around you, you cranky lizard.*

Oh. Those are fighting words.

You know I love you. She faced the wall and grinned, just in case someone was watching her. *It's so good to hear you're all right. I was so worried.*

I can't say it was easy.

How did it go with the crystal?

It was an exercise. Not only was it heavy, but I had to

drag it through the streets to the tunnel entrance Loys had described then follow the tunnel to the palace.

I hope you didn't leave it below here.

Honestly! I thought you'd know me better than that. No. I dragged it into these tunnels to look for the tunnel the dwarves supposedly rescued the princess through.

Samara sucked in a breath. *Did you find it?*

I think so. Ulrieg sounded excited. *Although it took a while. First, I went down into an underwater lake area, followed the paths out of there, and eventually ended up a long way out of town.*

Really?

There were literally no houses anywhere, only large trees and boulders.

Oh. And you didn't see any centaurs out there?

Nope.

Hm. Interesting. What did you do with it?

I found a spot I would recognize, and I buried it.

Samara wanted to clap her hands and jump up and down with joy, but she was too scared to move in case she was being watched or she woke the others. *That's fantastic!*

But now I'm exhausted. It took me ages to get it there, as I also covered the hole to the palace in case anyone checked out the tunnels. And after I buried it, it was a bit of a flight to return.

Samara patted a patch of hay close to the wall. *Curl up here and get some rest.*

She felt the straw move around her and squash down in the spot she had indicated near her thigh. When she thought he was settled, she reached out to him and felt for a talon, feeling the warm air from his nostrils instead. Gently, she stroked his nose and left her hand touching his soft skin, allowing her energy to flow into him and help him recuperate.

The excitement of having him safely back with her was enough to revitalize her spirits. *Ulrieg?*

Hm, he said sleepily.

Rest up for now, but tomorrow, we have much to discuss.

She heard the soft, satisfied clicking of his tongue against the roof of his mouth.

Ulrieg?

Hm.

Did I tell you how happy I am to have you back and know you're safe?

Yeah, yeah. Now shush, or you'll have an extraordinarily grumpy dragon in the morning.

Samara chuckled softly.

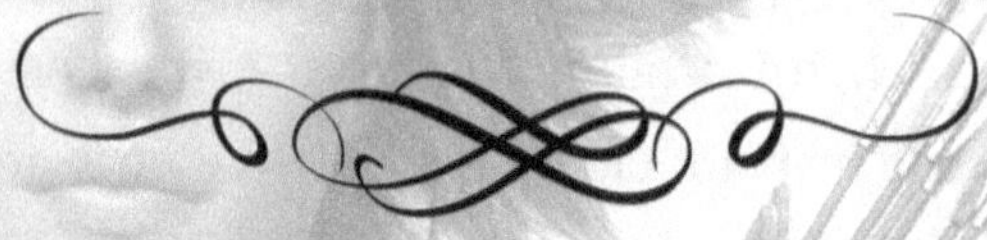

CHAPTER TWENTY-EIGHT

Samara, get up!

Something touched her hand, and she opened her eyes to see the gray-stone wall of the palace room, an invisible Ulrieg nudging her with his nose. She raised her head, brushing away the straw stuck to her face. Daylight dimly illuminated the room, and she rolled over to find Luna collecting the last of her things and placing them in her bag.

"Oh, look. You're finally awake. I trust you slept well." Luna eyed Samara as she scooped up Coco and hugged her to her chest.

Sitting up, Samara cleared her throat. "After a while, yes. How about you? You look well rested."

"With Coco by my side, getting a restful night's sleep is easy." There was no aggression in Luna's voice, yet there seemed to be an underlying message.

Samara resisted the urge to roll her eyes. Yet another dig about her familiar not being close to her.

Ah, the ignorance. If only she knew, Ulrieg sniped. *Actually, we really don't want her to know.*

Samara adjusted her pinafore, packed the few items she had removed from her bag, and slung her quiver and bow on her back. With every movement, her bones ached from tension and the lack of a comfortable, padded mattress. Although the straw in the room was thicker than in the troll dungeon, she longed for her more comfortable bed at the coterie building.

Movement caught her eye, and she looked up to see Mystique watching them from the door, her nose lifted and flaring as though she had found an odd scent. Samara tensed. The cat must be smelling Ulrieg.

Callista stood at the door behind her familiar, her face blank and chin lifted. "Are you both ready?"

"Absolutely ready to do your bidding, great sorceress." Luna stood tall in front of Callista, Coco tucked in the crook of her arm.

Standing beside her, Samara kept her spine straight and used her most sincere voice. "I'm also ready."

Callista peered around the room, her hand

resting on Mystique's head. "Is your familiar still not going to join us?"

Samara shook her head. "I'm sorry, but he's still uncomfortable being close to other coterie members."

"Hm." Callista's mouth formed a thin line, and she turned to the door. After a few steps, she faced Samara again. "Did he at least see if anyone took the crystal?"

Samara closed her eyes and pretended to contact her familiar, opening her eyes moments later and shaking her head. "I'm afraid not. He didn't see anything."

The impatient expression remained on Callista's face as she led them out of the palace. When they exited the remains of the front entrance, they were met by the centaurs lined on each side and behind the gathered people from the entire town. The villagers' faces portrayed their disappointment and even horror as they glanced at the bodies of Sela and Loys. No one had taken the care to bury them. Their lifeless forms remained as a reminder of what could happen to any of them today if the crystal wasn't handed to Callista.

Oh, Ulrieg. This is horrible. These poor people. Samara clasped her hands together tightly, trying not to let her guilt give her away.

What happened?

Callista killed them because they couldn't tell her where the crystal was. Not once did they give away that you took it, even under Luna's siren questioning.

Do you mean to say that Callista showed her true colors last night, and I wasn't here to tell you I told you so?

Samara knew she deserved the smugness in his voice. *Yes, she did. And now, even though these people have searched all night for the crystal, some are about to face the same fate. I feel so terrible.*

I know. But we must think of the bigger picture. If we give this crystal over to Callista, many more people will die, making it near impossible to defeat Callista and the coterie.

Samara felt him brush up against her leg, and she reveled in the brief contact.

Standing at the top of the stairs, Callista spread her arms. "Where is my crystal?"

The crowd fell silent, the dark circles under their eyes seeming to deepen. It was clear that the crystal hadn't been found.

"Did you not hear me?" Callista walked down a few steps. "I asked for my crystal."

Many in the crowd looked to the ground, wringing their hands in front of them. They looked exhausted and scared beyond comprehension.

Callista's hand twitched, and Samara caught a glimpse of crystals within her palm. All feeling dropped from her limbs. Callista was drawing energy from the crystals. These people were doomed.

"Do you not know what I can do?" The head sorceress raised her chin and waved one arm.

An elderly woman at the front crumpled to her knees, her hands held in prayer. "Yes, great sorceress. We know what you are capable of. Your power is shown in the deaths of this couple." She indicated the deceased. "And the power your coterie holds is shown in the destruction of the palace of the grounds you stand upon." She bowed her head. "We have spent all night tearing our town apart looking for your crystal and have turned against one another to spare us all from your wrath without success. I beg you to spare us, if only because of our commitment to keeping you satisfied."

Callista clasped her hands, the crystals between them, before thrusting a palm forward at the woman. "No! I won't spare those who disappoint me."

The woman's gray hair was blown over her face when a great force thrust her backward and into several other people, toppling them all and breaking their limbs, until finally, she hit the wall of a building. A loud crack sounded as her head hit the stone, and blood oozed from her wound and down the back of her body.

Still tied to a post near the palace, the horses shifted and snorted restlessly, unsettled by the disturbance.

Teeth clenched, Samara gazed over the destruction from one burst of power. Her knees wobbled. *Oh, Ulrieg. How awful!*

And I'm pretty sure she's not done.

The sorceress paced the stairs, working the crystals in her palm, her face set and unreadable.

A few people at the back tried to leave, but the centaurs herded them back into the crowd.

Callista whispered a madness spell, *"Manictium,"* several times, aiming her palm at different offenders. The people hit with the spells grabbed their heads, their eyes bulging and panicked as the madness spell took hold.

The remaining villagers folded to their knees and lowered their faces to the ground. Their trembling was visible from where the apprentices were standing.

Too afraid to show the horror she felt, Samara gazed over the heads of the people, determined not to watch the evil that unfolded. She badly wanted to defend the people, but she and Ulrieg were no match for the head sorceress alone, and Callista had help from Luna, their familiars, and the centaurs. She wanted this nightmare to be over. *No wonder why the kingdoms follow her rules. Many must have seen the punishment Callista and her Sacred Flame coterie inflict. This must be stopped, Ulrieg.*

That's what I've been trying to tell you the whole time. She's acting like a spoiled, evil toddler, all because she didn't get her crystal.

How are we going to end this? Samara glanced at Callista's unreadable face. There was no sign of sympathy for the people in front of her. There wasn't even rage. The head sorceress showed no emotion, as though she did this kind of thing daily. Luna was no different. If anything, the buxom elf looked more elegant than ever.

Suddenly, Callista paused and straightened, her fingers no longer working the crystals. "Let this be your lesson for now. I will never forget how this village lost my crystal, and I will undoubtedly send more of my coterie members in search of it. Bring them the crystal upon their arrival if you wish for a friendlier visit. This is the only thing that will save the rest of you." She raised her chin and marched to her horse, calling over her shoulder. "Come, apprentices. We are done here for now. They have plenty to ponder. Let us hope they have learned their lesson."

Samara released the breath she had been holding. *At least she didn't make us curse the people.* She made her way to her horse, attached her bag, and climbed on.

Do you really have to go back to the base with her after what you've seen?

Samara heard the concern in Ulrieg's voice. *Honestly, Ulrieg. If it weren't for the few beings I cared about at the coterie and their families, I'm certain I'd be trying to escape right now. And don't forget all those dragons that the coterie has been capturing and torturing.*

I really don't like this, Ulrieg warned.

Just remember what you said. We're only a couple of individuals compared to the kingdoms that could be saved if we risk our lives a little longer.

Ulrieg released a hot breath over her neck as he flew over her. *Let's hope our efforts are worth it.*

CHAPTER TWENTY-NINE

Several hours after they left the Paddosha Palace, a large branch in the copse of trees not far from Callista shook dramatically. Perched on the top of the bouncing branch was an owl that looked like Gray.

Seeing it brought the first smile to Samara's face that day. Almost pointedly, the owl looked at Callista.

The head sorceress gazed over her shoulder at Samara. "I see your owl has finally decided to come closer to us."

Samara's smile grew. "I hope this means he'll learn to remain near me."

"If he doesn't, then you won't be progressing higher in the coterie." Callista's tone was firm.

Samara inclined her head. "I understand, great sorceress." Although this news was not surprising, her stomach fluttered. She no longer felt as though she knew Callista at all. Even though she was treading on dangerous grounds within the coterie, the thorns had grown stronger.

Callista's eyes remained on the owl for quite some time as they passed, and Samara wished she could hear the sorceress's thoughts. She was still unsure what Kaine had told Callista in the past— only Ginger had witnessed Ulrieg sitting around the campfire with Daena and Byzarid.

A chill ran down Samara's spine. Was Callista leading her back to the coterie building to punish her, maybe even sacrifice her to the orb? Her knuckles turned white around the reins. No matter how much Callista knew about Ulrieg and Samara's loyalties, Samara knew she was in deep trouble. Still, she would sacrifice herself if she could save Paxton and Forgrac. Callista had made it clear to Paxton's family that Samara was his close friend, and that alone would put him in danger. Paxton had such a good heart. She couldn't let him be hurt by Callista.

Fantastic display of a strange owl, Ulrieg. I don't know if it's enough to get us out of trouble, but nice try.

I'll try almost anything to make you safer.

Look out, Ulrieg—you're sounding nice. Samara chuckled. *I love you too. Hopefully, your effort will keep both of us and our friends safer.*

After Callista passed by, the owl took off awkwardly, much the way Gray had flown with Ulrieg's help in the early days, earning a strange look from the head sorceress. Samara would rather the head sorceress think she had a peculiar familiar than know the truth.

After several hours of it clumsily following them, the owl flew normally in another direction.

I've let the owl go.

Thanks, Ulrieg. I still don't want to put another owl in danger.

I know. But I'll try to find another one soon. The evil sorceress will occasionally need to see more owls like Gray to believe your familiar is still around. We can't risk her having more suspicions.

Samara knew he was right.

Rivulets of sweat trickled down her back as they traveled back to the border. Every bit of faith Samara once had in Callista taking her side against the senior sorcerers had been stripped away in one short night.

A noise sounded behind her, and she turned, spotting Zoltos and his small army of centaurs trotting behind. The thought of them back there made her uncomfortable, knowing they constantly watched her movements. When she saw the destructed buildings near the border, she felt an equal amount of relief that the centaurs should soon leave them and despair that she had to face Kellam.

The centaurs left, turning back to their practicing grounds, when the ogre Glikag stomped out to greet the small group of sorceresses.

The ogre stooped low. "Great sorceress, Master Kellam be glad you back."

Callista raised her lilac eyebrows. "Is that so? It has only been one night."

Before Glikag could answer, the senior sorcerer came out to meet Callista, his long dark-brown cloak billowing behind him. He ran a hand through his short orange hair, knocking the hood from his head and exposing his pointed ears. A deep scowl marked his face. "Your return could not come soon enough."

Callista straightened her back as Luna and Samara caught up to her. "And why is this?" the head sorceress asked. "Our time away was shorter than expected."

The senior sorcerer hastily inclined his head to the head sorceress quickly. "I understand. But this human you left me to train is an immense pain in the backside."

"Kellam, are you saying that you failed to train a mere human?" Callista kicked her leg over the saddle and dismounted from her white horse.

Kellam looked taken aback. "Do you mock me?"

The edge of Callista's mouth curled up. "I'm merely pointing out that you often say the humans are beneath you, yet you seem flustered by this one."

"Indeed!" His body stiffened. "This one is disobedient and rarely does anything I request. She is untrainable!"

"Oh, and what has she done to make you believe that?" Callista grabbed her horse's reins and walked alongside Kellam. Samara and Luna dismounted, following close behind.

Kellam sucked in a loud breath. "Instead of doing what I ask, she disappears, and I can never find her."

"Well, that is her special gift and why she was brought to the border. She has excelled in using it," Callista explained. "You should be able to work with that and teach her to use it to the coterie's benefit."

The sorcerer thrust his hands out from his sides. "And how am I supposed to do that when she disappears when I ask her to do something? She lacks the discipline to excel in this coterie."

Henriette suddenly appeared between Luna and

Samara, her turquoise hair hanging loose and Pixie cradled around her neck. "I do not lack discipline. You threatened me and Pixie when I refused to set an ogre on fire. Just because they serve us doesn't mean I'll set them on fire for no reason. That's just cruel, and I won't do it."

Callista faced the young apprentice, amusement sparkling in her eyes. "So, you turned both you and Pixie invisible instead?"

Henriette nodded. "Well, I actually turned my cloak invisible and covered us with it."

Samara suppressed a laugh, wrapping an arm around the younger apprentice's shoulders.

And to think we were worried about Henriette being mistreated by Kellam and his monkey. Ulrieg chuckled.

The head sorceress turned to Kellam. "The apprentice was simply practicing her more powerful magic. I see that as a win, despite it annoying you. If you're honest, you would admit it's not difficult to annoy you."

Henriette huffed and stuck out her bottom lip. "And you said that you would do something horrible to Pixie. Callista said that we are to protect our familiars if someone threatens them, especially if the aggressor is part of the coterie, for a coterie member should know better."

Callista stroked her horse's nose. "I believe the

girl has done nothing wrong and has exercised her abilities and rights as a coterie member."

Samara's chest filled with pride, as it would have for one of her sisters. There was hope for the mischievous human girl yet. Her fondness for Henriette also made her heart ache. She hoped the girl would never follow the coterie's destructive ways. In a flash, panic filled Samara. She didn't know how she would keep everyone she cared about safe.

Kellam's eyes narrowed on Samara although he spoke to Callista. "And what about you? Did you get the halfling to bring her familiar down and show itself?"

Callista pulled back her shoulders, standing almost as tall as the sorcerer. "Do you question my rule?"

Kellam slouched and bent his knees, bringing his head lower than Callista's. "No, of course not, great sorceress. I merely know how troublesome this apprentice has been with her familiar. I didn't mean to question or offend you."

Callista's posture eased slightly. "The familiar has come closer to us during our travels home, although it has only been a day or two. I will keep an eye on their progress. I agree that this must improve, or it will prove the apprentice is gutless and unsuitable for our coterie."

Samara struggled with them discussing her as though she wasn't there, although she held her tongue. In so many ways, she didn't care to impress this coterie now that she had seen Callista's true colors.

Kellan nodded. "Will you be leaving her here to be trained?"

"No. I will be returning to the coterie training building with all the apprentices. There's more work to be done." Callista sighed. "It has been a troublesome trip to Paddosha Palace."

Kellam looked the horses over. "Didn't you find your crystal?"

The sorceress tugged harshly at the white horse's reins. "I believe we barely missed it. It seems a husband and wife managed to dispose of it somehow, and no amount of questioning exposed the truth of its whereabouts."

A sly look passed over the sorcerer's face. "I trust you dealt with them accordingly."

"Of course. Them and a few of the townsfolk. Hopefully, I have instilled enough fear into them that they will inform us if the crystal's whereabouts are brought to light."

"I'm sorry the rumors I heard about the crystal didn't pan out as we expected." Kellam gazed at the ground.

Callista's expression was grim. "I believe your information was true, but somehow, those people managed to move it before we could act. The crystal should arise again soon, and I will investigate further."

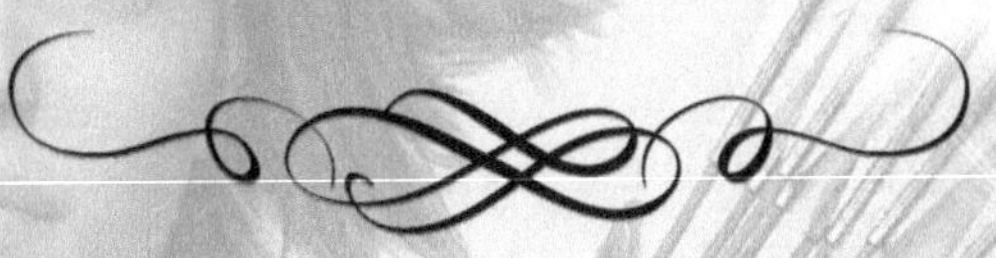

CHAPTER THIRTY

S amara gazed over her shoulder at the village of Tradedale, glad to be past the racist group of elves. At least the villagers remembered Callista's lesson from their last visit, so the group had been left alone.

It had puzzled Samara that they didn't stop in to visit Paxton's family. She had hoped to warn them about the coterie somehow, although she knew it would be impossible with the other sorceresses nearby. She didn't know how things would go when they returned to the coterie building, and on top of that, she was worried about how her friendship with Paxton would affect him and his family.

A breeze pushed down at her from above. *How did it go, Ulrieg?*

It was interesting, to say the least.

Why? What happened? How did Paxton's family act?

How did you think it would go when I exposed myself to people who have never seen a dragon before, let alone one with red eyes and abundant horns? Not only that, I was also in their house.

That well, huh?

Let's just say that the kid had to change his pants. He sounded disgruntled. *I even made an effort to smile.*

Samara pictured Ulrieg's tooth-baring smile and chuckled, ensuring she turned her head in the opposite direction from her companions. *You frightened the poor kid by exposing so many teeth.*

I was trying to be friendly, as you so often tell me to do.

At least you tried. Did you manage to talk to them?

It took a while for them to calm down, but eventually, I got them to listen. But only because I told them that I noticed how apprehensive they seemed around Callista, despite their gratitude for her intervention with the villagers. They seemed to listen more after I said that, and also when I told them I'm your secret familiar and my kind is an enemy to the coven. Not only that, but they know that Paxton knows about me and has been helping to save dragons with you. I explained that Paxton may be in danger because of these actions, and so are they. Ulrieg paused.

What did they say? Samara asked impatiently.

They said that they would prepare to leave, but they didn't know where to go that would be safe. I told them about the spot you opened the night you snuck out with Henriette to get into Slosiaran, then I suggested they go near the Merciless Sanctuary desert and see if they can find a safe place to live, since the coterie thinks that area is a lost cause and is less likely to go there.

Samara nodded. *Are they going?*

They're going to try. They have a small amount of funds saved since Paxton joined the coterie, but it's not much.

Let's hope they manage to stay safe. Samara watched Henriette's back. *I wish I had the gift of invisibility. I'd find it extremely useful.*

I must admit, it's been advantageous.

By the time they reached the coterie building, darkness had surrounded them for many hours, and the quarter moon shone down on them from the sky's apex. Seeing where they were going had been challenging for the last part of the trip, but Mystique was leading the way, the black jaguar barely visible in the darkness.

Leaving the horses tied up under the staircase, the sorceresses and their familiars entered the building, greeted by Jet at the door. Little was said as they parted ways, adding to the tension between them.

Each step up the stairs burned in Samara's thighs and backside, sore after the long ride, and every part of her body ached. She entered her room, ignited the sconce on the wall with a spell, and opened the window, allowing Ulrieg access that wouldn't accidentally let the breeze from his wings brush against another coterie member.

She collapsed on her bed, her back muscles aching with relief against the comfortable surface, and gazed at Gray's empty perch. Her heart filled with longing. She didn't realize how much she missed the adorable owl that had played along with their facade. The owl had become another companion.

Talons scratching on the windowpane alerted her to Ulrieg's presence, and she sat up and faced the window just as he turned visible. *I miss the little guy too,* he said after catching her forlorn expression. *I'm sure there's someone else you've been missing as well.*

She gave him a look of disbelief. *Of course there is, but it's not like I can just go over and see him. It's the middle of the night. However, I do worry about how everything went around here while we were gone.*

Well, I have some good news for you.

What's that? She pulled off her leather shoes,

giving her feet some much-needed relief after balancing on stirrups all day, and fiddled with the straps of her pinafore, readying to take it off.

I flew around Paxton's window, and his light was on.

Her hand dropped to her side. *Really.*

Absolutely. Perhaps he's awake. He grinned.

Standing, Samara walked to her door, ignoring her shoes. *Then I'm going to see.*

I'll come with you. His talons clacked on the floor as he followed her.

She opened the door, and Ulrieg turned invisible before launching into flight. Quickly, they crossed to the other side of the level. She balanced on the balls of her feet, tiptoeing over any wooden planks. Although no one seemed to be up, she didn't want to attract unwanted attention.

Standing outside Paxton's door, she lifted her hand, knuckles poised to knock.

Wait! That'll be too noisy. Ulrieg stopped her. *Paxton! If you're up, we're outside your door.*

Only a few moments passed before the door unlocked, and Paxton drew it open, his face unreadable as the dim light of the room framed his body. He reached for Samara, gently grabbing her wrist and drawing her in then closing the door once Ulrieg announced he was inside.

Paxton hugged her close. His dark-green hair

hung loose around his shoulders, and he was shirt-less, with loose pants tied around the waist.

Samara melted against his firm chest, soaking up the comfort of his heartbeat, and held him close. After the tiring trip, this embrace was precisely what she needed. "I wish you could've come with us."

He stroked her hair, the motion soothing her tangled nerves. "I know it was only a couple of days, but I missed you." He smiled at Ulrieg when the dragon turned visible in one corner of the room.

"I've missed you more." She tightened her arms. "It was a nightmare of a trip, although I did meet your family. I didn't realize they lived close to the border."

He pulled back to look at her face. "Are they all right?"

"They were." She squeezed his hand. "It must be harrowing for them to be so close to Kellam and his influences. The town is horrible to humans and half-bloods. It's no wonder your family needed Callista's protection."

"What do you mean 'they were'?" Paxton asked, concern washing over his face.

Samara rubbed her thumb over his large knuckles and moved to sit on his bed, avoiding the boxes of potions he had stacked on his floor. He sat next to her. "Callista introduced me as your close friend at the coterie."

"Well, that's correct." But he still looked puzzled.

"That was fine until we went to Paddosha Palace. Callista changed personality to some kind of evil creature I didn't recognize, and during our time with the Paddosha Palace's people, different things happened, and Callista's reactions seemed to place me in a suspicious light."

"Did you deserve to be treated that way?"

"I would have to say that if she suspected I worked against her when she was looking for the crystal, she wouldn't be wrong." Fiddling with her hands, Samara filled Paxton in on everything that had happened while she was away. "I had a feeling Callista was becoming suspicious of me, and I don't know how much longer we'll be able to stay here. I sent Ulrieg to tell your family that it would be best to leave the village and find a place where Callista wouldn't know where they were. I didn't know how much longer we would both be here."

Worry filled her as she looked at him. "I'm sorry if I overstepped, but I was only thinking of their safety. If we end up having to leave here, I didn't want them to have to deal with Callista."

He rested his head in his hands. "I hope they find a safe place."

Samara laid a hand on his thigh. "Me too. I'm surprised just how wide the coterie's reach is and how it's affecting the different areas. You should have seen the people of the village near the Paddosha Palace. They were horrified and frightened, surrounded by centaurs, and forced to betray their fellow villagers to keep safe."

"I think you've done the right thing for my family." Paxton drew his knees to his chest, pressing Samara's hand between his thigh and chest as he hugged them close. "And I'm afraid that's not all that's happened."

"What do you mean?" Samara shifted closer.

"While you were gone, things changed rapidly around here." He gazed at her, his eyes filled with worry. "It's no longer safe here either."

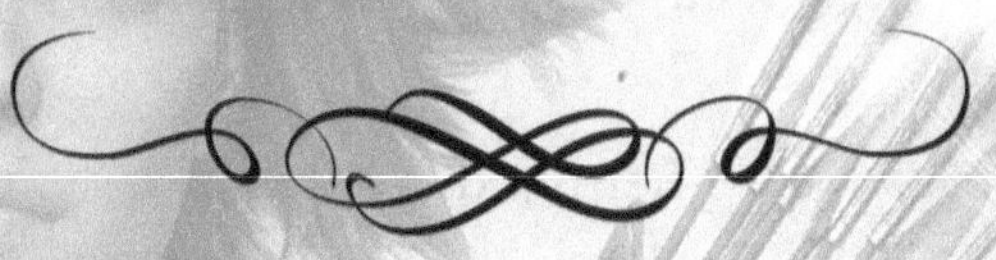

CHAPTER THIRTY-ONE

What's happened? Ulrieg sat on the floor before them, his red eyes dangerously bright. *Is that why you're still up?*

Paxton nodded. "It's been horrible. I've been trying to work out what to do." A deep frown creased his forehead, and Samara wrapped an arm around his shoulders. "They have Forgrac."

Samara stiffened. "What do you mean? He's basically been a slave here since he arrived, trying to work for his passage to cross the border and go home."

Paxton shook his head. "It's worse than that. While you were away, Forgrac wanted to see this big orb thing we've been talking about, and he wanted to see the cave where they have been capturing the dragons and torturing them."

All feeling drained from Samara's cheeks. "He didn't go, did he?"

"I told him not to, but the day you left, he was cleaning Artemise's potions room, and he found the key we had been talking about. That night, he used it."

Samara wrung her hands. "I should have kept my mouth shut. It was just so nice to have someone else to talk to." She tamped down her fear for the dwarf. "Did someone catch him down there?"

Paxton shook his head. "He had a good look around before he got out of there, but at the same time, he found a guardian dragon tied to one of the benches." His voice dropped to a whisper. "And he set it free."

Samara's eyes lit up. "That should be good news, shouldn't it?"

Paxton raised a hand to stop her. "Forgrac pulled me aside at breakfast to tell me, and as I left the kitchen, Kaine walked in and charmed him into telling the truth. It was horrible! Zofia and Vexx marched into the kitchen and forced Forgrac into the catacombs. We haven't seen him since."

"But he does so much around here."

"It doesn't matter. Artemise has been cooking our meals. And let me tell you, they are ordinary compared to Forgrac's. I've tried to sneak down to rescue him or at least to see if he's all right, but I can't get in there. They have had Vexx's snake guarding the entrance to the catacombs outside, Jet's been at the front door, and Tabitha has been guarding the entrance down to the tunnels. It's impossible to get down there without being caught and endangering my family."

He paused then continued, "But then again, if my family has moved to a safer location that Callista doesn't know, then I can risk going down." He began to rise.

Samara grabbed his arm and secured him to the bed. "Oh no, you don't. I'm not going to let you risk your life like that. For one, your family may not have moved yet. I didn't think it was that urgent. And if they have, you want them to have a head start. Two, we have other methods to use. Ulrieg can find a key."

"But even if Ulrieg gets a key, you can't turn invisible, and I imagine the key is tricky for a dragon to use. And even if Ulrieg can sneak down unseen and open the door, he can't make Forgrac turn invisible, so he will be seen trying to leave."

Samara smiled.

Paxton shifted on the bed. "This isn't a smiling matter."

"No. It's not, but do you know what Henriette's special gift is?"

Paxton shook his head.

Her smile grew broader. "She can turn things invisible."

Paxton's eyes widened. "We're not getting Henriette involved in this. I couldn't do that to her or anyone else. Dealing with the catacombs is definitely dangerous."

"I'm not going to involve her. But I can borrow something from her that will help."

"What's that?"

"Actually, she likes pranks, so I'll just ask her to turn my cloak invisible when I'm ready to go down. It only works for half an hour, but I know my way around, so I'll be quick."

"But Forgrac will still be visible."

"He's small. I'll wrap my cloak around both of us."

"I see." For the first time that night, Paxton grinned.

Samara climbed onto his lap and kissed him, her body warming at his touch as he held her close. She sighed. "I'd love to stay here, but I'm worried about Forgrac. And maybe Henriette is still up."

Pulling back, Paxton cupped her face in his hands. "Is there anything I can do?"

"Get some sleep. I might need you to sneak him some food at breakfast."

He pursed his lips. "I doubt I'll get much sleep knowing you're putting yourself in danger."

"I'll be careful. Besides, Ulrieg and I are getting good at sneaking around."

Hey, I've always been good at sneaking around, Ulrieg retorted.

CHAPTER THIRTY-TWO

Quickly, Samara tiptoed back to her room and grabbed her cloak, folding the long black fabric over her arm before making her way to Henriette's door. She tried to think of an excuse for needing Henriette to turn her cloak invisible.

Standing outside her door, Ulrieg called to the younger apprentice. *Henriette! Henriette, are you awake? Samara would like to talk to you. She's outside your door.*

Soft mutterings came from behind the door, followed by faint footsteps heading toward the door from inside. When the door flung open, a bleary-eyed Henriette partially filled the frame. Her turquoise hair was in disarray, hanging loosely around her torso. She blinked into the dim corridor as though trying to make out who stood before her. "Samara, you're still in your travel clothes. What're you still doing up?"

"I'm sorry if I woke you, but I really needed your help."

Henriette looked both ways down the corridor and beckoned her in. "Come in before you wake the whole building. Who called me, by the way?"

"That was Gray. He's been practicing talking to others." Guilt washed over Samara at the lie.

Henriette gazed at Samara's empty shoulder. "Where is he?"

"Still outside."

Frowning, Henriette shook her head, looking too tired to worry about something she didn't understand. "Anyway, why do you need my help in the middle of the night? Or should I say, early hours of the morning?"

Samara lowered her voice further. "I heard that Kaine is back, and I wanted to sneak in and frighten him. He wasn't very nice to me before he left, so I thought I'd spook him a little." She hid the cringe she felt over lying to the girl again. "Can you pleese make my cloak invisible?"

A slight grin pushed aside some of the tiredness on Henriette's face. "Sure. He was being nasty to you before he left. I don't know how you have the energy after such a long trip, though. Not even I've been thinking about causing mischief."

She reached for the cloak and whispered an incantation over it. Within moments, it turned invisible. "All right. You have half an hour. Good luck, and let me know how it goes tomorrow. I hope you get him good."

Samara gave her a quick hug. "Thank you. Sorry again if I woke you. Go back to bed."

As soon as Henriette closed the door behind her, Samara put on the cloak and descended the stairs.

Ulrieg. Are you nearby?

Almost. I'm just leaving Artemise's room. I have the key.

The cloak is invisible. I'll meet you at the top of the indoor stairs near Tabatha. If I go out the front, it'll grab Jet's attention when I open the door.

Quietly, she made her way to Tabatha. The cat's ears pricked, and her slitted eyes searched different areas as Samara got closer. Samara stopped several feet away, watching the cat search for something she couldn't see, before she edged her way past her and closer to the entrance of the stairs. Samara remained close, watching the cat's tail flick back and forth with agitation as Tabatha stared into the common area, looking for whatever she smelled.

A breeze brushed over Samara. *I've passed you,*

and I'm over the stairs down to the catacombs. So far, I can't see anyone other than a few familiars.

I'm on my way. Samara tiptoed toward the stairs, glancing briefly over her shoulder to check that Tabatha remained in her spot. She was glad she had left her shoes off. It made sneaking around the building much easier.

You know, you really are difficult to see. I wouldn't have known you were near Tabatha if I hadn't caught a glimpse of your face under your hood.

Samara grinned despite their situation. *That's kind of the point. But it's good to know.*

Moving through the corridor took longer than she expected, or perhaps it was her nerves making her feel like it was taking a long time to reach the cave door. She passed a few doors on her right, and she wondered if these were doors to the opposite side of the additional strange rooms they had found, the ones where she had discovered Byzarid's body. The thought gave her shudders, and she hoped Forgrac wasn't in there—or in the same condition. She decided to check these rooms if they didn't find Forgrac in the cave.

Most of the underground tunnels on this side were very similar to those outside, minus the puddles left from rain. Sconces shone with dull light every ten yards until, finally, the path finished at the door. A sconce burned on the right a few feet above the door handle, accompanied by the coterie's emblem keyhole on the left of the handle.

Still invisible, Ulrieg produced the key he'd stolen earlier, letting the leather necklace dangle from his talon as he hung from the lit sconce.

Grabbing the key, Samara pressed the emblems together and whispered, "*Aperti.*" The lock clicked softly and the door cracked open, setting the light of the orb free into the corridor. Samara quickly peeked in, checking for people inside the room, then pushed inside when she didn't spot any. Closing the door, she pushed the hood off her head, giving her full peripheral vision, and Ulrieg turned visible.

The orb pulsated with its orange glow, and remembering all the dragon hearts sacrificed to the evil power sent shivers down Samara's spine. *How many more are they going to sacrifice to this horrid thing?* She moved protectively between Ulrieg and the orb, not wanting anything to happen to her familiar. As far as she was concerned, the orb had tasted plenty of dragons.

The orb felt alive and buzzing, leaving Samara to think that the additional dragon hearts it had been fed must have powered it further, making it stronger. That couldn't be good for the future of the kingdoms.

Their feet rapidly crossed the large cave to investigate the twenty smaller caves leading off its sides. The place seemed empty, but they weren't leaving without checking every single one. Forgrac wouldn't take up much space.

Each empty room they observed lifted Samara's spirits slightly, as it meant no dragons were being held captive there, either. Still, worry had eroded her resolve by the time they had searched the tenth room. Maybe they had already killed Forgrac and disposed of him, feeding him to the orb. Or perhaps he was being held somewhere else and being tortured. However, that seemed unlikely, considering it was the early-morning hours. Samara would be a tired mess if it wasn't for the adrenaline pumping through her veins.

They searched another two rooms before Ulrieg called to her. *I've found him. He's in the next room from you.*

Heart thumping loudly in her chest, she hurried to the next room to find Forgrac secured to a gurney table, his face pale and clothes torn and bloody from cuts on his arms and legs. She ran to him, placing a hand on his forehead. "Forgrac, are you awake?"

The dwarf startled, his eyes opening wide. She realized drool had pooled in his beard and down his bushy moustache. The dwarf's breathing was staggered as he searched the room for what had woken him. Samara yanked the cloth gag from his mouth.

His eyes met hers, his panic lessening momentarily before coming back stronger. "Love. What are ya doing 'ere? Ya gotta get outta 'ere. It's not safe."

Samara's heart melted. Here he was, in danger, and he was worried about her. She smiled despite the situation. "I'm here for you. I know this is dangerous, and that's exactly why I'm not leaving you here." She quickly worked to unfasten his restraints. "Paxton told me what you did. That was very brave and stupid."

"Jus' like ya, then!" the dwarf sniped, then he caught sight of Ulrieg. "An' it's even more dangerous for ya. Ya both need to get outta 'ere."

Not without you. Ulrieg yanked the restraints away. *Can you walk?*

"I 'ope so." Forgrac sat and draped his legs over the table's edge. His brow furrowed when he looked at Samara. "Where's the rest of ya body?"

She looked down, having forgotten she was wearing the invisible cloak. "Henriette spelled my cloak to be invisible, but it only lasts half an hour. So we must get you out of here before it wears off." She grabbed him under his arms. "Excuse me." Then she lifted him off the bench and placed him on his feet.

The dwarf kicked his legs to the side as if to test

their ability then took a couple of steps. "It's all good. Let's get going."

She grabbed him gently by the wrist, directed him into the main room with the orb, then headed for the external door. "I'm so glad to see you alive. I was worried they had fed you to the orb."

Waddling slightly, Forgrac fought to keep up with her. He shook his head. "They wouldn't do that. They don't want the likes of me in the orb. I'm a dwarf. A creature too lowly for their tastes an' definitely not sacrificin' material. I ain't got dragon blood, an' I ain't got a magical power. Me understanding is that's what the orb needs. Which means 'at ya lot are in more danger than me." He stopped short. "'Ay! Wait a minute. If you're back, does that mean Callista is too? If so, then ya should probably leave me, an' maybe Callista will set me free once she finds out an' let me return to me duties so I can go 'ome."

Samara held tight to his wrist. "That's a lovely thought, but I'm afraid it's not going to happen if Callista finds out you've been down here."

"What makes ya say that?"

"Let's just say she showed her other side while we were away, and everyone who is in favor of the dragons and withholding anything the coterie wants are enemies of the coterie and Callista. I'm afraid there won't be any going back for you."

Forgrac tripped and landed on the floor.

Samara stopped to help him up. "Are you all right?"

Dusting off his knees, Forgrac rose to his feet. "I'm jus' in shock. I've worked so hard to please Callista, 'oping she'll let me cross the border to me family. All of 'at has been thrown away in an instant."

"I'm sorry. Hopefully, we'll figure something out. But right now, we need to get you out of here." They reached the door leading to the external corridor, and she opened it, Ulrieg leading the way as they brought Forgrac through. They secured the door behind them and hurried along the dank corridor, past several doors, and climbed the stairs to the hidden bush.

Ulrieg abruptly stopped, and Forgrac ran into one of his horns.

"Ow!" The dwarf rubbed his forehead where the tip pierced the skin.

Shh! Ulrieg spun to face him, his red eyes glowing. *Mystique is waiting near the bush.*

CHAPTER THIRTY-THREE

They froze where they stood on the top step. Callista must've placed Mystique there after seeing Samara in the catacombs, suspecting she would try to rescue Forgrac. Confusion washed over her. She didn't understand why Callista didn't get upset when she discovered Samara in the corridor that day, especially after how she acted at Paddosha Palace. Maybe it was because there weren't any dragons to save then. But surely, Callista thought Samara must've been involved with the escape of the dragons and dragon elf.

Then again, if Forgrac was busted for releasing a guardian dragon, he's probably being blamed for all the past missing captives as well.

She shook her head, trying to think straight. *Is there anything we can do?* Samara asked Ulrieg through their bond. *It's going to be too risky to take Forgrac through the building. I can cover him with my cloak, but I can't stop Mystique from smelling him if the wind blows the wrong way.*

Ulrieg turned invisible. *You two wait here. I'll see if I can get past and distract her.*

Samara bit her bottom lip. She didn't know if he would be able to make it past the bush without making it move too much. It always sat securely over the top of the hole.

Placing her feet on different steps, Samara braced herself for a quick escape either way. She then pulled the hood of the cloak over her head and wrapped Forgrac inside its layers, instantly hiding him from sight. She didn't know how long it had been since Henriette charmed the cloak, but she was sure time was running out quick. If the invisibility spell wore off before they were back in her room, it would be obvious what she was doing down here.

Careful not to knock into Ulrieg, she raised her head just above the hole and saw Mystique's back through the bush. Her tail whipped from side to side as she took in the surroundings in front of her. Parts of the bush moved very slowly as Ulrieg inched out of the hole, heading to the opposite side of the jaguar. Although Ulrieg was a dragon who would give a significant fight, he was smaller than a full-sized jaguar. That was a battle Samara didn't want to see.

After long, slow movements, the last of the bush softly dropped back over the hole, and after a few breaths, Samara heard the soft sound of beating wings. Under the half moon, Mystique's back stiffened, and she peered over one shoulder, her yellow eyes eerie in the moonlight. She leaned to the left to see behind the bush, giving up soon when she didn't spot anything unusual.

Keeping her face and head covered, only exposing enough of her eyes to see, Samara stuck her head out farther, feeling Forgrac shifting underneath the cloak.

Suddenly, the branches of a tree across the wildflower-strewn plain in front of the large cat bounced dramatically, instantly pulling Mystique's attention back to the front. The cat's tail twitched, and she stalked several yards in that direction before parking herself in a seated position, her eyes fixed on the moving bush.

Move now! Ulrieg instructed.

Quickly, Samara helped Forgrac and then herself out of the hole, the task of remaining hidden and silent simultaneously proving challenging. Ulrieg kept up his loud branch rustling, holding Mystique's attention.

Forgrac and Samara ran to the pine forest, staying on their tiptoes to eliminate any possible noises. A stick jabbed into Samara's foot, and it was an effort not to cry out. Her shoes would have been useful just then. Still, she pressed on, doing her best in the dull moonlight to avoid any more twigs.

They passed the line of the forest, heading several trees deep into the darkness before pausing behind some tree trunks out of earshot of the large cat's acute hearing.

"Where are we goin'?" Forgrac whispered.

Samara panted. "I don't know. Honestly, I don't know where it's safe anymore."

"What're ya goin' to do, love? It's not safe for ya 'ere." Forgrac rested a hand on her forearm.

"I have to go back. I can't leave Paxton there on his own. On top of that, my family is still at the mercy of the coterie. It's all become too dangerous." Samara checked the bottoms of her feet, feeling the pain from the rocks and sticks she'd encountered during their mad dash.

"Exactly. Not much point in ya hangin' 'round if ya can't go against all the senior coterie members. Ya should probably come with me, and we should head to ya family an' tell them they 'ave to find different accommodation."

"My family has six children. It's not going to be easy for them to hide and take care of themselves."

"Six children!"

"Plus me." She gave him an awkward smile.

"That's a lot of responsibility."

"I know. That's why I joined the coterie. It was supposed to be our safety net."

"I'm sorry, but they're goin' to 'ave to move. They're better off learning to look after themselves where no one knows 'em than having a chance against the coterie." He peered past the trees to see if Mystique was still being entertained by Ulrieg. "Tell me the name of ya village an' ya parents, an' I'll find 'em an' warn 'em."

He leveled his gaze at Samara. "Then, I'm comin' back for ya, and ya better 'ave Paxton safe by 'en 'cause ya comin' with me whether ya like it or not. We'll find another way to save the dragons an' any dragon elves before they can get caught."

"My parents are Hamon and Abigail Wren, and Callista set them up on a farm to manage it just out of Pearlmire the last time I saw them." She told him about the hole in the border to Slosiaran and how Paxton's family might be heading that way.

Forgrac fixed his clothing and tamed his hair with his hands. "Right! I'll be off. I 'ave a long way to go in a short amount of time, an' ya need to get back inside before ya get caught. As much as I long to go through 'at hole to see me family, I'm comin' back for ya an' that nice lad Paxton first. Take Paxton an' ya familiars to the nearest village. A few friends there should look after ya. Check in with the local tailor."

Nodding, Samara squatted down to his height and brushed her hood off her head. "Are you going to be all right out there by yourself?"

He grinned. "I've made a few friends in a nearby village. I'm pretty sure they'll lend me a horse an' some food for me travels. 'Sides, I'm a master at disguise. That's 'ow I lasted so long before. I'm small, an' I learnt to blend in. The only thing I couldn't do is cross the borders without the coterie's permission."

Contemplation filled the dwarf's face. "I was so lookin' forward to seein' my family again. Now, 'cause of ya, I might 'ave a chance—as soon as we get ya outta 'ere." He laid a hand on her shoulder. "Now 'urry back. I want ya to stay safe while I'm gone."

Samara hurried back toward the coterie building, glancing back to see Forgrac's small form tottering steadily in the opposite direction. Then she covered her head with her hood again and kept her chin down as she darted for the bush, hiding the hole to the underground.

On the far side of the clearing, Ulrieg continued to entertain Mystique with his antics, jumping from tree to tree and ensuring they swayed violently.

Samara smiled. *I'm returning to the underground now. You won't have to entertain the kitty for much longer.*

Finally! This was getting rather tiresome. I'll come back in by the window soon.

See you soon. Careful not to make any noise, she climbed into the hole, hurried back through the cave, past the pulsating orb, and out the door into the coterie. Her eyes darted wildly in every direction, ensuring no one was around.

When she exited the cave and walked along the sconce-lit corridor, her heart pounded loudly when she didn't see Tabatha sitting in the same place. Panic bloomed as she passed the area, searching every dark corner for signs of the cat. She hoped the familiar didn't realize something was happening and report it to Artemise.

Quickly, Samara climbed the stairs and slipped into the common room, heading for the kitchen. She hadn't eaten in quite some time and wanted to grab extra food for their escape, but it was also a good excuse for wandering the building if the cloak lost its invisibility.

Pushing the kitchen doors wide, she lit a sconce

before searching the benchtops for any sign of food. Her cloak caught on a bench, and she decided to take it off at least until it turned visible again. If someone came in to see things moving without someone holding them, it would raise suspicions.

She brushed her palm along the mostly empty benches. It was unbelievable how different the kitchen looked after only a couple of days without Forgrac in charge. Bread rested on the bench as before, and she picked it up, feeling its rock-hard crust. It must be the last loaf Forgrac baked before being captured. Her nose crinkled at the thought of sniffing the stale bread. She returned it to the bench and searched for something else to eat.

The fruit boxes remained on the floor, and she hurried to them, dragging them into the open, only to find just three apples, all with large bruises marring their skins. Still, she grabbed them. She was too hungry—she would have to cut the bad pieces off and eat the rest.

Searching the shelves, she was unable to find any leftover food from dinner. Forgrac always used to have something around that she could eat. Eventually, she found some pieces of salted meat in one corner and clutched them in her hand.

Sighing loudly, she was about to give up her quest when something entered the kitchen. She spun to face it, only to find Tabatha eyeing her through the entryway. Samara held up her findings. "I couldn't sleep because I was starving, so I've come looking for something to eat." She showed off her bare feet, as if that would prove she hadn't been outside, then bit into the salted meat. "There's not much here, so I was about to leave."

Tabatha's eyes didn't leave her, and Samara hoped the cloak draped over her arm didn't make her arm disappear and raise the cat's suspicions. She casually looked down and thanked her lucky stars to see the cloak had turned visible.

"All right, then," Samara chirped. "It was lovely chatting. I'm going to take these to my room to eat then hopefully get some sleep." She wandered past the familiar, doing her best to look unfazed and hoping the cat wasn't smart enough to realize she was still wearing her traveling pinafore.

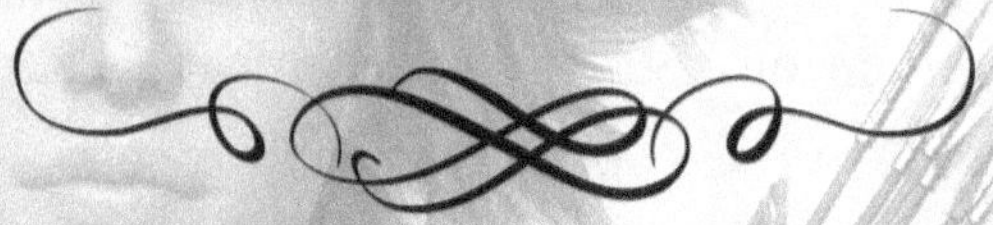

CHAPTER THIRTY-FOUR

A knock woke Samara from a deep sleep. Blinking, she took in the early-morning light shining through her window. Ulrieg slept beside her on her bed, curled up near her legs. She rubbed her eyes. It surprised her how quickly she must have fallen asleep despite all her anxiety. The exhaustion must have won the battle.

All the events of the previous day crashed back into her memory, and she stiffened, cursing herself for not being more prepared for an emergency exit. Looking at the amount of light in the sky, she had even missed breakfast. She cursed herself again. She was supposed to sneak out extra food from the breakfast buffet to take with them when they escaped later that day.

The knocking sounded again, and she wondered

if the person at the door was there because she'd been discovered helping Forgrac escape or if it was a friend.

Another knock, this time more impatient. "Samara, it's me."

She exhaled a sigh of relief at hearing Paxton's voice. Throwing off the blankets, she kicked her feet to the floor, realizing she had been so tired the night before that she hadn't even changed into her sleeping shift. Running a hand through her hair, she opened the door.

Paxton smiled and held up a bowl of porridge, and Jojo stuck his head out of his bonded's tunic pocket. "I've brought you some breakfast. I figured you'd be worn out and probably hungry."

Samara ushered him in. "Thanks. I went looking for some food when I got back, but there wasn't anything fresh to find. Forgrac always kept a little fresh food where I could find it easily."

"Forgrac added more love to his food than Artemise does. You would think that the potions master would know how to cook. She probably does but doesn't care enough to make good food for us." He shrugged. "At least it's edible."

She nodded, taking the bowl from him and sitting at her desk, ensuring her window was shut securely. "Is breakfast finished?"

He nodded.

She groaned. "I was hoping to raid the buffet for some additional rations."

"I'm afraid Artemise doesn't put out extra food for the apprentices who can't make it to the next meal, either."

"Really?" Samara's shoulders sagged. "I guess there's no surprise there. She doesn't strike me as the caring kind."

Paxton sat on the end of her bed and acknowledged Ulrieg with a smile. "How did you go last night?"

Samara scooped a spoonful of porridge and blew on it. "Henriette was more than happy to help when I said I wanted to play a trick on Kaine for what he did to me in the past." She shoveled the porridge into her mouth.

Paxton grinned. "I'm sure she was. Did you manage to find Forgrac?"

Samara nodded and swallowed, screwing up her nose slightly. Paxton was correct—the porridge was edible but not much else. "He was tied up underneath. He was hurt, but not too badly. He said they didn't want the likes of him to feed to the orb because he's not a dragon or a magic wielder." She stirred her porridge. "We escaped through the outside tunnels, and Ulrieg distracted Mystique so she wouldn't see us."

Paxton rubbed his hands along his pants. "Where is Forgrac now?"

She took another spoonful of porridge. "I honestly don't know. He said he would visit my family and tell them to leave and find safety elsewhere, then he was coming back for us." She turned to face him. "We must leave. You know that, don't you? He wanted me to leave last night, but I said I wasn't leaving without you, and I also wanted to make sure Henriette would be all right. That's also why I was hoping to grab some extra food. I think we need to seriously think about leaving today."

"What about all the dragons they might catch and torture?"

"We'll have to find a better way to help them." She scratched her leg. "There must be a better way. Maybe we'll be able to find Dragoria. Maybe there's a way to let the dragons go home and a safe place for dragon elves and guardian dragons to bond. We're not strong enough to beat the senior coterie members, even with two of us against one of them. And there are more of them, plus they have apprentices like Kaine, Mist, and Luna. I'm certain they will fight for the coterie."

She quickly finished her porridge and sat beside

Paxton on the bed, resting a hand on his thigh and feeling warmth travel up her arm. "What are you thinking?"

Paxton focused on her, his dark-brown eyes filled with compassion, making her body tingle. She didn't care that he didn't have Kaine's looks. This care and compassion he poured out to her stole her heart more thoroughly than any attractiveness and experienced charm could muster. Paxton had shown her so much more of himself over the last few months, coming a long way since simply being a scholarly, quiet male who barely spoke to anyone. She cupped his cheek with her hand.

He leaned into it before encasing her hand between his larger ones. "How was I so lucky to win your affection?" He ran the back of his fingers down the side of her face. "You are so beautiful and caring, and you're passionate about protecting those who can't protect themselves."

Her cheeks warmed, and she shook her head before resting it on his chest. "I'm the lucky one to win a heart as good as yours. Besides, I'm the one who may have placed you in danger. If you or your family get hurt, I'll never be able to live with it."

He stroked under her chin, lifting it so her eyes met his, which were filled with longing. "If anything happens to me or my family, it's not you who would be to blame. It's the coterie and me, for I knew full well that what I was digging into was taboo in this place. And if you remember correctly, I'm the one that came to you with secret information."

"Yeah, but I'm the one who came to you with the emblem to research."

Gently, he grabbed her chin between his thumb and forefinger. "Don't. I was more than aware it was dangerous, even after only a little research. This library hides books about all kinds of taboo subjects. While you were away, I read stories worded like nursery rhymes about how dragons and dragon elves overcame evil powers to bring peace to the realms."

Her jaw dropped. "They have those kinds of stories here in the library?"

Paxton tilted his head from one side to the other. "They're in the restricted section and are mostly inked out, so they're difficult to read. But nobody guards the library anymore, so I spent time deciphering the words behind the ink." He squeezed her hand between his. "The stories say the dragons and dragon elves had enslaved the evil power, binding it within a powerful ward and hiding it in a cave deep in the earth. It was safe for many years until one day, it disappeared. Somehow, they couldn't remember where the cave was and couldn't find it. It was like their memories had been altered any time they tried to remember the location."

Paxton took a deep breath and continued, "After many years, it was rumored a building had been built over it, but the building was also magically hidden from everyone but a select few. Within this select few, a strong magic wielder communed with the orb, giving it what it wanted, in exchange for teaching how to overcome the rule of the dragons and their elves. The more the magic wielder fed the orb what it wanted, the stronger it became, and it bestowed small portions of its power on the magic wielder, making them stronger and more evil, helping them defeat the dragons and their elves."

He gazed at her. "Despite the dragons being contained to a point, the evil power is still entrapped. It needs the blood of its enemies and the power of magic wielders to release it. The fact it's still trapped means the dragons are still too strong."

Samara gasped. "That sounds exactly like the orb in the catacombs. There are too many similarities to be overlooked."

Glumly, Paxton nodded.

A magical pulse radiated through the building, and they pulled away from each other.

"That feels like Callista's calling. I guess it's time to see if they have noticed Forgrac has gone." Samara gazed down at Ulrieg. "Perhaps you should stay away today. I have a bad feeling about our future here, and I'm not certain that Callista doesn't know about you."

Ulrieg's red eyes narrowed. *If you think I'm leaving you alone to face her wrath, you have another thing coming.*

"Please, Ulrieg. I couldn't stand seeing you get hurt." She reached for his talon.

And you expect me to sit back in the distance and watch you get hurt? No way. I'll hang around in my invisible form, as always. He stamped his feet, the effect lost on the soft mattress.

Samara's shoulders caved. "Well, we don't have much choice. We need to see what this meeting is about." She looked at Paxton. "Maybe we should go at different times or at least a few minutes apart, to give the impression we're not together."

"I see what you're trying to do, but it sounds like the damage has already been done. Still, we'll try the safer approach." Paxton turned to leave then quickly kissed her on her forehead and wrapped his arms around her. "I'll see you very soon." He gazed over her pinafore. "Perhaps you should change to make it look like you've been in your room all night."

Samara nodded and, as soon as she closed the door behind him, pulled out her leather pants and sleeveless fitted leather tunic. At least these clothes made her feel ready to take on whatever might come her way.

Gazing down at Ulrieg, she took a deep breath. "Did you put Artemise's key back?"

Of course.

She breathed a sigh of relief. "Good. Are you ready?"

He turned invisible. *As ready as I'll ever be.*

Pulling the door open, she saw Kaine, with Ginger standing behind him, and Mist, with Okak on her shoulder. Mist's fist was raised as if ready to knock.

Samara flinched, cringing on the inside, before putting on the most cheerful voice she could muster. "Oh, hi. I was just heading down to the hall. You didn't need to come and get me."

Kaine reached for her arm, his charmed touch instantly washing away her apprehension. "Where were you last night, my sweet Samara?"

Her resolve melted, and she opened her mouth to answer him.

Samara! Don't you dare! Ulrieg's gruff voice pierced Kaine's hold on her. *I can't believe he can still charm you so quickly after all this time.*

Samara blinked, realizing she was about to tell

him the truth of her freeing Forgrac. She changed her answer. "I was here catching up on some sleep."

Kaine frowned and shook his head slightly at Mist as if to answer a question.

Mist's mouth pursed, and Okak cawed. "Tabatha said she saw you in the kitchen."

"Oh, yes. I woke up hungry because we missed dinner, and I got up and searched the kitchen for something to eat. I was disappointed with how little I found."

Mist clasped Samara's other arm, and both she and Kaine turned with her. "In any case, Vexx has commanded your company."

Samara's face tingled and went numb. "Isn't Vexx in the hall where Callista is about to address everyone?"

"He is there, but you'll be meeting him elsewhere." Mist's grip tightened, and Okak flew downstairs.

"Come with us, please." Charming magic oozed out of Kaine, and Samara found herself willfully walking with them to wherever they were taking her, Ginger padding behind them. They passed through the empty common room and the far side near where Tabatha was sitting last night.

Luna swayed over to meet them, her face peaceful, a broad smile filling her lips as her eyes connected with Samara's. "You'll join us willingly as we take you to the cave," she sang. She petted Coco's head, the rabbit nestled in her arms.

The need to obey built higher in Samara, and her footsteps quickened.

I don't like this. When Samara didn't answer, Ulrieg tried again. *Samara! Wake up and fight against them.*

Samara blinked and looked from Kaine's hand grasping her arm to Mist's on the other side then at the mesmerizing sway of Luna's hips as she led the way. Something strange was happening.

Samara, you need to get away from them, Ulrieg urged.

Her mind felt clouded, although a vague light of reason shone through. *And go where? I won't get far from three powerful magic wielders, even if they're only skilled apprentices.* She gazed toward the front door. *Besides, Mystique and Jet are guarding the entrance. I won't get far.*

Looking back at the three, she remembered Mist's ability to strike with lightning shocks, and she cringed. There was no way she could combat that kind of power. Maybe if she had Peadar's ability to block spells, she would survive it.

The three senior apprentices directed her into the catacombs toward the cave.

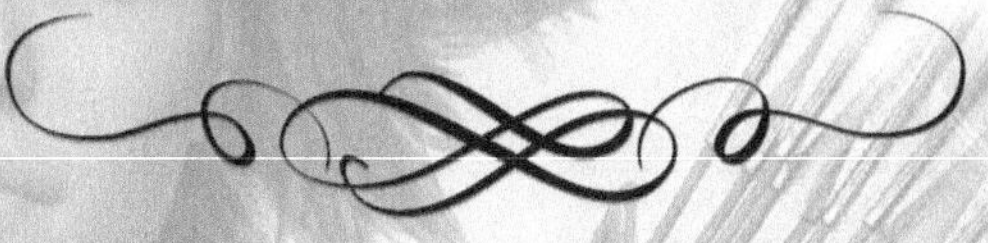

CHAPTER THIRTY-FIVE

Mist and Kaine threw Samara onto one of the gurneys. Her weight was nothing for the muscular, tall male and the warrior female. Samara kicked and squirmed, but Mist sat on her legs as Kaine and Luna secured her hands. Their familiars circled around them, eerie and watchful.

"Wait! What are you doing? There's no need for this. I'm not going anywhere." The chains chafed her skin as she struggled. But her efforts were ineffective, and judging by the expressions on their faces, so were her arguments.

When they finished securing her hands, they then worked on her feet. Images of the dragons she had found tortured in these caves flashed into her mind, and her panic increased. It was impossible for her not to think the same outcome might be intended for her.

Then a thought crossed her mind. Perhaps if she stopped fighting them, they would leave her alone, and she could escape the chains. She ceased her struggles.

Once her feet and hands were chained, Mist relieved Samara of her weight, her shoes thumping on the hard floor as she slid to the ground.

A soft touch caressed Samara's arm as Kaine pressed close to her side. "Where is your familiar?"

The charm clouded her mind, enticing her to cooperate with her handsome ex and give in to his requests. Her body betrayed her, curving into his touch. She gasped, the words forming in her head, ready to spill from her tongue.

Samara. Stay with me. Don't give in to his magic.

Ulrieg's voice pushed a thin line of clarity through the fog, and her body stiffened. *Oh, Ulrieg. You should get far away from here. I don't want to betray you. The last thing I want is to put you in danger.*

I know. It's all the more reason for me to stay and break you free from their influence. Hurt colored his voice, and she hoped it wasn't because of her. She hadn't betrayed him yet. He had made sure of that.

He continued, *The last thing you want is to betray anyone helping you and the dragons.*

Are you disappointed with me?

No. Of course not!

I can hear hurt in your voice.

That's because of what they are putting you through and what they potentially have planned for you. We should have just run from this place.

You know I wouldn't leave Paxton behind. There's a strong chance that Callista has connected us in plotting against the coterie. She paused. *I need you to warn him as soon as you can.*

I'll see what I can do. But you're my priority.

When the three captors realized she wouldn't tell Kaine what he asked, Mist wrapped a scarf around her head and over her mouth, gagging her. "This way, you won't be able to undo the lock on your cuffs."

Samara's one sliver of hope diminished. That was her last option to get out of here without involving anyone else. Cuts wore into the edges of her mouth from the tightness of the gag.

Realizing he wasn't needed, Kaine grabbed Luna's hand. "Let's go up top to let Vexx know his orders have been accomplished."

The beautiful elf didn't waste any time taking him up on his offer. She scooped up Coco and called over her shoulder to Mist, "Are you all right to watch her by yourself for a while?"

Mist grunted. "Of course!" As the two disappeared from the room, Ginger followed close behind, sniffing the air.

Tears leaked from the edges of Samara's eyes as different tragic scenarios played in her mind. She played with the hope of Callista becoming involved and telling them that there was a mistake, that they were to release her, but the memory of what happened at Paddosha Palace squashed such a fickle dream.

Time ticked by slowly as everything fell quiet. Neither Mist nor Ulrieg chatted with her to pass the time, and Okak sat on the back of a chair, peering at her with alternating beady black eyes. *Ulrieg, are you around?* she asked, but when he didn't answer, she didn't try again. She didn't want to interrupt him if he had managed to sneak out with Kaine and Luna to warn Paxton.

Samara wouldn't blame the dragon if he changed his mind and left her to fend for herself. Even though they were bonded and their friendship had blossomed quickly, they hadn't known each other long. This only made her care for him more, almost wishing he would leave her and save himself.

Ulrieg would be more important to help find Dragoria and to bring the dragon elves and guardian dragons together. She hadn't even learned the extent of her magic yet and knew for sure that she wouldn't have a chance against one of the senior members of the coterie, let alone the apprentices like Mist and her lightning energy. Samara would be completely singed in a few of seconds if Mist chose to attack, with Samara unable to stop her even if she saw it coming.

The orange light of the orb pulsed brighter. It almost seemed it was thriving, knowing that the person responsible for denying it some of its magical meal would be punished. A sickness filled her stomach. Maybe it thought that she would be another meal for it soon. Bile rose in her throat, burning the lining of her esophagus as she attempted to force it back down.

Fog grew around her, evidence of Mist's temperamental magic as her impatience increased, and Samara watched as the stocky female apprentice attempted to control her emotions. If she knew Mist as well as she thought, the warrior female would likely be battling with a wish to destroy Samara before Vexx came to talk with her. For once, Samara had a reason to be thankful that the sinister senior sorcerer had control over the apprentices, or else she might have already been a pile of ash.

Even though the apprentices had only asked her about Forgrac, she suspected this was much more than that. She was suddenly glad that she had set him free and that he would warn her family.

She didn't know how much time passed then, as minutes seemed to take hours. Her back ached from lying on the solid gurney with no padding underneath. Being forced to lie on her back on a cold, hard surface for hours was punishment enough, although she felt this wouldn't be the worst of it. Her eyes glazed as the stress of the situation became her norm, and the lack of sleep from the last few days began to catch up with her.

A door clicked loudly in the background, and Samara's muscles stiffened, instantly draining her of all sleepiness. Mist shifted from her seat near the door and checked the main room for the source. Several footsteps inched closer, and the apprentice stood straight just outside the doorway.

A dark-brown cloak filled the entrance, and Samara felt all feeling drain from her body as she took in Vexx's thin, tall frame, his snake familiar slithering around his shoulders, its black tongue tasting the air.

Vexx's thin hand stroked the snake's yellow scales. "Mara tells me that there is a taste of betrayal in the air." His grin was sly, almost sickening, as he brushed his hood off, exposing his short, spiky red hair and rounded ears. "I hear you have been sneaking down here and releasing many of my captives, including a dwarf only last night." Strangely, it was the first time Vexx had referred to his familiar and used her name.

Samara cringed, unable to say anything to defend herself. She didn't think that betrayal could be tasted by a snake. Shaking her head, she attempted to deny the accusations even though it was a lie.

Amusement crossed the senior sorcerer's face as he turned to Luna and Kaine. "Can you believe she is trying to argue that she is innocent? How bizarre. I could have sworn the familiars on guard said they smelled you and your elusive familiar last night."

Samara frowned, attempting to feign confusion, and shook her head. She felt so helpless. She couldn't speak any spells for defense, and having her hands and feet tied left her utterly useless.

Vexx lifted a red eyebrow, his eyes narrowing. "Are you accusing your senior coterie members' familiars of lying?"

Eyes wide, Samara shook her head.

The senior sorcerer leaned over her, holding his cynical, mocking face close to hers. "Clearly, you don't have a familiar with the ability to smell, or else you would know that you can't trick them by simply avoiding being seen. I don't know how you or your familiar got past them, but they didn't smell anyone else."

Samara attempted to speak, only to expel a combination of useless muffled sounds.

Vexx yanked the edges of her gag down, tearing at one side of her mouth as he did so. "Go on. Tell me the truth."

Samara wet her lips with her tongue. "I am telling the truth. Why are you treating me like this? You don't have any proof."

"I have the proof of Mara and Tabatha."

"Two familiars who are biased against me," she accused.

Vexx smirked. "That's hilarious. Why on earth would they conspire against you or any apprentice unless it was necessary?"

"Because you don't like me, and Artemise isn't known for being logical. She's a little crazy. Just ask the majority of the students."

The amusement didn't leave his face. "I must agree the old human sorceress is a little eccentric, but her cat is not and wouldn't lie about an apprentice's smell. And neither would Mara." He stroked his snake gently with the back of his hand, and the snake coiled closer to his neck.

"And what does Callista say about you holding one of her apprentices without proof?"

The sorcerer straightened, and Samara heard soft footsteps entering the main cave, coming closer. Vexx turned and backed away, granting access to the thin form filling the entrance. All kinds of emotions whirled within Samara as her eyes beheld Callista, with Mystique's black body slipping through the gap to stand guard in the corner.

The light of the orb pulsed behind Callista's thin frame, turning her lilac hair a tinge of red and emphasizing a rare scowl on her face. Samara's toes curled as she cringed away from the head sorceress, recognizing the look of madness she'd witnessed at the Paddosha Palace. No empathy showed in Callista's expression, a far cry from the sorceress who brought Samara to the coterie, kept her under her wing, and cared for her family's welfare.

Callista pressed her diadem against her forehead before twisting her golden bracelet, her fingers caressing the purple stone. The orb pulsed methodically behind her, almost like a heartbeat that powered the sorceress. Perhaps she had just finished communicating with the orb. Samara wasn't sure, as it remained just out of her sight.

She swallowed, relieved that Vexx had left off her gag. "Callista. What is going on?" She wanted to say she had done nothing wrong but couldn't muster the courage to say what they would consider a lie. As far as her conscience was concerned, Samara hadn't done anything wrong.

The head sorceress sauntered closer, and the air seemed to turn to ice as Callista gazed at Samara. She barely contained the shiver her body screamed to execute as cold blue eyes fixed on her.

"I brought you into the coterie for you to learn to restore the peace and defend the kingdoms from the evil threatening to rise again," Callista said. "I took you under my wing and looked after your family."

Samara clenched her fists and steeled her nerves. "I thank you for your generosity, great sorceress. And I have been working for the peace and order you recruited me for."

Callista's chin rose, and all expression left her face. "There has been evidence of late that proves the opposite."

Frowning, Samara mustered sincerity. "I promise I have been working for the good of the kingdoms."

"In your distorted view, perhaps." The sorceress moved closer to Samara's head.

Samara opened her mouth to speak.

Callista raised her hand to quiet her. "First, we need your familiar to join us so we may see him."

The coldness froze Samara's bones. She wasn't going to bring Ulrieg here, and Gray was gone. "My familiar showed himself many times during our trip to Paddosha Palace."

Callista scowled. "I didn't physically see him."

"You know he was in the distance a lot because he has lost faith in being treated well here, but he showed himself while traveling," Samara argued.

"Not in a satisfactory way. He must mingle with the other familiars, or he isn't worthy." She whirled sharply, her movements turning harsh. "I demand that you call him here where we can see him."

A movement caught her eye in the corner, where she couldn't miss the satisfied grin that filled Kaine's face. Ginger sat beside him, her nose working overtime.

"I'm afraid he won't come. He still doesn't trust the coterie to treat him well." Samara wouldn't budge.

Callista paced around her. "Tell your familiar to come and show himself and any oddities about him, or I will feed you to the orb."

Eyes wide, Samara glanced out the door at the pulsating light. "You're going to kill me?"

Callista waved a hand dismissively. "If I give you into the orb while you're alive, it'll feed off your magic until your soul gives everything to its will. Then you won't have a choice but to serve. So far, I have given you apprentices a choice. But if you don't adhere, I'll strip you of that privilege and force you to serve within the orb." She paused. "But at the same time, I'll strip your family of their privileges. No longer will they be under my protection. And over time, you will be stripped of your free will, and the orb will rule your soul."

Samara froze. The idea of losing her will and being forced to comply rocked her to the core, but there was no way she would betray Ulrieg on purpose. Her sacrifice would be worth it if the others could help Dragoria, the dragon elves, and dragons.

Callista muttered something under her breath, and Samara was instantly overcome by a terrible urge to scratch. Her skin felt like it was crawling, and she could do nothing about it. She writhed within her restraints but clamped her mouth shut. She refused to give in just because things became a little uncomfortable.

"Tell your familiar to join us," Callista demanded when Samara didn't give in.

Grasping firmly at her resolve, Samara said, "I've

already said that he won't come down because he doesn't trust how you will treat him."

"Not even to save his own bonded?" Callista's voice raised.

"I wouldn't expect him to. I care for him too much," Samara cried, fighting the words Callista wanted her to say.

The sorceress increased the intensity of the itching. "Now, let's be honest. I have it under sound authority that your familiar isn't who you said it is. And I demand to see him now. Is he what I think he is?"

It took all of Samara's will to feign shock. "I don't know what you're talking about."

Callista grunted in frustration. "I've tried to be civil with you, nice to you, in hopes that you would trust me enough to expose your familiar, but now, I've run out of patience, especially after you cost me my crystal."

Samara! What's going on? Ulrieg's voice coming through their bond brought a mixture of relief and terror.

Ulrieg, stay away. If you're in the cave, get out now! I hoped you were busy warning Paxton to leave.

Ha! You really don't know me well if that's what you think. I went to see him, but for help, not to tell him to abandon you. Besides, you should've seen his face.

There's no way he's leaving you here to be harmed or killed.

Suddenly, Ginger and Mystique's noses lifted, their nostrils flaring.

Ulrieg, get out! Samara screamed through their bond.

Callista's shoulders straightened, and Mystique abruptly left the small cave. "I've been informed that your odd-smelling familiar has entered the cave. He's in here somewhere. I knew he wouldn't be able to stay away. Your bond is too great." She rushed to the door, searching the larger cave for any sign of Ulrieg. "Show yourself, familiar. I know you're not the owl."

The eagerness in her voice unsettled Samara further. *Ulrieg, she possibly knows you're a dragon. Get out! I wouldn't be able to live with myself if I lost you to the orb.*

And you expect me to live with you being thrown into the orb? That doesn't seem fair.

The sorceress's eyes were slitted. "Show yourself. I want to see if the image Kaine painted in his description is true."

Samara froze. It truly was possible that Callista had known the truth for a long time and was just biding her time, waiting for them to slip up. *Ulrieg, please get out. I know you're concerned for me, but from what Callista said, there is more chance of us surviving if you leave and get help.*

What makes you say that?

It sounds like she feeds magic wielders to the orb alive, and it possibly takes time before it kills me or takes me over. But from what we've found in the past, they kill the dragons before feeding their hearts to the orb.

His silence seemed to extend longer and longer, and she held her breath, not wanting to miss any noise or word he might make.

"Where are you, familiar?" Callista made her hand into a claw and shoved it toward Samara. *"Needleprenora!"*

The itching that took over Samara's body intensified, making her skin feel like it was on fire. She writhed, attempting to use anything to scratch and relieve the torture. Then she stopped and blocked off the pain she was feeling from her bond. A bead of sweat trickled down her forehead. She didn't want Ulrieg to know what she was going through. She didn't want to give him any excuse to stay here and be caught.

"If you don't show yourself, familiar, your bonded will be put through worse, and for as long as it takes." Maliciousness tainted Callista's normally inexpressive voice, destroying all Samara's efforts to convince Ulrieg to leave.

Ulrieg, please. Go. A tear trickled down her face onto the table beneath her.

Ginger and Coco moved out of the room and into the larger cave, with Kaine and Luna following them. Okak on her shoulder, Mist went with them not long after, trailed by Vexx and Mara. The whole group had turned its attention to finding Ulrieg.

Callista called from the door to the smaller cave, "If you don't show yourself soon, these familiars and their bonded will sniff you out. You will be outnumbered, with no one to protect you."

Filled with pain and longing, Ulrieg's voice cut through Samara's pain. *If something happens, always remember I have not regretted one moment of being bonded to you. Although it was initially a mistake, I'm proud to be your familiar.*

Dread filled Samara, and she felt like her heart was being torn. More tears trickled into her hair. *Don't you dare show yourself. It's not worth it. You could do so much more for your realm than I could.*

Don't downplay your importance to my kind. You've done more than you realize, and if you don't have the magic needed to go against these terrible beings, you have other skills that will ensure their downfall, even if it takes longer than you want.

Ulrieg, please go. It will kill me if you don't leave. I don't know if I'll ever recover. Her hair grew wet from tears, strands of hair clinging to her scalp as she shifted, spilling more.

A deep, heartbreaking groan crossed their bond, and Samara choked on a sob, almost drowning Ulrieg's voice. *Hold strong, my sweet bonded. Don't give up. There is much for you to live for. I'm still with you even if I go silent. Remember this.*

So much love poured through their bond that it almost made the pain she was going through bearable.

Then something hit her, dulling her senses, and everything went black.

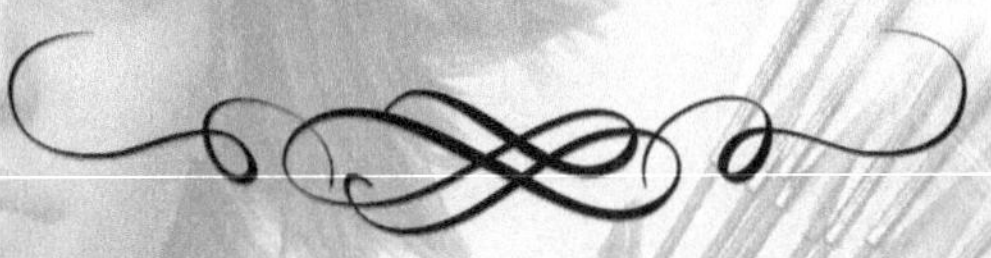

Samara's head throbbed, and her body ached. Orange light pulsed behind her eyelids, and she cracked them open, peering through the slits. Her cheeks felt numb, and when she lifted her head slightly, she saw her shackles were still fastened. Worst of all, she wasn't dead. She was still in the cave under the coterie building. Horror filled every pore in her body.

This can only mean one thing.

A sob rose in her throat, and tears spilled from her already-puffy eyes. Ulrieg must have given himself up. *No! No! No! No! No! Why would he do that?* So many horrible scenarios ran through her mind. She didn't even know if he was still alive. Her chill deepened when her mind shifted to

Paxton. *Have they also captured him? Is he also in danger, along with Jojo?*

Her mouth parted in a cry as heartbreak rocked her to the core. She didn't even care when someone shifted in the corner of the cave and began to speak. "Honestly, you're so weak. I don't even know why Callista picked you in the first place."

Samara swallowed her grief and blinked rapidly until, eventually, her vision cleared enough to see Mist, who was still guarding her. "What do you care? You still have your familiar."

Mist glared down her nose at Samara, disdain distorting her face as she stroked Okak's chest while he sat on her shoulder.

Samara tugged at the restraints, the chains clanking loudly against the hard surface. Wrecked, she lost all pretense of her loyalty to the coterie. "Why are these still on me? You lot never keep your promises unless it suits you. My familiar has given himself up, knowing he was under threat, yet the promise of letting me go hasn't been kept."

Mist crossed her arms. "It was never promised that you would be let go. The only promise was that you wouldn't be thrown into the orb." She smirked. "As far as I'm concerned, you should already be in there."

Growling in frustration, Samara gritted her teeth. "What has been done with my familiar?"

Placing a finger below Okak's chest and torso, Mist encouraged him to step onto her hand. "Your familiar clearly never cared for you."

"He gave himself up to save me!" Samara yelled.

Mist shook her head. "No. He never showed. Instead, he remained hidden wherever he found a little hiding space. That's how little he cared for you. What a warped bond you two had. Clearly, he didn't share the bond love."

Samara blinked, her heart jumping for joy, and she no longer heard what Mist was saying. Ulrieg had listened to her. When she replayed what he said to her before she passed out, it was clear it pained him to do so, but he did it. Her heart swelled with pride. He had actually done what she asked.

Samara suddenly ached to see his harsh exterior and hear a snarky retort. Still, it comforted her to know he was not in the coterie's hands. As to why they had yet to throw her into the orb, she would have to wait and see.

Ulrieg, if you can hear me, I'm so happy you did as I asked.

Samara, you're all right? His voice was strangely timid, as though he couldn't believe what he heard, but it also carried hope.

She was relieved that he was still near enough to hear her but scared that he hadn't gotten to safety yet. *Yes, I'm all right. Are you leaving this area soon to stay safe?*

I had a couple of things I wanted to do, but now I know you're still all right, I will add you to the top of my list.

Instantly, she regretted reaching out to him. Again, she had placed him in danger. *No. You need to leave. I don't know what they have planned for me. It's too dangerous for you. Just make sure that Paxton and Jojo are safe, that Henriette isn't in danger, and leave.*

Look at you, basically at death's door and still giving me orders, Ulrieg sniped. *Get your energy back and look for a way to escape. You being fed to that orb isn't something that should happen. If you can't find enough reason to fight back, just remember—if the orb gets your magic, that will only make it stronger. It's not something we or the dragons need. And most of all, I need you to be safe.*

The feeling's mutual. I'm fine. I don't know what they've planned for me, but I'll handle it. So get out of here.

I'll be fine. Resignation filled his voice, and Samara hoped she had won the argument. *You need to rest up and recoup your strength.*

Footsteps sounded in the large cave, and Samara

stiffened. *I've got to go. Someone's here, and I'll need to deal with that. Take care, Ulrieg.*

Likewise. The bond fell silent, but knowing Ulrieg was fine helped build Samara's strength. She rubbed the toes of her shoes together and stretched as much as she could while secured in the lying position. Her muscles screamed from the stiffness. However, the pain didn't seem as bad now that she had confirmation that Ulrieg and Paxton were all right.

Callista and Vexx filed into the small cave where she was being held, followed by Mystique. Their faces were somber and unreadable, and Vexx caressed Mara as she slithered over his cloaked arms and shoulders. Samara's insides stiffened with each step they took, waiting for another attack.

"Samara. How nice to see you awake and logical again. You had me so worried." Callista ran her fingers gently around the edge of the table.

Samara's brow pinched into a frown. This Callista was entirely different from the one who'd attacked her last time she was conscious. She studied the head sorceress, looking for some sign that she was someone other than herself, but everything looked the same.

Callista placed a hand on Samara's chafed ankle, and it took all of Samara's effort not to recoil. The head sorceress smiled, throwing her off even more.

Samara glanced at Vexx to see his reactions, trying to get some bearings. She wasn't disappointed. A deep scowl lined the senior sorcerer's face, and nothing remained in his eyes. Strangely, this comforted her. He was showing her the face she was used to, grounding her emotions. Callista's friendliness wasn't to be trusted.

"What's going to happen to me?" Samara looked from Vexx back to Callista, gauging their reactions.

Callista's mouth almost formed a smile. "Well, later, we're going to hold a meeting with the senior apprentices and senior coterie members to see what your fate will be."

Samara couldn't believe it. Callista made it sound like nothing sinister would happen to her, but judging by Vexx's reactions, this was far from the truth. It seemed like Callista was trying to gain her trust and get her to let down her guard.

Callista clasped her hands in front of her. "You know all of this will be forgiven, and you and your family can come under the coterie's protection again —if you just clear up a few things."

Samara tilted her head awkwardly to the side, seeing the irony, since she was still cuffed and secured to the top of the table like the next experiment. "Oh. And what would they be?" she asked sweetly. Two could play this game.

"You just need to tell me the location of the crystal and your familiar." Callista's gaze was soft. "That's it, and all will return to how it was."

Samara scoffed. "I don't know where my familiar is. Like I said, he doesn't trust you. And what makes you think I know where you'll find the crystal?"

Callista's facade broke, and her eyes turned icy, her words snapping out. "I know you were with the people who held the crystal just before it disappeared. And if your familiar is what I think it is, he probably helped you hide it."

Despite knowing she was in danger, it amused Samara just how easy it was to get Callista to turn back into her true self. "I honestly don't know where the crystal or my familiar are."

"Then perhaps I should get Kaine and Luna back to question you. I'm certain the only reason they couldn't get the truth out of you before was because your familiar helped you overcome their powers."

Callista's fingers ran over the bare skin on Samara's arm, and she could feel the tingling of a spell on the edges of those fingers. She knew that meant she was only a heartbeat away from being hurt again. She wiped away the smile playing at the edges of her mouth and looked Callista directly in the eyes. "If they come to question me, they will find out nothing more, because I honestly don't know where they are."

Callista turned abruptly and nodded at Mist. The muscled female stood and touched Samara's bare skin, sending shockwaves through her. Samara cried out in pain as tiny barbs of electricity seared her body.

"You may think you are above us, but we can make you live in a world of pain, misery, and grief for your loved ones," Callista hissed near her ear. "What you have experienced so far is merely the tip of the iceberg. I can make you wish you were dead yet force you to live on." She marched around the table, while Mist remained close to Samara, waiting for her next order to inflict pain, face filled with gleeful anticipation. "You will face the coterie's judgment tomorrow as to what your punishment will be. We don't treat situations like this lightly, and anyone discovered to have helped you will face the same fate, as will your familiar if found. Or perhaps they will fare worse."

Callista circled the gurney one more time. "Think about your actions, and any cooperation will be considered for a lighter punishment. Bear in mind, if it is ruled that you spend the rest of your miserable life inside the orb, it will be a far-from-pleasant experience. It will mean having your power slowly drained from you until you wither and die—or join our cause wholeheartedly."

Callista marched to the door with Vexx and nodded once at Mist. The apprentice's face lit with enthusiasm as she penetrated Samara's skin with several more shots of lightning bolts until Samara screamed, hoping for the relief of unconsciousness. Her wish went ungranted.

CHAPTER THIRTY-EIGHT

Pain and numbness sapped the energy from Samara's limbs. She blinked, trying to clear her vision, still clouded from the intense pain she was dealt earlier, remembering horrible images of Mist grinning as she kept shocking Samara without mercy, not relenting until sweat poured down Mist's face.

Blinking again, Samara searched the room for Mist, surprised that the apprentice was no longer in the room with her. She must have left when Samara's vision failed temporarily. They must have ruled Samara out as being capable of escape when she was barely conscious.

Her attempts to lift her head and then her arms to see if she was still restrained failed. Fighting through her brain fog, Samara could understand why they had left her. Her body remained useless. Even her magic was probably dulled along with her cognitive functions, leaving her unable to concoct an escape plan.

The orb still pulsed as though waiting to devour her magic, and there was nothing she could do. A shiver rippled down her spine. If she understood correctly, when the orb was powered up, it helped Callista wield her magic, making her stronger. Adding the power of the crystals to the high sorceress's magic, she would likely be unstoppable.

She remembered how they counted twenty smaller caves off the larger one and wondered if that was for the number of apprentices they took in at one time. If none of them did as Callista required, there were plenty of rooms to secure them all, throw them into the orb, and drain them of their powerful-yet-untrained magic.

Samara's breathing quickened. What a perfect way to take advantage of strong magic holders, pretending to help them but using them to make the coterie stronger, either by serving without restraint or being drained of their magic to serve the cause.

She tried again to pull against her restraints, but her arms were too weak. Groaning, she cursed her inability to move. Now was the time for her to escape, when no one was around to stop her. It was difficult to believe that she didn't even have enough energy to lift an arm, let alone walk herself out of there. Her chest heaved with rapid breaths as frustration built, soaring through her body where she should have power. Usually, this amount of frustration or anger would transform into power. This time, her strength still eluded her.

Another noise sounded near the door to her small cave, and she shifted her head, angling it, trying to see if her wardens were back. She couldn't see anyone. Shortly afterward, it sounded like a shoe scuffed on the floor only a few feet away. Again, she tried to find the source without luck. Maybe she was imagining things after the pain that Mist and Callista had put her through.

Something moved again, and she shifted her head to see in that direction. Her eyes nearly dropped out of her head. Paxton's head, his body not visible, moved around the end of her bed. When she met his eyes, they were awash with concern, softened by a smile just for her.

"Paxton?" Her eyes searched for his body, which appeared as he shifted, pushing off what must have been an invisible cloak. "What are you doing here? You're supposed to be leaving the coterie and finding safety. That's what I sent Ulrieg to do."

His smile widened, and he came closer and

gently stroked her face. "As if Ulrieg and I were going to leave you here. You should know us better than that."

Jojo peeked over the top of the invisible cloak and croaked.

Samara's heart melted with happiness as Paxton began removing her restraints.

His concerned eyes studied her. "How come you haven't undone these locks yourself?"

Samara swallowed the lump in her throat. "I can hardly move. All my limbs are weak and exhausted and seem to weigh more than a ton. Mist shot me with several bolts of her lightning. I guess they knew I was robbed of all my strength, so they left me alone for the first time."

Paxton laid his hands on one of her arms, and she could feel the healing power entering her, slowly mending her muscles and nerves, returning her ability to move. He then moved to her other arm.

Her eyes watched him as he worked. "Did Henriette spell the cloak invisible for you?"

Paxton nodded. "Don't worry. She doesn't know why I needed it. She didn't seem to mind as long as it caused some kind of mischief." He chuckled. "That's certainly the perfect special gift for her."

Some feeling began returning in the limbs

Paxton had worked on, and he moved to the next. "Where's Ulrieg?"

I'm right here, by the door. Ulrieg's gruff voice brought with it all kinds of comfort. *I knew you'd be in a bad way, and I didn't want to hinder Paxton from healing you. We need to get you out of here quickly.*

"How did you get in? I imagine they guarded this area to prevent anyone from helping me escape or in case I somehow gained enough energy to escape."

"Oh, they definitely have guards around the whole area." Paxton stroked her bare arm.

Tingles traveled up and through her chest. "Then how did you get past them?"

"Mostly because of the invisible cloak, and Ulrieg 'borrowed' the key from Eliphas. I don't think he will ever realize it's missing unless the others make him look. He doesn't seem to like anything to do with the underground. I don't know if it's because he doesn't like what they do in here or because he's simply antisocial and wants nothing to do with them aside from his teaching."

"Possibly both," Samara said. "The guards. Were any of them familiars with strong abilities to smell?"

Paxton paused. "We came through the outer tunnels, and Mystique and Zion were near the bush. Mystique was doing more prowling, while Zion was lying close to it." He seemed deep in thought. "Now that I think about it, I did see Zion's nose twitch like he was sniffing something. He looked at Mystique at one point, although I didn't notice any changes in Mystique's mannerisms."

Samara's mouth went dry. "Maybe Zion smelled you. But if he told Mystique, I'm sure she would have reacted." She frowned. "Devi seems so genuine. I hope she's not on Callista's side. If she isn't, then Zion may have kept the information to himself." She groaned. "I don't know. But you need to get out of here, just in case. Familiars like Mystique, Ginger, and Tabatha have been reporting to their bonded about my strange-smelling familiar. They would recognize Ulrieg's scent by now. It's too dangerous for you to be here."

I'm going over by the entrance to keep an eye out. I'll let you know if someone is coming.

"Thanks, Ulrieg." The joy of hearing his voice still whirled through Samara. She hoped their rescue gamble wouldn't backfire on them.

His mouth forming a thin line, Paxton moved to Samara's leg and began healing it, bringing back her energy and ability to move. "I'm not going anywhere without you. If it wasn't too hard to carry you while hiding you under this invisible cloak, I would have already gotten us out. But to keep you hidden, I'll need you to be able to walk."

Samara attempted to lift her arms, excitement raging through her when they lifted, feeling a little sluggish but moving. Slowly, she pushed herself up to sit, watching Paxton as he finished healing one leg then moved to the next. His face turned paler as he used his power, and Samara felt guilty. At the rate he was going, she hoped he would have enough energy to execute their escape.

She pulled the healed leg to her chest and reveled in the slight feeling slowly returning to her other leg.

We have to get out of here!

Paxton and Samara met each other's gaze, eyes wide. The urgency in Ulrieg's voice was unmistakable, and it was followed shortly after by his talons clacking on the hard floor.

Mara is slithering to the door, and I hear Vexx following her.

Free from all restraints, Samara swung her legs over the side of the table. "It's going to have to do. You can help me limp out of here, and maybe the movement will bring the circulation back."

Paxton nodded and helped her off the table then wrapped his cloak around both of them. He pushed her head under the sides. "You're going to have to squat under the main part of the cloak, since both of our heads won't fit under the hood."

Samara complied, holding Paxton's waist tightly. His closeness sent pleasant jolts through her body, especially when she caught a whiff of his soap-kissed skin. He must have had a bath just before he came.

The embarrassment of how she must smell overcame her. She was sure that she must stink of sweat and possibly even scorched skin after the jolts Mist had shot into her. Quickly, she pushed away the distraction. She could do nothing about it right now, and their safety was more important than her dank body odor. If they got out of here, she would make up for it later.

They hurried out of the small cave and past the large orb, slowly spinning on its axis, then they headed toward the door to the external tunnel. The clacking of Ulrieg's talons led the way, and he swung the door wide just as the lock to the internal door clicked and the door cracked open.

Hurry! Ulrieg hissed.

Scurrying to get through the door without tripping over one another, Samara and Paxton made it to the other side.

Ulrieg quickly closed the door behind them with the slightest click as it locked behind them.

Dragon moon! That was too close for comfort. Let's hope they didn't hear us.

CHAPTER THIRTY-NINE

Paxton heaved, trying to catch his breath. Healing Samara must have taken more out of him than he'd admitted. They broke away from each other for a while, Paxton removing his hood so she and Ulrieg could see him. Samara leaned against a wall away of the invisibility of the cloak.

I realize you two are struggling right now, but we need to get away from the door in case they heard or saw us. Ulrieg stood between them, turning visible long enough to get his point across.

Samara nodded, straightened, then stretched in an attempt to get her blood circulating quickly and regain fluid movement in her limbs. With only one sconce on the wall, it was difficult to see if Paxton was coping in the dimness.

She moved closer to him, hooked her body under his shoulder, and wrapped her arm around his waist. "We'll help each other and work out a way to cover us up with the invisible cloak when we get to the hole. Besides, the invisibility cloak will only last for half an hour. We'll be cutting it close, so we don't have time to waste. And I'm certain that once they realize I'm gone, they'll be looking everywhere for me."

Paxton grabbed her hand and squeezed it. "I'm fine, honestly. I get a bit weak when I heal a lot in a short time. It'll come back soon." Paxton grabbed the torch from the sconce with his spare hand.

Remaining under his arm, Samara continued to help him along. Her arms and one leg were almost working like normal, and the last leg was gaining more movement and feeling the more she used it. After a few minutes, Paxton recovered slightly, and their pace increased.

Several times, their shoes scuffed on the hard floor, and they consciously tried to be quieter, listening closely for any sounds of opening doors or movement coming from their exit ahead.

When they reached the stairs, Paxton placed the torch in the nearest sconce, and they tiptoed up the stairs.

I'll scout ahead and make sure it's safe for you to come

out. Ulrieg turned invisible and climbed out as Samara and Paxton prepared to exit.

Paxton covered his head with the cloak's hood and ensured every part of his body hid under the cloak. "I think the best way to do this is if I go out first then stand over the hole with the cloak draping around it. That way, you should rise directly into the cloak's protection when you climb out, and no one outside will see you."

Samara nodded. "That's actually a clever idea."

All right! You're good to come out quietly. Mystique is farther away from the hole, and I've rocked some branches near her. She's a little distracted. Amusement colored Ulrieg's voice. *And Zion doesn't seem too interested in the hole. The wind is blowing any scent from the hole away from them.*

Sunlight shone through the bush's branches as Paxton levered himself out and set up the plan for Samara's exit. Samara grabbed onto the hole's edges, ready to pull herself up, when the sound of a door opening echoed down the corridor. She startled then pulled herself through the hole, squatting awkwardly over the hole with her legs on either side while under the cloak, as planned. Paxton's strong hands tucked under her arms and held her steady as he shifted forward, away from the gaping space beneath them.

The bush hiding the hole rustled as it swung back into place, and Paxton and Samara froze, squinting against the brilliant daylight as they watched for a reaction from the two familiars on guard.

When nothing happened, they moved forward, limbs intertwined, edging their way toward the forest. There was no going back for Samara, and if the coterie had any suspicions about Paxton helping her escape, there would be no going back for him, either.

Very carefully, they crossed the field of wildflowers, careful to avoid twigs. Only a few more feet, and they would be within the boundaries of the pine forest. At least then they would have large tree trunks to hide their thin bodies from view.

Suddenly, a thick veil blocked Samara's sight. She paused for a moment, causing Paxton to slightly trip over her.

"Are you all right?" he whispered.

"Yes, but I can't see the way before me," she whispered back.

Paxton twisted one way then the next. "Prickly ferns!"

"What is it?" Samara looked up, unable to see his face through the tightened neck of the cloak.

"Jojo has just pointed out that the invisibility spell has worn off."

Fear shot through Samara's veins. "Have they seen us?"

"I don't think so, but it wouldn't take much now."

Ah, guys? Mystique has suddenly lost interest in me and is heading your way. And you're visible.

Dragon moon! Samara cursed. Readying to bolt for the trees on tiptoes, she steeled her nerves and stepped out of the security of the cloak and into the open, only to stop two steps away from Paxton. Mystique sat in the shadows of the first line of trees, her yellow eyes locked on the two apprentices.

Clenching her teeth, Samara cursed under her breath. *Ulrieg, we've been caught. I doubt we're going to get out of this one. I want you to promise me that you'll fly away, live your life, and never look back.*

Pfft! As if I'm going to do that.

Mystique hissed in pain, jumping away from her position. Samara thought she caught sight of long gashes down her back.

Run! Ulrieg screamed.

Samara dug in her toes, her leather boots groaning a protest with the added pressure. As she ran, thumping footsteps sounded behind her, and she glanced over her shoulder to find Paxton close behind. In the distance, Vexx's head peered out of the hole in the ground to the catacombs.

"Quick, Paxton!" she yelled, turning back to see

Mystique's shadowy form following up the sides. Instincts had her reaching over her shoulder, looking for her bow and quiver, only to remember she didn't have them with her. She shoved her palm toward the jaguar. *"Elevorto!"*

The cat lifted off the ground, yowling a protest as she was suspended in the air, her legs working helplessly underneath her.

Samara's heart pounded, hopeful they would keep their head start against Vexx. They might have a chance now that Mystique had been taken out of the chase. She peered over her shoulder, looking for Zion, only to see the wolf seemingly watching the commotion uncommittedly while heading more slowly in their direction. It almost felt like Devi's familiar was more amused over the action playing out before him than wanting to get involved.

Samara dodged several trees, branches cracking with every twig they trampled. They would have to be quieter when they lost sight of their pursuers. She headed toward the boulder where they had hidden Daena and Byzarid.

Paxton's footsteps started to catch up with her and keep pace. She hoped it was a sign he was getting his energy back after all the healing. She increased her pace, peering over her shoulder after a while to no longer see anyone else behind them.

Slowing, she enabled her lungs to grab much-needed air and softened her steps, trying to be as silent as possible. Paxton followed, both of them shadowing different trees and using their trunks as cover.

A breeze pushed down from above Samara, and she glanced up, following the faint trail of branches that swayed differently from the natural breeze. *How are we doing, Ulrieg? Have we lost them, or are they still catching up?*

Nope. They're still following you and speeding up. Callista has joined them, and Devi is standing guard near Zion, but those two seem to be staying behind.

Samara still didn't know if Devi supported the coterie and their terrible actions against the dragons. The thought of the kindhearted instructor being as nasty as Vexx, Kellam, and Callista was disturbing. She hoped it wasn't so, although she knew it wasn't something she could rely on. Both she and Paxton increased their speed.

The pine forest ended, and they moved into the regular forest, which was thick with evergreens. The sunlight peeking through the leaves grew dull. A streak of orange flashed several feet before them, instantly invoking horror as thoughts of Kellam and his monkey joining their hunt haunted Samara. She slowed, becoming more cautious with her next steps, indicating to Paxton to also slow down.

She stopped and crouched, her eyes darting everywhere, looking for signs of other coterie members. She couldn't see any, so she stood and began moving again. *Ulrieg, have you checked for any coterie members in front of us?*

A moment passed, and she realized the forest had turned silent. *That's never a good sign.* A crow darted toward them from the right, and a fox charged out of the shadows.

Look out! Ulrieg yelled.

Samara and Paxton ducked the attack from Okak but didn't have enough time to bolt from Ginger, who approached with her fangs bared.

Dragon moon! I didn't see them in time. I'm so sorry, Ulrieg moaned as Kaine, Mist, and Luna marched their way, each holding their weapons, Coco hopping to catch up with Ginger.

Kaine smirked. "I told them we should wait close to where Ginger spotted you that night. Looks like some people never change their habits."

Mist and Luna separated, and they formed a semicircle, cutting Samara and Paxton off from their escape.

Samara's knees felt weak. They were surrounded. The three older apprentices closed in around them as the noises from behind confirmed that senior coterie members were closing in.

Samara didn't have her weapons, and her magic without them wasn't nearly as impressive as that of the other apprentices. She wasn't worried about Kaine and Luna's magic, as long as she didn't let Kaine touch her or listen to Luna sing. But Mist was a different story with her lightning and fog plus being an excellent swordswoman.

Backing closer to Paxton, Samara spun to find Callista, Mystique, and Vexx with his familiar, Mara, coiled around his shoulders.

"Samara, it's lovely to see you again. I feared

you would miss your judgment day before the senior coterie members and our special older apprentices." Callista's voice oozed with fake sincerity, grating on Samara's nerves. "And Paxton, such a shame to discover you involving yourself with Samara's traitorous ways. I had great hopes for you and your future in the coterie. Powers like yours would make two of my less-worthy instructors look foolish, showing them to lack the skills needed to be members of the Sacred Flame coterie."

Callista's face remained unreadable, but after what Samara had experienced in the cave and at Paddosha Palace, she knew the blank face wasn't a sign of indifference. It was an expression of not caring enough to show praise when warranted and to hide her evil thoughts and intentions, especially from the naive apprentices.

Samara shifted to stand before Paxton, maneuvering until his back was against a large tree trunk to protect him. He shouldn't have come with Ulrieg to rescue her, although she was grateful for them and for how much they cared for her. But now, they were both in danger, especially Paxton and Jojo. Ulrieg still had a chance to get away.

Suddenly, Callista thrust her palm at the branches above, shouting, *"Petra!"* A moment later, a thump sounded on the ground several feet away from Samara.

Samara's eyes widened as the head sorceress sauntered toward the sound then reached down and touched something she couldn't see that was about a foot off the ground. Her heart stopped as she realized what Callista was doing.

Leaning over with her palm pointing to the ground, Callista muttered something no one else could hear. Samara's knees buckled as Ulrieg's black form turned visible, his body stupefied, his eyes open. Samara gasped, and so did Kaine, Luna, and Mist.

A sly smile distorted Callista's face as she gazed up at Samara. "There he is. There's your real familiar. I'd hoped you would open up and tell me the truth if I continued to be nice to you. Clearly, your loyalties never were with the coterie and what we stand for." She shook her head. "How could you bond with such a despicable creature? And after everything we've done for you."

Kaine, Mist, and Luna looked curious, like they wanted to move closer to have a better look, but they had to remain on guard in case Samara and Paxton bolted.

"Leave him alone!" Samara cried. "He's done nothing to you or your coterie."

Callista squatted closer to the helpless Ulrieg, focusing her hard, crystal-blue eyes on Samara. "Oh, so he didn't work against me and hide my crystal?"

Samara opened her mouth to speak but failed to force out a denial of his involvement. There was no point. Callista would hate Ulrieg and accuse him even if he was innocent, simply because he was a dragon. "What did you expect him to do?" she asked instead. "You would use the crystal to get stronger, oppose the dragon race, and try to snuff them out forever. Every creature deserves a chance to live and to have a place to call home."

Callista's chin rose. "They have a home. It's their forefathers' fault they're not living there."

"It wouldn't have anything to do with the fact you have hidden their realm from them and everyone else and cut it off from the rest of the world?" Samara's voice rose an octave.

A self-satisfied look passed over Callista's face, mirrored by Vexx's. The sorcerer moved closer to Samara and Paxton, his hand cupping Mara as she slithered around his shoulder. "They got what they deserved." Vexx sneered. "They thought they were better than us and were put in their place. Just like you two and your familiars will be."

Samara backed up, wanting to protect Ulrieg from Callista, but Paxton was closer, and she didn't want either of them to be harmed. Her back pressed against Paxton's side, and she realized he was shaking. She glanced unobtrusively over her shoulder at him, checking to see if he was all right. His body trembled slightly, and she spotted his arms close to his sides, his palms facing out. She had seen that stance before—he was working on something. She tried to block his body from the senior coterie members' view.

Callista faced Samara and Paxton as though emphasizing Vexx's point until Ulrieg shifted slightly. But the dragon was only twitching under the spell and didn't appear to be coming out of it.

Samara stared at Ulrieg, her heart breaking. He shifted again, this time not attracting the head sorceress's attention. Samara hoped he was waking up from her spell, then she saw some roots growing underneath him and extending their way toward the two senior coterie members. She looked away, trying not to draw attention to what Paxton was doing, but when her gaze fell on the apprentices boxing them in, they also had roots slowly sneaking up on them, out of the sight of their familiars. All the coterie members' attention was focused on Samara and Paxton, not what was happening on the ground around them.

Paxton jerked, suddenly forcing all the roots

higher and wrapping them around the coterie members, holding them hostage and securing their arms by their sides, lifting their feet off the ground.

Frustrated cries filled the air as the roots' captives wriggled in an attempt to free their arms and counterattack. Despite her semi-healed gashes, Mystique attacked the root holding Callista with her teeth and claws. Callista and Vexx uttered spells that they couldn't aim properly, and Samara shifted away from Paxton toward Ulrieg now that there was no need to hide what he was concocting. She bent over Ulrieg and attempted to negate the stunning spell, but it didn't dissipate, and her heart froze. Callista must have used something stronger or secured the spell so Samara couldn't undo it.

Panic filled Samara. She didn't know what to do. Something caused movement of the dried leaves not far away, and they drifted gently out as though something invisible was coming closer to her. She prepared to defend herself and her dragon before a soft whisper barely reached her ears.

"It's Devi, Samara. Relax. I'm going to help him."

Samara didn't move, doing her best to act as though no one had spoken to her, although her mind was whirling with questions, not the least of which was how Devi had gotten an invisible cloak. She hadn't thought her defense instructor could turn things invisible.

"You need to remember the spells you learned in our classes. I know you haven't been able to practice them much, but surely, you remember them," Devi whispered.

Ulrieg started to move, slowly rising to his feet and getting his bearings. He still seemed a little stunned as he nudged Samara. *Attack these horrible coterie members, and let's get out of here.* He launched into flight, heading for a secure branch before turning invisible, the leaves on the tree rustling heavily not long after as the dragon changed his position.

Samara stood and mouthed, "Thank you," at where she suspected Devi might be standing then lifted her hand toward Vexx. *"Manictium."* The sorcerer thrashed wildly within the roots, his face distorted with madness, bringing a smile to Samara's face. She did remember some spells. The longing for revenge welled in her, and she aimed for Kaine, casting the same spell before moving on to Luna.

Slowly, she raised her hand. *"Needleprenora."* The beautiful elf cried out with rage, desperately wanting to scratch the itchiness that had engulfed her. She started toward Mist, only to get distracted when Callista began to yell at her.

"You'll pay for this! You will never find a place that is safe for you again!" the head sorceress vowed.

Changing her mind, Samara went toward the head sorceress. For the first time, Callista could not retaliate against the spell about to be cast upon her, and satisfaction swelled in Samara's chest. She had a chance to finish this.

Then a crackle of electricity buzzed through the air, and she whirled around. Paxton's face was blank with the shock, and Jojo flopped off his shoulder to the ground, landing upside-down, unmoving, his white belly exposed to the sky. Samara screamed, but not loud enough to block the second strike as Paxton was electrocuted again. A stream of smoke left her beloved's body before his knees crumpled and he collapsed to the ground.

Samara screamed again, charging toward him, but at the same time, she saw the roots dropping away from their captives as his spell evaporated. Callista and Mist were still in their right minds and being released. Despite her heartbreak, she realized she had to dodge and duck for cover as both a spell from Callista and a bolt of lightning from Mist came her way from the opposite direction. Both barely missed her as she darted behind a tree.

Another bolt of lightning hit the ground not far from her feet, and a spark ignited the dried leaves into a small flame. She dashed to the next tree, dodging another attack from both sorceresses, as Okak flew over her head. Samara continued to scramble away from the attacks, using the trees as a shield, although she didn't think she could keep this up for much longer.

Sucking in a breath, she darted to another tree, rapidly pulling her foot up as another bolt of lightning hit the spot it had been a split second before.

CHAPTER FORTY-ONE

A cry sounded behind her, and she sneaked a peek around the tree in time to see Callista arch her back and hurl spells into the treetops.

The branches above her swayed and rustled as Ulrieg charged through the leaves on the tops of the trees. *Don't you dare give up! You keep going,* he urged Samara, cheering her on.

As another bolt of lightning struck the tree she hid behind, she dived to another.

"Why don't you come back and face us? If you don't like what we're doing to the dragons, why not come and fight us?" Callista taunted her.

A branch cracked to the right of her, and when she turned, there was no one to be found, not even a familiar. "Devi?" Samara whispered, hoping that it was someone who would help her.

She was about to give up and dart to the next tree when a small voice stopped her.

"It's me. Stay still."

Samara searched for Henriette until she felt something wrapping around her shoulders.

"I've made your cloak invisible. Devi told me you needed some help," Henriette whispered as she secured an invisible cloak around Samara's shoulders. The younger apprentice was clearly wearing her own cloak, also turned invisible. As a final touch, she lifted the hood over Samara's head. "Now, you need to get out of here. I'll walk with you a little way. Peadar will block the spells for a while, but I'm sure you'll understand that we can't be caught. I'm going to miss you."

"Why don't you two come with me?" Samara whispered.

"Our families aren't protected, and so far, we haven't done anything to make the coterie mad. I don't know the full story, but I guess it has something to do with that weird creature that's your true familiar. I wish you'd told me."

Several more lightning spells and curses were sent their way, blocked by Peadar.

Samara's gratitude was tempered with sorrow. "I was trying to keep you safe." Samara made sure the words communicated her regret.

"I understand, but next time, trust me with the information. You know I thrive at causing mischief, and secrets are part of that."

Samara gently bumped shoulders with the younger apprentice. "Make sure your mischief doesn't get you into serious trouble."

Henriette shoved something underneath Samara's cloak. "Take these with you. The sprayer contains vinegar, and the bag contains pepper and ground chili. Any animal with a sensitive nose hates these smells, and they get up in their nostrils. Spray the vinegar and top it with a sprinkle of powder to throw off the tracking animals that will try to hunt you down."

Peadar blocked a few more curses.

"Please thank Peadar and Devi for me if you get the chance."

"I will. You need to go."

"Thank you. Stay safe." Samara heard the soft crackle of the leaves as Henriette left her side and headed toward the building.

"Oh, Samara," Callista taunted. "You should have come and fought us. While you've been busy running from us, you should have seen what has happened to Paxton."

Samara froze, barely daring to breathe.

"Aren't you interested in finding out?"

Mist's taunting laughter reverberated through the trees, echoed by Kaine and Luna in the distance.

"Leave Paxton alone!" Samara yelled before dodging to another location.

More spells were thrown at her along with lightning, still blocked inconspicuously by Peadar.

"Oh, we've done that already. But it's where we've left him alone. That's where the real surprise lies."

Samara wanted to run to Callista and rip out her voice box. She was sure what the head sorceress was gloating over would be terrible for Paxton.

"You're not going to ask?" Callista taunted.

Her breathing turned ragged, and panic began to set in. From the way Callista was acting, this couldn't be good for Paxton, but she was more interested to find out if he could be rescued before she ran. She shifted farther away from the approaching coterie members.

Callista rubbed her fingernails lightly on her dress and pressed her diadem against her forehead. "Perhaps I'll just tell you anyway." She sauntered closer to where Samara hid. "His familiar is dead, but he isn't. For how much longer, I don't know. But don't worry, his power will not go to waste."

Samara's arms turned numb and her cheeks icy as she realized the worst thing they could do to

Paxton aside from torture and death. *Surely, Callista hasn't...*

"I helped Vexx out of that little spell you put on him, and he set to work immediately. The whole time you've been running, Paxton has been dragged away." There was too much joy in the sorceress's voice. "Can you guess where to?"

Callista moved closer, tapping her finger against her lips. "Fine, I'll just tell you. Vexx dragged Paxton into the catacombs and threw his body into the orb. Now, despite your escape, the orb will still get its fill of strong magic, maybe even stronger magic than you could've given it."

The three apprentices laughed while fury and devastation roiled in Samara's stomach. Tears threatened to blur her vision, and she blinked them back, pushing down her emotions with great difficulty, just for the moment.

Her mind whirled rapidly. She didn't know how to get Paxton out if he was inside the orb.

"Slowly, his magic will be seeped away and fed to the orb until, one day, I'm guessing, his body will wither and die. Or," Callista added cheerfully, "he'll join us to fight you and any of the dragons that may come near. I'm hoping for the latter. That would be something I would like to watch."

This time, the tears did fall. Another few spells

were shot at her, blocked by Peadar as he made them hit the ground a few of feet away from her as inconspicuously as possible.

My heart breaks, too, Samara. Ulrieg's tone reflected his grief. *But you've got to run. You won't stand a chance to get Paxton out. Maybe we'll find someone in the realms who knows if he can be rescued. But you've got to go, or you're helping no one.*

She swallowed hard. Her familiar was right. Letting herself get captured would not help anyone, not even Paxton. Quickly, she headed farther into the forest without leaving her pursuers a trace of her direction.

SAMARA KEPT quiet as she ran and covered her tracks with vinegar, ground pepper, and chili. The combination seemed to work wonders in covering her tracks, especially when Ulrieg spread a false trail.

It had been some time since she had heard anything from her pursuers. Even though it seemed she had managed to escape them, her heart was heavy and filled with guilt. She had gotten away, yet others would need help to get out of the coterie's control and awful practices. The thought of the enormous task overwhelmed her. She had to get away and hopefully gather enough people to go against the coterie and its horrible deeds. Along the way, she would watch for any signs of Dragoria. There must be a way to release the dragon realm so they could build an army again and rise to protect the people of the kingdoms.

First, Samara knew she needed to learn more about what was really happening in the kingdoms. She was so naive, and although she'd learned more, she still had much to discover if she was going to be able to execute her plan to rally people together to rise against the coterie.

Forgrac had wanted her to join his theatre troupe and travel with them when they put on shows. She didn't know if that was still his plan now that he'd had to leave the coterie before he was granted access to Slosiaran. However, thanks to her brief trip to the border, she had discovered a way to get through the magical barriers.

This reminded her of her lack of weapons. She had no money to buy a new bow and quiver and would have to make arrows. This was a problem. Her cloak had turned visible some time ago, which made sense. She felt as if a vast amount of time had passed since she lost her pursuers, but she had no idea how long because she was constantly on edge, expecting someone who wished to do her harm to poke their head around a tree trunk in front of her.

Ulrieg, are you all right? I haven't heard from you for a while.

Physically, yes, I'm fine. I'd be lying if I said I wasn't grieving, though.

Me too. She took a few deep breaths, trying to calm the swell of despair threatening to overtake her. *Where are you?*

I'm just above you. I've been watching you from above the trees. He paused. *You've lost the coterie. Do you have somewhere in mind where you want to go?*

I thought I'd wait in that nearby village Forgrac mentioned. He said he has a few friends there. If I can, I will hide there until Forgrac returns. I wish I had my weapons, though.

Oh, wingless flight! I forgot!

Forgot what?

Paxton and I hid your weapons here in the forest. We figured you wouldn't return to the coterie if you managed to escape. We should go get them first.

The thought of having her bow and arrows back brought her some relief. She felt more secure with them by her side. *Lead the way.*

Turn to the right. I'll be with you shortly.

Samara did as instructed and heard the leaves above rustling as Ulrieg dived through them and then landed on the ground. He turned visible and walked the ground near her, directing her along the way. Before long, they came across a small boulder leaning on another with a thin gap underneath. Ulrieg indicated it. *We hid them under there.*

Lowering to her hands and knees, Samara slid her arm under the boulder and grasped the first hard thing her hand touched, dragging it out. Her eyes welled with tears as she saw Paxton's flail in her hands. A sob escaped her lips as the tears trickled down her cheeks.

Ulrieg pressed against her, and she put an arm around him, carefully avoiding his many horns. He nuzzled her cheeks and licked her tears, his red eyes deepening with sadness. *I worry for him too. Hopefully, we'll find a way to release him before it's too late. His* voice broke. *I don't know what else to do. He was very special, with a heart of gold and loyalty that put many others to shame. The best we can do is try to give that back to him.*

Samara wiped away the tears Ulrieg missed with the back of her hand, taking a break from twirling the flail in her fingers. It may have been Paxton's least favorite thing, but it was something that belonged to him. There was no way she was leaving it here.

Wiping away more tears, her eyes still blurry, she

reached under the boulder again, her fingers clasping her quiver and bow simultaneously. She pulled them out and slung them on her back, adding the flail to her quiver with the arrows. At least she had something to remind her of Paxton and fire up her commitment to free him.

EPILOGUE

An owl hooted close by, and Samara cracked an eye open, peering out the opening of the caravan and taking in the full moon that cut through the darkness. She stretched, and her toes touched something sharp. Pain shooting up her leg, she pulled her feet back and glanced at where they'd been. Ulrieg curled up in the back corner near the opening, his face turned toward the moon and his many horns protruding menacingly, one of which had pricked her toe. He was always on guard from intruders, even as they slept.

A couple of months had passed since they had escaped from the Sacred Flame coterie, and it was only in the last few weeks that they could finally stop looking over their shoulders for the coterie sorcerers. Samara was certain she and Ulrieg would forever be on their most-wanted list, which would make traveling through the borders almost impossible if Samara hadn't learned to create holes through solid barriers.

Little did Callista know that enlightening Samara about her most important magical talent would be the tool she used the most to escape the coterie members and their torturous ways. Because of this, she could even cut through the border areas that weren't guarded by Callista's senior sorcerers.

Samara peered around the semilit caravan, her eyes landing on her companions, the actors in the troupe. When they were traveling between the villages, the sleeping spaces were cramped. Some would sleep outside near the fire or under the caravan unless it was raining, and they all tried to cram into the small spaces inside the canopy and over top of their props and costumes. This caravan held the females of the troupe, while the other held the males.

They were many miles away from the Perpetual Vale, where the dwarves lived in the human realm, Slosiaran. Samara had spent several weeks meeting Forgrac's family and reuniting him with his wife and his grown children. Now it was time to travel and to find the last human royal—or royals. And they had to check on Daena's cousin, Tanila, to ensure she was safe from the coterie members, especially if she had dragon-elf blood.

A slight, steady rumble came from Forgrac's wife as she breathed in deep, even breaths. The dwarf woman had decided to join Forgrac's team as they set out on their tour to use their troupe to learn more about what was happening.

Samara curled into a sitting position, and Ulrieg lifted his head to look at her, his black face twisted with an emotion she couldn't read.

What is it? Samara crawled closer to him and peered out the opening between the privacy flaps. A breeze whipped through the leaves, rocking the branches of the trees.

Something is traveling in the breeze.

Samara stuck her head out and took a deep breath, only picking up the smell of damp leaves, tree bark, and dirt, typical aromas of the forest. She pulled her head back in and frowned. *I'm not picking up anything other than the scents of the forest.*

Ulrieg snorted. *It's not that.*

She took another whiff and shook her head, not finding anything different. *I thought you couldn't smell that well.*

He tilted his head, eyeing her as though she should know better. *It's not a smell I'm talking about. It's a sense.*

On the breeze? Samara echoed his look of disbelief.

Ulrieg nodded. *I can't tell what it is, but it seems to be calling me.*

Then why didn't you go and investigate?

Ulrieg huffed. *As if I'm going to leave you unprotected while no one is watching out for the coterie.*

Samara climbed out of the caravan and placed her hands on her hips as she squinted, trying to see as far as she could to find the origin of the breeze, yet even with the full moon, she could not figure out what would be calling to her dragon.

Ulrieg climbed out of the caravan after her, his talons scratching the wood on his way down. *Can you see anything?*

Samara shook her head. *How about you?*

He flew to the top of the tallest nearby tree. *No. But I still sense it even from up here. In fact, it seems stronger.*

The moon was high in the sky, indicating many hours left of night. *Perhaps you should follow your gut.*

We can't just leave the others unguarded.

Samara glanced over at the two caravans and spotted Forgrac sleeping by the fire. *If you're sensing it on the full moon, it must be important to us. The only dwarf they should be after is Forgrac, since he released the guardian dragon.* She hastened over to the sleeping dwarf and shook his shoulders.

The dwarf grumbled, muttering curses as he rolled to his backside. He rubbed his eyes and blinked at her. "What is it, love?"

She squatted beside him. "I'm sorry to wake you. But Ulrieg is having his full-moon sense, and we must follow it up. I didn't want to leave you unguarded while you were sleeping."

He roughly wiped his face with his arm as though trying to brush away the sleep. "All right, then. Ya betta go an' see what it is."

"Are you going to be able to stay awake?" Samara's brow pinched with worry, seeing how dazed the dwarf was.

Forgrac waved his arm at a bucket not far away. "'At water'll be cold. 'And me 'at with a cloth, an' I'll wipe it over me face an' eyes. Should do the trick."

Rising, she placed the bucket beside him then went to her caravan and retrieved her quiver and bow, along with a small cloth for Forgrac. "Here. I'm not sure how long we will be, but I'll return as soon as possible. We need to get our play to the next village to earn more coins for us and my family." So far, Samara hadn't acted in any plays. Forgrac had spent the time training her.

"Which way are ya travelin'?"

"Upwind." Samara indicated north with a nod.

Forgrac grunted. "Ain't it sad it's not in the direction we'd be travelin'. We could 'ave joined ya. Me only knowin' of that way is it be blocked with large mountain ranges 'at are impossible to climb, an' there ain't no dwarf tunnels under them."

Samara shrugged. "We're just following Ulrieg's hunch. It's never let him down before."

The dwarf's mouth bunched on one side. "'Is moon hunch shouldn't be ignored. It led 'im to ya, didn't it?"

Samara nodded. She reached back, grabbed Paxton's flail from her quiver, and handed it to Forgrac. "Just in case." The usual emotions of guilt and sorrow washed over her, and she longed for her beloved and his release. *I haven't forgotten you, Paxton. We're trying to find a way to release you.*

"Be safe. 'At's the main thing." He dunked the cloth in the water and wiped it over his eyes, releasing a satisfied moan. "This'll do the trick."

Samara squeezed his shoulder. "Watch over yourself as well. The others should be fine." She turned and traveled north, a strong wind pushing against her face. She was grateful it wasn't winter and the temperature of the gusts wasn't too cold.

Ulrieg landed beside her and kept up with her

pace. *It's times like these that I wish I was bigger and could carry you on my back. It would be a lot quicker.*

Why don't you fly ahead and see what you can find?

And leave you alone, without protection? You must be joking!

Samara tilted her head to one side, giving him an incredulous look. *I'm awake, and I have my magic and weapons.* She tugged at the quiver's straps. *I'll be fine.*

After huffing out a plume of steam, he launched into the sky and flew ahead. *I won't go too far. I still want to check that you're all right.*

Honestly, Ulrieg. We haven't seen anyone from the coven in weeks. We should be fine.

You never know when they'll decide to check on the occupants of this realm, or maybe we could run into some centaurs. They could stumble across us at any time.

Samara shook her head. *Go as far as you need. Maybe you won't need me when you get there, which'll make our trip much quicker.*

I have a sense you're wrong.

Samara sighed. *All right.* She had a feeling it was going to be a long night.

She focused on where she was going. Their camp hadn't been in a dense part of the forest, yet the trees were thinning quickly until they opened up, with only a few sparse trees and the plains scattered with many large rocks. She wondered if they were reaching the larger, rockier mountains Forgrac mentioned. Gazing at the sky, she thought she saw a flying animal several yards ahead. *Is that you up ahead? It's a bit hard to see for my human eyes.*

The flying animal swayed a little. *I can still see you, so it is possibly me.*

Is the path blocked ahead with mountains?

No, they're a little more to the west.

She squinted but couldn't see the mountains. *I believe you. Can you see what's pulling you?*

No, not yet.

An owl hooted and leaped out of the tree above her, startling her. One hand over her pounding heart, she watched it fly away, memories of Gray flooding her. He hadn't deserved to be forced into her world, and she wished the coterie hadn't mistreated him.

Samara scanned the sky, losing sight of Ulrieg, and quickened her pace, weaving around a large rock, her arrows shifting in the quiver in time with her footsteps. She knew the dragon wouldn't leave her behind, and she was fine traveling without seeing him as long as she was going in the right direction. They had been at this for a large portion of the night, and at this pace, they wouldn't make it back to their camp before daylight.

She continued for some time, passing a large

cluster of boulders on her left. *I've lost sight of you. Can you still see me?*

Yes. I've paused on the top of some pine trees. Can you see them?

Samara concentrated on focusing on the distance. There seemed to be fewer rocks on one side, and she turned slightly to the right. She thought she spotted a large copse of trees there. *Maybe. Are they on the east?*

Yes.

Changing direction, she jogged that way, heading for the trees as the moon cast her shadow under her feet. Out of breath and nearly at the edge of what looked like a forest now that she was up close, she gazed at the treetops, trying to spot Ulrieg. *Have you found it?*

Ulrieg landed on the ground in front of her, his black, spiky form a welcome sight. *Unfortunately for you, no. We're about to travel through the trees, so I wanted you to catch up to me.*

Bending over, hands on her knees, Samara sucked in a few breaths. *Right.*

It looks like you needed a little rest as well. Amusement flashed over his face.

Still struggling to breathe, Samara waved a hand. *I'll be fine. Keep going a little slower for a bit, and*

I'll catch my breath while we walk. I've never really liked running.

Ulrieg walked into the forest, and she fell into place by his side. *The good news is that the sense is getting stronger, so we must be closer.* He flashed his teeth, which she knew was his version of a smile even though it looked threatening.

The noises of nocturnal animals broke through the darkness under the cover of the tall trees as pine needles crackled under their feet.

Well, I guess that's good news.

They cut through the trees quicker than expected, and the other side opened into fields divided by several large boulders in what seemed like a barrier.

Samara scanned the rocks that blocked their passage. *Can we get through?*

Ulrieg took to the sky and scouted ahead, hovering over a section slightly off to the west. *There's a passage that looks large enough for a caravan to pass through right here beneath me.* He spun on the spot and faced the other direction. *That's odd.*

What is?

He didn't answer as he flew in that direction.

Samara groaned and quickened her pace to catch up with the dragon. She cut through the opening he'd indicated to the other side, only to see him flying in the opposite direction and halting abruptly as though he had hit an invisible barrier. He turned around and tried again, each time ending with the same result. Beneath him was what looked like a rock wall built higher than her head, although it was hard to tell because it was covered in purple flowering vines.

She stopped before the flowered wall, pressing her palm through the thick vines and working along it until her hand pressed into a void. Pulling away the vines, she attempted to peek through, only to run into something solid and invisible. She tore away parts of the vine until she revealed the gap, finding a stone archway that should allow passage to the other side.

Backing away from the opening, she looked up to find Ulrieg hovering above the wall. *Is this where your senses are telling you to go?*

Yes. I don't know how far in. I didn't want to tell you before, but I'm sensing dragons.

What do you mean?

I mean many dragons, like I've never sensed before.

Samara frowned. *Is there anywhere else that has lots of dragons that you know of?*

Only Dragoria.

Samara stilled. *So, you're telling me that this thing stopping us could be the powerful magical barrier that has made the realm invisible to us for four hundred years?*

Yes. Ulrieg sounded stunned. *I'm sure this isn't the border to Wraeyanor.*

Samara's blood thrummed through her veins with excitement. She tried once more to push through the opening in the wall, only to be blocked again. However, it didn't just block her entry like the other borders. This ward reflected what was on her side, obstructing her view through to the other. She could only see herself.

She backed up again, drawing an arrow out of her quiver. She gazed up at Ulrieg. *There's an opening that should let me through down here, but I'm also blocked off. Let's see how my spell works against the powerful ward.*

Ulrieg dropped to the ground, giving her space to work, his red eyes filled with hope.

Samara muttered *"Aperti"* while waving her hand over the arrow. She nocked it and took a large breath before releasing it into the gap. It bounced off.

Wingless flight! It didn't work. She lowered the bow, and her shoulders sagged, especially when she saw the disappointment on Ulrieg's face. She tried again, only to find the same result. Her boots clattered on the rocks before the opening as she began to pace, her mind whirling over what to do.

She eyed her familiar. *Surely, you wouldn't have been called here if you couldn't do anything about the ward.*

That's very unlikely, but my gut said I needed you to be with me.

After a few more moments of pacing, Samara stopped, her thoughts brightening. *Maybe you should be touching me as I spell and fire the arrow.*

Ulrieg shrugged and waddled to her side. *It's worth a try.*

Just to be sure, I'll roll up my pant leg so you're touching my skin.

When she felt his scales pressing against her calf, she enchanted another arrow and nocked it.

Wait! I've heard a rumor about how dragon's fire on a weapon will often make it stronger.

Samara lowered the arrow. *What are you suggesting?*

I should strengthen the arrow with my fire.

Won't it burn the arrow?

It'll only be brief, and I'll focus on the tip.

I guess it's worth a try.

She lowered the arrow tip toward him. Ulrieg expelled a plume of fire, bathing the tip of the arrow, before pressing himself against her exposed leg again.

Samara nocked the arrow once more, and after a few deep breaths, she released it into the gap below the archway. This time, it penetrated, and her heart skipped a beat.

Samara glanced down at Ulrieg in disbelief. *It stuck. That usually means it worked. I'll try the other side.* When it also stuck, she fired one more enchanted and dragon-kissed arrow into the upper middle. *That should make a bigger hole.*

Ulrieg approached the opening apprehensively, gradually pushing through the other side of the vine. He stuck his head back through to look at her, his scaly face filled with excitement. *Come on!*

Samara's limbs tingling, she stepped through, and her jaw dropped. On the other side was a worn path speckled with grass that seemed to lead up to the ruins of a castle.

Did I honestly just break through the powerful ward that has hidden your realm for hundreds of years?

Eyes glowing, Ulrieg indicated the building. *From the tales I've been told, that fortress used to be home to some of the best pairs of dragon elves and their guardian dragons. So yes.*

ACKNOWLEDGMENTS

The last year has been a big rollercoaster ride. My hereditary kidney disease has decided to throw me into the end stages. Thankfully, modern medicine has progressed over the last two generations, and kidney disease is no longer terminal. However, it is a lifetime of treatments, including dialysis and hopefully a transplant for a fuller life. Because of this, my story production has been slower. But thankfully, the editors can help me produce quality stories when my brain lacks the alertness that comes with health.

Hopefully, I'll receive a transplant soon, along with the health benefits and energy that come with it.

As always, my husband and sons have been tremendous supporters. My husband has been a helpful first reader and, at times, been an excellent motivator.

A huge thank you to my editor, Mary M., for her editing and writing tips and my proofreader, Kim H., for picking up the things we missed.

Thank you to all my readers who have loved my work and continue reading my stories. I'm looking forward to writing many more.

BOOKS BY KATRINA COPE

Pre-Teen Books

<u>The Sanctum Series</u>

JAYDEN'S CYBERMOUNTAIN

SCARLET'S ESCAPE

TAYLOR'S PLIGHT

ERIC & THE BLACK AXES

ADRIANNA'S SURGE

~~~~~

Young Adult Urban Fantasy

<u>Afterlife Series</u>

FLEDGLING

THE TAKING

ANGELIC RETRIBUTION

DIVIDED PATHS

TRUTH HUNTER

<u>Afterlife Novelette</u>

THE GATEKEEPER

~~~~~

Young Adult Urban Paranormal Fantasy

<u>**Supernatural Evolvement Series**</u>

(Associated with the Afterlife Series)

WITCH'S LEGACY (Prequel)

AALIYAH

~~~~~

Young Adult Norse Mythology Fantasy

<u>**Valkyrie Academy Dragon Alliance**</u>

MARKED (Prequel)

CHOSEN

VANISHED

SCORNED

INFLICTED

EMPOWERED

AMBUSHED

WARNED

ABDUCTED

BESIEGED

DECEIVED

<u>**Thor's Dragon Rider**</u>

SAFEGUARD

PURSUIT

ENTRAPMENT
~~~~~

HOODWINKED

RELINQUISHED

SHROUDED

ASSIGNED

ACCOSTED

DESTRUCTION

~~~~~

Young Adult Epic Fantasy

<u>Dragoria: the Lost Dragon Realm</u>

DRAGON MOON

DRAGON HEART

DRAGON BREEZE

DRAGON'S ROYAL

ROYAL ALLIANCE

ROYAL RESISTANCE
~~~~~

ABOUT THE AUTHOR

Katrina is an author of several books in epic fantasy, young-adult fantasy, and a middle-grade sci-fi thriller series.

Her series include:

Dragoria: The Lost Dragon Realm - Coming of Age Epic fantasy

Valkyrie Academy Dragon Alliance - YA High fantasy

Thor's Dragon Rider - YA High fantasy (Spin-off of Valkyrie Academy Dragon Alliance but can be read separately)

The Afterlife - YA fantasy (contemporary)

The Sanctum Series - Middle-grade Sci-fi thriller

She often talks to creatures of all kinds and has a passion for animals, nature, and travel. She lives in Queensland, Australia, with her husband and has survived teaching her three children how to drive.

Katrina's online home is at www. katrinacopebooks.com

You can connect with Katrina on:

tiktok.com/@katrinacopebooks

facebook.com/Author.Katrina.Cope

instagram.com/katrina_cope_author

bookbub.com/profile/katrina-cope

x.com/Katrina_R_Cope

pinterest.com/katrinacope56